Dec. 4, 2001

Dear Nancy,

Before its public release Dec. 6, 2001, I wanted you to have your copy of this first book. I hope you realize you were a major part of our success and in many areas aside from the business. Family wise, vacation wise, health wise, oh so many ways you were always there for us and we were able in recent years to be relaxed when we were gone knowing you and Julie were the best guards, managers, family dedicated like humans anyone could ever have. We miss you beyond belief. You always have been and always will be in my prayers daily and ask God to bless you always and Mom. You are a gift from God and we thank him for loaning you to us. We will always be here for you.

Respectfully,
Carland Dolores
D'Aquila

Count the Pickets in the Fence

COUNT THE PICKETS IN THE FENCE

BY CARL D'AQUILA

WITH AL ZDON

MOONLIT EAGLE PRODUCTIONS
2001
ST. PAUL, MINNESOTA

Count the Pickets in the Fence, copyright 2001 by Moonlit Eagle Productions. All rights reserved.

Printed in the United States of America by Stanton Publication Services Inc.

Published by Moonlit Eagle Productions
5064 Irondale Road, Mounds View, MN 55112

No part of this publication may be reproduced in any form without the prior written permission of the publisher except in the case of brief quotations within critical articles and reviews.

ISBN 0-9711940-0-9

Photos on page 42 are from the Minnesota Historical Society. All other photos and clippings are from the author's personal collection.

Contents

1. Prologue
2. Mom and Dad in North Hibbing
3. Growing Pains
4. On the Campaign Trail
5. The Best Room in St. Paul
6. The Politics of Losing
7. Back in the Real World
8. Back into the Fray
9. Fighting for Taconite
10. Just the Guy They Were Looking For
11. My Good Friend Rudy
12. Trying to Preserve Reserve
13. Staying Rational with National
14. Hundreds of Ways to Lose Money
15. Political Connections
16. Stories about Friends
17. Family Ties
18. The Equation of Life

Dedication

When our kids would head off to school in the morning, Dolores would remind them of the number of challenges they would face and the obstacles they would have to overcome. "Count the pickets in the fence," she would say. That phrase has become part of our family lore, and it applies, I think, to my life too. The challenges and obstacles along the way have been as numerous as those white pickets that surround our home in Hibbing. I could never have made it without my family.

I dedicate this book to the memory of my mother and father and my two brothers, and to the future of my children and grandchildren. And, most particularly, I dedicate it to Dolores whose beauty, intelligence, energy and love have made my life worthwhile.   -- C.M.D.

Special Thanks

There's a crew of people who work for me who not only make the business go, but have also allowed me the time and freedom to do many of the projects I refer to in the book. They are my extended family. I offer special praise and thanks to my invaluable, longtime secretary Julie Olin, to the man who does everything in our office, Gaylord Chapin, to super-secretary Nancy Payne and to Louis Paul, Larry Unger and Kerry Warzecha. They are employees, but, more importantly, they are my good friends.

There are other special people who are not employees but who help us keep our business and our lives straight. Steve Jarvi is our trusted outside CPA, financial advisor and consultant who has always led us in the right direction. Carol Blomberg does the same for our personal banking. Our legal wizard, Ed Matonich, has been both advisor and faithful friend. And it's been a privilege working with Dave Ellefson on one of our ventures. And a very special thanks to dear friend Cindy Johnson whose final editing of this book was both consummate and invaluable.

Chapter One
PROLOGUE

It was an absolutely gorgeous day in St. Paul. It was the first morning of the legislative session. I had arrived a couple of days earlier, taking the Great Northern Railroad from Hibbing to Duluth, and then down to St. Paul. I was staying at the Ryan Hotel, a beautiful old place in the downtown area.

That morning, January 4th, 1947, I got up about 6 a.m. When I got down to breakfast at about 7:20 a.m., the place was already bustling. I was wearing one of my brother's suits, a really fashionable number with wide pin stripes. It was a hand-me-down that he had given me.

The sun was shining as I left the hotel, and I didn't even wear a topcoat. I walked the six blocks or so up to the Capitol.

As I walked up the Capitol steps on that first day, I was thinking about my parents. I was thinking of the fact that I was very, very lucky to be elected, and I had to succeed. I just wanted to do everything right.

I thought, too, about those people who had written in my high school yearbook predicting that I would end up in public office. Some classmates had even suggested that I might be President of the United States someday. But I didn't have a thought about what I would do next, where I would go from here. I only thought about getting the job done, about succeeding, about making the area, my parents, my older brothers, and teachers and everybody proud of my accomplishments.

As I reached the top of the many steps, Gov. Luther Youngdahl, known in those days as "the crime buster," came down to meet me. He greeted me warmly and said, "I'd like you to come into the office."

Prologue

The Speaker of the House, Lawrence Hall, was there as was Roy Dunn, the majority leader. They all told me of the tremendous opportunity I'd have. I was exhilarated.

I had caucused with the conservatives beforehand, and George McKinnon, a congressman who had served in the Legislature, came up to me and said, "How did you ever pull this off on the Iron Range?" The conservatives offered to do everything they could to make me look good.

I came out of the governor's quarters, and before I went over to the House chamber, I walked up to the Senate right at the top of the stairs. Sen. Elmer Peterson was there and he took me around and introduced me to all the senators. There was all the pomp and ceremony anybody could ever have as a first termer.

I even was introduced to the legislative postmaster. He came up to me and said, "I've got mail for you already."

It was really something.

I was 22 years old.

Chapter Two

Mom and Dad in North Hibbing

My mother was Concetta Vendetti and my father was Pasquale D'Aquila. They came from a small town in Italy named Vinchiaturo. They grew up in that town, and the two families knew one another. I guess at that time you didn't look very far for a suitable partner.

The more you got to know somebody, the more you knew the family background. It was simpler world. They knew each other, and they knew each other's qualities. I think that's why the marriages lasted. I can never remember a divorce of those people from Italy.

Vinchiaturo was a poor town. It was located in a hilly region, about 125 miles southeast of Rome. There were farms, and some people had vineyards. It was just south of the province in Italy that bears our name. "Aquila" means eagle in Italian.

While nearly everyone in Vinchiaturo farmed, my father got away from that. When he was 16, he left with his uncle to work in the mines in Brazil. Two years later, in 1900, he returned to Italy.

There was a large landowner named Gianotti who had vast amounts of land with vineyards, and my father became his steward. In particular my dad became very pro-

Mom and Dad in North Hibbing

Vinchiaturo is where my family came from. It's a beautiful town about 125 miles from Rome.

ficient in the art of timing the picking of the grapes to make the best wine.

From the beginning, my father had his eyes on coming to America. Everyone was beginning to realize that America was the land of opportunity. Dad was of that mindset. It wasn't something unique to him. There were a lot of people who had the same idea, and that's why so many people from that same area settled in Hibbing.

In 1910, he and mother got married, and two years later he went to Canada, again as a miner. Over the next few years, he went back and forth from Canada to Italy. My brother Mike was born in 1911, and brother Frank was born in 1913 in Vinchiaturo.

In 1914, dad finally made it to the United States, going through Canada and settling in Montana. It was easier to enter the U.S. from Canada than to try and get past all those quotas and rules if you were from Europe. He never returned to Italy after that.

He came to Hibbing in 1916 at the age of 34 and lived in a boarding house. My mother was still in Italy, as were all the wives at that time. He started at the Albany Mine, and he became a foreman there. Later he moved to the Scranton Mine where he worked the remainder of his life. In fact, he was so well-regarded that they asked him to stay on after retirement age, and so he worked until he was almost 69 years old as a track foreman. They didn't want to let him go.

It took him five years to get enough money to send for his family. It was a big event among the family in Vinchiaturo in 1921 when my mom and my brothers finally left for America. My uncle, Salvatore, killed a steer and used the hide to make hobnailed shoes for my brothers so they would have something nice when they came to the new world.

When my mom arrived with the kids, they settled in Nassau Location, a few miles north of Hibbing and about a mile east of the small community of Kitzville. Nassau was just a little place with a dozen or so homes clustered together. In the summer, the residents all drew water from one common well, a block or so away, but in the winter that well froze over, and they had to walk a mile with their pails for household water.

There were no basements and no insulation in the houses. The homes were heated with woodstoves. Of course, there was no indoor plumbing, just a pot in every room. In the outdoor facilities, the toilet tissue was the paper that had been wrapped around the fruit they bought by the case.

A passport photo shows Concetta D'Aquila with her two sons, Michael and Frank, in 1921.

The only thing they really had an abundance of in Nassau was bedbugs.

The family then moved to 110 Granite Street in the Brooklyn neighborhood, a part of Hibbing they called Little Italy. I was born there just before noon on August 1, 1924. My dad was 42 and my mom was 43 when I was born.

During that time, my mother took in boarders. We later moved to 416 McKinley Street, which was in North Hibbing. The house wasn't that big, maybe three bedrooms, and it had a little basement. Some of the houses had basements and some didn't. We paid $15 a month to rent our house.

Mom and Dad in North Hibbing

My dad always said, "We've got to get our own home." But it was pretty hard during the Depression to come up with that kind of money.

C.A. Nickoloff had worked for my father in the mines when he first came from Bulgaria. Nickoloff would burn the midnight oil every night, and each payday he would buy a lawbook or a real estate management book. When he came home from work, he would always change into nice clothes.

My father saw that he was ambitious and said to him, "Why don't you think about

Pine Street in North Hibbing before the time the D'Aquilas moved there. Note the buses passing each other. The Hull-Rust Mine is at the end of the street.

getting out of the mine, get out on the street, and find homes for these people who are coming over here? You could take care of their finances for them." And that's what Nickoloff did. He would take care of other miners' finances for them, cash their checks, send money back to the old country for them. He also got into the real estate business.

One day in 1934, my father and I were in South Hibbing, and we ran into Nickoloff. It was just before noon, and the banks were closing at noon because it was Saturday. My dad banked at the First National.

"I've got a house for you, Pasquale," Nickoloff said. "I want you to buy it. It goes tax forfeited at 12 noon today unless you sign the papers. It's really a great house, and you've got to trust me. Take out money right now from the bank."

So my dad withdrew $1,800 right there. Mr. Nickoloff drove us up to the house in North Hibbing because we didn't have a car. The house was at 418 Mahoning Street, and it had been owned by G.H. Alexander. Alexander owned the Mesaba Lumber Company. He was one of the elite of Hibbing, but he had suffered financial losses.

It was really a buy. We had probably the nicest home in North Hibbing and there were many, many nice homes in North Hibbing. It had an amusement room with a wooden dance floor and a cloak room. It had two beautiful glass porches. It had four bedrooms, a fireplace, built-in china cabinets, and chandeliers. It was an elegant home. There also was a really big yard, and my mom would be able to have a much larger garden.

We were very happy with what we saw, and my dad agreed to buy it.

When they bought that home, my dad bought a Montgomery Ward Airline radio. We had an RCA Victor phonograph for the music records. That was it for home entertainment. People just liked to visit each other. It was very unusual if you didn't have two or three Italian families calling on you, or you calling on them on weekends.

If you went into any of these Italian homes, out would come the Italian bread, the cheese and the proscuitto and the wine. The kids mixed in and all hung around. They listened to their parents, and they picked up quite a bit of the heritage.

Winemaking was a big part of North Hibbing. It's sort of like trying to figure out who was the best bocce player, but if my dad wasn't the best winemaker in Hibbing, he was probably one of the two or three best because of that experience he had in Vinchiaturo.

John Fena, a beverage and liquor dealer, used to import the grapes from California to Hibbing to sell to the local people to make wine. My dad would go over and look at the grapes for him. In every railroad car, there had to be a certain kind of wood. It was like a cherry wood. If you took the skin of the grape, and squeezed out the innards, and just brushed it across that wood, the tannic acid in that grape skin would stain the wood. By looking at the stain, a trained eye could determine what the best blend of tannic acid and sugar content would be in order to make the best wine.

My dad would reject the railroad cars until he was satisfied that he had just the right tint. There were times when it wasn't quite up to his standards, but Mr. Fena would say, "I'm not sure I'm going to get another car." And my father would reply, "Okay, I'll take it. Give me a ton and a half."

Winemaking used to be so much fun. At first we didn't have a press, just had big tubs, and we would wear clean, rubber boots. We would squeeze the grapes by stepping on them in our boots. We never used our bare feet which was the way they did it in Italy. Then the presses started to come into existence. My father bought his press from Chicago.

We had the torchio, the wine press, bolted to the floor in the basement. We would put the mash in, and two big steel bars, each moving from the opposite direction, would compress the juice. It would take at least two people, and it would become increasingly difficult as the juice was crushed out of the grape. It was tremendous exercise. One night my brother and I went back and forth 135 times.

You'd either throw away the mash after all the juice was gone, or put it in an open barrel to become what we'd call an aquatiche, or a rose . There was still something left in the mash, and, if you'd add a little water, it would ferment. Today, it's called white zinfandel.

The rest of the juice we'd pour in open barrels and wait for it to ferment with some of the grape skins still in it. Later we would pour it into other barrels, making sure that all the rings around the barrels were waxed. They had to be air tight, and then we would pound the cork into it. The cloak room in our house, when you cut off the heat, became a very cool room, perfect for the cultivation and preservation of wine.

We would make the wine in September or October, but nobody would ever touch it or even sample it until Palm Sunday or Easter Sunday. Then we could start looking to see what we had. My dad would get about three barrels, or about 150 gallons, from a ton and a half of grapes. Sometimes he'd also make a little muscatel, or sweet dessert wine.

Almost everybody sold wine during those times without the blessing of the federal government. Because my dad had a good job in the mine, he was afraid that somebody might try and frame him. So if people came to the house, whether they were good friends or people from the mine, if they wanted to buy wine, he'd simply give it to them.

It paid dividends, because I remember when the Federal agents came in on a raid, and broke up all the barrels of wine in everybody's basement or crawl space up and down the street, our home was the only home on the block that was left untouched. They knew where they were going, and they didn't touch us. They knew dad was "clean."

Can you imagine what that was like for those people when the agent would break up those barrels of wine and it would flow out of the basements? Those were very shallow basements, and the wine would run out in rivers.

My mother's life was her garden. She would tie the bandanna around her head, and would spend most of her days outdoors. She was just a workhorse. She would plant all the Italian spices. She would have potatoes, tomatoes, beans, carrots, beets, cabbage, just about everything you could think of. She would can hundreds and hundreds of bottles that would last us all winter.

She also had chickens. They were thin and had no fat on them because they'd run all the time in a large fenced-in area. Today, they call them free-range chickens. The city didn't have the codes or restrictions then, and there was never any complaint from the neighbors. Sometimes, they'd escape, and I'd have to chase them for two or three blocks before catching them. It would be a disaster if I didn't. If I didn't bring the chicken home, you'd think I'd lost the world. Maybe that's how I became such a proficient runner.

All the women from Park Addition and Brooklyn and North Hibbing, including my mother, would gather at the Farmer's Market.

You hear about how hard it is to find a soup hen today. Well, in those days the farmers would bring the fresh hens into the market. They would bring in eight or ten at a time, and the women each wanted to buy two or three and make up a huge batch of spaghetti sauce or "sugo" and keep it on the ice to where it was virtually frozen. There were no refrigerators.

These women would start arguing. A woman from Park Addition had the head of the chicken, and a woman from Brooklyn would have the feet. They'd both be pulling on it, yelling, "It's mine, it's mine, it's mine."

You had to feel sorry for those poor farmers because sometimes these women would pull the head right off of the chicken. The farmer had to figure out in Solomon fashion whose it was.

That's when my mother started raising her own chickens.

                                                 ುಙುಙುಙ

Hibbing was "The Town that Moved." Before 1920, the mining companies realized that much of the town was actually sitting on top of the iron ore body. Even the part that wasn't would be much too close for blasting and mining.

The companies picked out a spot about three miles south and began laying out a new town. They financed the construction of a new downtown, a new high school, new hotel, new everything. Around 1920, the move was on, and hundreds of buildings were rolled south to the new Hibbing. The old Hibbing became known as North Hibbing, and the new city was called South Hibbing.

The move took years. Even by the time my folks moved to North Hibbing, much of the town had already been moved. Still, into the 1940s, there still was quite a bit left of the old town. It had a self-sufficient business district, its own schools, the St.

Mom and Dad in North Hibbing

Louis County Courthouse, the county garage, and even the Palace Theater so families could go to the movies.

Then came the Dyer Appraisal.

The legislature passed a law allowing the mining company to buy up what was left of North Hibbing. It was an eight-year law, during which the mining company could purchase all the homes. The maximum you could get would be the Dyer Appraisal, named after a local tax appraiser. In the first years, the people probably got 40 percent of the appraisal. But some people, like my dad, waited until the very end. I did the negotiating for my dad. We told them we didn't want money, we just wanted a smaller home in South Hibbing where my folks could be comfortable.

The Dyer Appraisal on our home was $8,800, and I think my dad got $25,000 in 1955. By that time, there were only three or four homes left in North Hibbing. We obtained a lot from U.S. Steel in the Courthouse Addition in South Hibbing, and we hired Erickson Lumber to build a smaller, three-bedroom brick home. I think there was even a few thousand left over to buy new furniture.

A classmate of mine by the name of Clayton Johnson bought our old house and had it moved to some property south of Hibbing. Later, I heard that it burned down.

My dad stands in front of the house at 418 Mahoning Street in North Hibbing. This was the house I grew up in.

ଔଓଔଓଔଓ

My dad was a very gentle man. In an emotional Italian family, I'd have to say he had a sense of inner peace, and he was also the peacemaker. My mother was much more emotional and high strung. My brothers and I would contribute to the conflagrations, but

10

South Hibbing in 1924. Some of the homes were built new, while many others were moved south from the old North Hibbing. The empty lot at front, left, is where the future D'Aquila home was constructed.

my dad would listen. When he spoke he would start with a very soft voice, but then he would elevate it, and he'd finally say, "Shut up." Everything came to a standstill, and you started over again from there.

Both my parents were very religious, and they prayed endlessly. My father was very interested in other people. He was almost saintly in the way he respected and treated people. He and my mom in later life walked to the Italian church every single day. We still have the relics, the prayerbooks, rosaries and scapulars they had. They're worn to a frazzle. They're Scotch taped. They're just like relics you'd want to put in a museum.

I find myself doing the same thing as dad with some of the important prayers I have today. If I lose them I spend hours trying to find them. My days are very, very upset if I don't have those companions with me.

Dad was an incessant reader. When he came home from work, he'd do the chores, either the garden or chopping wood or something around the home. Then he would bathe. When he was ready to relax, he'd light up his pipe and read the Hibbing paper first.

Afterwards, he would have dinner, and it was a ritual to him. He was a little bit on the portly side. The evening meal was a time of reward and a time of togetherness. There was a lot of conversation at that table and a time for a lot of good information that we exchanged

My mom, Concetta, with some of the mushrooms she picked on the mine dumps.

Mom and Dad in North Hibbing

The Hull-Rust Mine just outside of Hibbing is the world's largest open pit mine. It is three miles long, a half mile across, and covers 1,200 acres. Over a billion tons of ore and overburden have been taken out of the Hull-Rust-Mahoning series of mines. At the top, you can see North Hibbing peeking over the edge of the mine. The closeness of the mine and city forced the city of Hibbing to move three miles south.

whether we were alone or had guests or relatives. Then after, before he went to bed, he would read the *Il Progresso*, the Italian newspaper that came in the mail, and that became an everyday part of his life.

    They were a saving people. It's amazing that on a very small paycheck what they were able to save and do. I think those lessons have been lost today. My dad was the one who was very generous, but it was my mom who was the saver. My father would always want to send money back to his brother, Salvatore, and he and mother would have great arguments about that. As I said, my mother's and father's temperaments were completely different. My dad was more of a Dag Hammarskjold, and my mother was more of a Rudy Perpich.

As Hibbing moved south, so did the public buildings, one by one. Hibbing High School was then and still is one of the finest public school buildings in the nation. It was under construction in this photo circa 1920.

My mom was a hard, hard worker and had an incredible drive. She was a beautiful lady. There's one picture I remember seeing of her when she was younger. Many people commented that she looked like Jackie Kennedy. She was thin all of her life. She fed everybody else meat and pasta and vegetables and salad and proscuitto and all, but she ate very little. She'd eat very few desserts, but if she was at someone else's house, she'd eat them by the ton.

She didn't bake much, but she could really bake bread. We tried to get the recipe, but, of course there was no recipe. She could make bread better than any bakery could even think of making. She would get up at 4 in the morning and knead that bread for hours, pound it with her fists. She kept the loaves ready for the oven by covering them with a woolen blanket. Of course, it always had to be baked in the wooden oven.

She loved to pick mushrooms, and she always had her own garden and chickens. Her religion was very important to her. People would ask me how my mom lived and was so healthy for so many years.

I would say, "Well, she never knew about Vietnam, she never knew about the deficit, she never knew about any of these things." All she knew about was her God, her garden and her family. She learned how to dial a phone, and every day she would call her family and find out if they were all right. If her children were all right, and she had gone to church, and there was food on the table, then her world was complete. She died when she was 96.

Mom and Dad in North Hibbing

We spoke both English and Italian with my dad, and always Italian with my mother because she never learned to speak English well. My brothers and I always spoke English to each other.

Chapter Three
GROWING PAINS

I was born in Brooklyn, an old neighborhood on the northeast side of the new Hibbing, but my first real friends were in old North Hibbing — the original Hibbing.

North Hibbing was a unique place, dating back to the 1890s, and the street we lived on, McKinley Street, was a little nation all of its own.

The kids would play all kinds of games on the street including kicking the can and stealing the bacon. We used to take baseballs or tennis balls and throw them over roofs. There would be teams of guys on each side of the roof, and you could throw the ball anywhere along the roof. There had to be an honesty system as to whether you had missed the ball. Of course, if it took a long time coming back, you knew the other team had missed it.

I started my education at the Washington School on Mahoning Street. I knew English pretty well, and it came to me easily. I was always near the top of my class in spelling and math and English.

The McGolrick Institute for Catholic children was right around the corner from our home, and my mother wanted to send me there. But my brother Frank was opposed to it. He said there was enough religion in our house, and he was a firm believer that I should get right into the public system where I was going to have to spend the rest of my life. He didn't want me in a protected environment. I was probably one of the few Catholic kids in that neighborhood who didn't go to the parochial school.

Church was a very, very important part of our lives. The old, wooden Blessed

Growing Pains

Sacrament Catholic Church was only a half-block from our home, and I used to be in the choir at church. Between songs, I'd run down from the choir, and, with Jim Gleason and Joe Dragich, help take the collection.

I started working for money at an early age.

Hibbing began moving south in about 1919, and the process continued for another 30 years or so. As they started to tear down North Hibbing, there were these beautiful, beautiful brick buildings like the St. Louis County Courthouse and all the schools. These bricks were so well-made that they didn't crumble when the buildings were demolished. The Remington Yards would hire kids to clean the bricks for a half cent each. We would do it with a paint scraper and a hammer.

When I started out, I was so careful and methodical, that in the time between school and suppertime, I only cleaned 90 or 100 bricks. I'd tap the mortar off with a hammer or scrape it off. Later I would try to break my own record every day. Pretty soon I was doing 300 to 400 bricks in three hours, and I was able to bring home a few dollars.

You could buy Pocahontas Coal on credit during the Depression. In the early days, I think it was about $10 a ton. My dad had steady employment, but the wages were low. He always paid on the bill, but I think it was years before he fully retired it. He'd give Erickson Lumber and Coal two dollars or four dollars or eight dollars or whatever he could. Those merchants were so great, there were no interest charges. There was trust, and the merchants never lost anything from their customers.

My dad bought me a Montgomery Ward Airline red wagon. Part of the deal was that I was to pick up tar blocks everyday and bring them home. The tar blocks, about eight inches by four inches by four inches, were from the streets in North Hibbing they were abandoning as the city moved south. In the

The great white hunter. I was probably about 14 when I bagged this dangerous predator in the wild country around North Hibbing.

house, you combined those tar blocks with the Pocahontas coal. Two chunks of coal and two tar blocks would keep the furnace going all night. I read once that Jeno Paulucci, Hibbing's most famous entrepreneur, used to scavenge for tar blocks too, but I never saw him out there.

After that I got a newspaper route. The Star Journal of Minneapolis had a prize, a trip to the World's Fair for the person in the state who obtained the most subscriptions. That's probably where my political career began, because I would go from house to house asking people to take the paper. Every week the standings were published in the newspaper, and, lo and behold, with a couple of weeks left in the contest, I was in second place in the state.

I had this scheme. I thought I could enroll some of the older people in town who weren't going to subscribe and pay for the subscriptions myself. It would be worth it because there were only a couple weeks left, and I could win this trip. So I did it. I bought about 24 subscriptions, and I won the contest.

There were some screams when the newspaper people found out how I had won, but there wasn't much they could do about it. The ironic part was when all was said and done, my mother wouldn't let me go on the trip. She thought it was too much for a 13-year-old boy.

I did get my picture in the paper as a consolation prize, and I got to meet Charlie Johnson, the sports editor for the Minneapolis Star, and Halsey Hall, the legendary sports broadcaster for WCCO Radio in the Twin Cities. Hall also wrote a column for the newspaper. Holy Cow, Halsey Hall. I kept up that relationship with Halsey through the years, and he invited me into the booth to watch him broadcast three or four Gopher games. That was an awful lot of fun.

Another way I made money was guiding the tourists that came to the area. By meeting groups early in the morning, I could get more trips during the day. I'd take them to the mines, the high school, the Glass School, or maybe the Memorial Building. People would give you two or three dollars, although some big spenders would toss me a five dollar bill. I remember a fellow giving me $20 one time. I even remember his his name -- Dr. Eastvold from Minneota, Minnesota.

Another tourist scheme involved going to the dentist's office and getting discarded novocaine tubes. I'd crush different kinds of iron ore to get different kinds of colors. I'd call them ore samples, and I sold them for 50 cents a tube. Inside the tube, they'd look just like a rainbow.

My dad was making $8.40 a day as a foreman in the mine at that time, and, so help me, it was not uncommon in those days that I'd come home from tourist guiding, and my mom would say, "Quanta oggi?" (How much today?) and I'd have $20 or so in my pocket from a day's work. Only later could I imagine how it was for dad to have his kid coming home from a day's work with several times as much as he was making. Here my dad had to walk to the mine, two miles every morning, through every

Growing Pains

Hibbing was a city of about 20,000, but the mining taxes paid for magnificent schools and public buildings. Two of the schools I attended, about two blocks from my house in North Hibbing, were the Jefferson and Washington Schools.

The Lincoln School was a marvel of modern architecture and school construction for its time. It had modern science classrooms and dozens of other features schools were lucky to have in the early part of the century.

COUNT THE PICKETS IN THE FENCE

The St. Louis County Courthouse reflected some of the splendor of North Hibbing's architecture. It was one of the last buildings to be torn down when the city moved to its present site.

Andrew Carnegie built dozens of libraries across America, and Hibbing's was one of the most spacious and beautiful. It was close to where I lived, and this was where I spent a great deal of my time in my youth.

19

kind of weather. Sometimes it was 40 below zero. When he got to the mine, he'd have to go down 235 steps. Then, after working all day, he'd have to go up 235 steps and then walk back home two miles every night. My dad never owned a car.

The tourist guiding got to be such a lucrative business that the Chamber of Commerce wanted me to conduct a training program for the rest of the guides. That's how I got involved in the Chamber. I was always working with people much older than I was.

Helmer Olson asked me to join the Junior Chamber, and I went to all the meetings and whatnot. I was on a committee with Olson, Nick Berklacich, Dyke Manella, Alex Steele, Gus Ekola, and John Blatnik when they were pushing for the taconite tax and the creation of the Iron Range Resources and Rehabilitation Commission. By this time I was 16 or 17 years old.

※※※

Very close to my McKinley Street home in North Hibbing were the beautiful St. Louis County Courthouse, the Lincoln School, the Jefferson School, the Washington School, the Palace Theater, the Royal Cash Market, and an eight-block long business district. The area was gorgeous. We had the tourist cabins, the city comfort station, the general headquarters of the Oliver Iron Mining Company, the Andrew Carnegie Library, four beautiful churches, the Catholic school, and Hibbing's only baseball park. It was a tremendous park, and the home of the Hibbing Outlaws. The Outlaws team was made up of guys who didn't sign for the Major Leagues, the holdouts. They would come to Hibbing and the city would pay them. They had an outstanding baseball team.

The baseball park was really something. It had a beautiful grandstand and a well-kept diamond. Way out in right center field was a clubhouse which in later years became a warming shack for an outdoor skating rink. The rink was large with a couple of nets set up for the hockey players. I took a stab at playing hockey, and they assigned me to the goalie position. I didn't do too well. I couldn't skate, but I tried bringing the puck up by myself and, of course, the other team took it away from me and scored right away into the open net. That didn't make my teammates very happy, and I didn't last very long.

When we moved to Mahoning Street, we were only a block from the library. It was always reputed that if I wasn't at the baseball park, I could be found at the library. I can remember Miss Helen Prahl, a wonderful English lady who was the librarian, and Isabel Thouin, her assistant. The library was so refreshing a place, with cork floors, beautiful wooden furniture, and many original painted murals on the walls. Any book that you could get at any library in the world you could get there. It was such a place of meditation and quietness.

Most of us didn't have space in our homes to study, and so we'd go to the library. There were reference books and the Encyclopedia Britannica and the like. There really wasn't anywhere else to go. We were too young for the saloons.

I liked to read Shakespeare. And I like to read biographies, particularly those about the presidents and world leaders. I remember reading about Huey Long and Woodrow Wilson, Teddy Roosevelt and Mussolini. I read Tom Sawyer and Huck Finn and Honore De Balzac. The library had the *New York Times*, the *Christian Science Monitor* and the *London Daily News*, and I would read them as well. There were religious books and lives of the saints, and W. Somerset Maugham. I read John Steinbeck's "Of Mice and Men," and Og Mandino's "The Greatest Salesman in the World." Now and then I would read a best seller if it had to do with business or politics.

Another great book I found when I was practicing for my First Communion was called "Bible History," and I was more than entranced with it. In fact I just devoured it. It contained the Bible stories, all in color pictures. Just like other people read mystery novels, I was mystified by these stories of the Bible.

꽁꽁꽁

One day I was riding my bike, going down the Brooklyn Road from North Hibbing to Brooklyn, and there was a group of boys playing baseball along the road. Mish Sachs was the great recreational director for Hibbing, and he yelled out to me, "Hey kid, what are you doing?" And I said, "I'm just riding my bike." "Well," he said, "we need one more player. Take this glove and go and play first base." That was my introduction to baseball.

I had played unorganized ball many times — the neighborhood pick-up games. But we could never play at the baseball park because that was pretty well watched and protected for only league playing. We would play in the fields, and mostly we would play softball.

I played well enough in that baseball game that Coach Sachs said, "Why don't you try out for the American Legion baseball team?" I did and earned a spot at first base as a reserve. The first year I was very young, and Packy Schaffer was the regular first baseman and Jim Gleason Jr. also played first base. Packy also pitched, and when he did, I'd alternate with Gleason at first base. When the older guys graduated, I became the regular first baseman. For the next two seasons, I batted cleanup. I had a .428 batting average my last year and I tried out for the New York Giants. Their farm team was the Duluth Dukes. Some people thought I had that much ability, and I thought maybe it would work out, but by then I was starting to broadcast athletic events and was getting paid for it. The Dukes' salaries were about $45 a week with the top guy getting $90 a week. I was doing that well without playing baseball, so I decid-

GROWING PAINS

This was the Hibbing American Legion Baseball Team around 1939. I'm the player standing at the far right whose uniform doesn't quite match. I was the youngest player on the team at that time.

ed not to pursue organized baseball.

Our Class B softball team won the state championship. We played a swanky Minneapolis team in the finals, and they almost scared us off the field just with their uniforms. Al Nyberg, our manager and hard-hitting outfielder, was our inspiration.

Al Taddei was on those baseball teams, and he was phenomenal. We didn't have speed guns in those days, but I'm sure he could throw the ball 90 miles an hour. If he had lived in a warm climate, he would have gotten a baseball scholarship and become a Major League star. But all we had were city teams and the American Legion — no high school teams yet. There were no scouts for the colleges.

ℰℭℰℭℰℭ

My political career started in school.

I attended Washington School for the elementary grades and Lincoln School for junior high. In my first try at politics, I ran for president of the seventh grade and was elected. It wasn't easy because there were three or four people running all the time. There were signs and campaigns. I was president of the seventh, eighth, ninth and tenth grades. We really had a machine.

Joe Taveggia, who later became mayor of Hibbing, was the office manager at the school. He became my informal political advisor, at one point telling me to, "Give 'em hell, kid." I'll never forget the ninth grade election. We used to have a monthly assembly with some kind of a presentation. Everybody would go to the school auditorium and be excused from class for an hour or two. So I ran on a campaign that there would be an extra assembly every month. The principal, J.G. Hegstad, called me in after I got elected and said, "How do you expect to do that?"

I said, "I don't know. I made the commitment. I guess I'll have to do it." I told him I would try to arrange to have something. "We'll bring in speakers or we'll do comedy using talent from the school." One time I undertook to do a musical, "Alexander's Ragtime Band." I put together an orchestra, singers and comedians. We did it all with our own class talent, and the show was a barn burner.

When I began high school, my friends urged me to run for class president again. Well, I had been in North Hibbing, but now I was in South Hibbing. The only time I came to South Hibbing was to go to the grocery store with my folks, or to go to church after Blessed Sacrament moved from North Hibbing. The only time I had stepped into the big, beautiful high school in South Hibbing was to attend my brother's graduation.

Hibbing High School was the greatest monument to education built up to that time in any town in America. It was built as a memorial to those who fought in World War I. It cost $4 million to construct, and you could never recreate it these days for any amount of money. This photo was taken about 1923 shortly after it opened. The house we purchased in 1960 is the large, white house just across the street.

Growing Pains

This family portrait was taken about 1943 or so. In the front row, my brother, Frank, is in uniform and Mike is on the right. Mike's wife, Lucy, is in the middle. I must have been about 19 at the time, and I'm standing with my mother, Concetta, and my father, Pasquale.

In 1979, my brothers and I posed for an informal portrait. Mike is at center and Frank is on the right.

I probably went to a few football and basketball games, but I had never walked through the whole high school.

In the election, I ran against students who had enjoyed the same kind of political success I'd had in South Hibbing. I was defeated in both the 11th and 12th grades, and that was the beginning of the realization that I wasn't always going to win in life.

When I got to high school, I started to run into teachers who had taught my brothers. Mike had been an honor student, but he came home in the 10th grade and announced, "I'm not going to go to school tomorrow." My dad said, "What?" He said, "I quit today. I'm going to get a job in the mine. I want to work in the mine, and I don't want to go to school."

My dad couldn't talk him out of it, and he was very disappointed. Mike started as a laborer, and he eventually became chief iron ore sampler for all the Pickands Mather mines. You really could give him credit for prolonging the life of some of the mines because of his knack for mixing ores.

When PM sold all its natural ore mines and switched to taconite, Mike lost his job. Hanna picked him up, and he worked at the research lab at Cooley until he retired.

My brother Frank was very athletic and a very good student. He was the only person I ever knew who earned 12 letters as a regular on the football, basketball and track teams for all four of his high school years. He won the American Legion Award in 1933, which at that time was the only major award at the high school for being the top athlete and scholar. Frank was offered a football scholarship to the University of Southern California, but he decided to hit the books. He went to Hibbing Junior College for two years and then to the University of Minnesota for two years. He then attended St. Olaf for two years and became a classmate and roommate of later-to-be Governor Karl Rolvaag. Frank did post-graduate work at Georgetown University in Washington D.C. and earned his PhD in foreign service. After military service, he joined the Coca Cola Company with Jim Farley. Farley had been the postmaster general under Roosevelt and then had become chairman of Coca Cola. My brother's job was to open up plants in Mexico, Central America and South America.

I ran into teachers in the school who would say to me, "Are you going to be as outstanding as your brother Frank?" I really didn't apply myself in school until the 11th grade when they dropped that challenge in my lap. And then I really tried. There were some students there then who were really brilliant, like John Miettunen, Ben Owens, Jay Shapiro, Keith Blumhardt, Sigrid Bantarri, Connie Nickoloff, Marian Chocos, and Helen Rantala. They all carried 4.0 averages. At times I did too, but not always. I had to make a deal with the teachers. I told them there was no way I could keep up with these people unless they let me do extra work. One teacher, Lillian Hurley, let me do a book report for the class every week, and then there would be a class discussion. It really became an exciting dialogue.

They were tremendous teachers, and I wouldn't trade my high school experience for anything. I was editor of the paper, vice president of the Hi-Y, and was voted the most popular student in the senior class.

☙❧☙❧☙❧

I began doing radio broadcasting during my sophomore year. I was on the track team, and I went out for the high school basketball team and didn't make it. Hud Gelein, who was the coach, told me that if he could have one more on the team, I'd be the one. I felt bad, but it was a good break because as it was I started the next week broadcasting games on WMFG radio. It had its studios in the basement of the Androy Hotel.

I was doing basketball games, and WMFG allowed me to have a program on Wednesday nights at 6:30, prime time, called Sports Chatter.

I had never done hockey, but Hibbing had a semi-pro team called the Monarchs. They were a tremendous team, and they'd fill the arena every single game. They were owned by Sandy McHardy and Alipio Panichi who owned the Monarch Bar on Howard Street. It was a very valuable franchise. There were Canadians playing, and many players who later went on to the big leagues. That's how Bibbs Miller, later a prominent businessman, came to Hibbing.

I was doing the color work for Jack Hirschboeck. Hibbing had tremendous announcers, and Jack was one of them. One night, though, when it came to the end of the first period, Hirschboeck stood up and said, "I'm going down to the Crystal Lounge at the Androy Hotel to see Louis Rocco and get a couple of drinks. You take over. I'm not coming back." And that's how I started broadcasting the hockey games. That was my introduction. Hirschboeck never broadcast another game, and that was my big break.

Later, I had my own color man at the games. His name was Sanford Berman. Later he was known as Michael Dean, who became one of the top hypnotists in the United States. He still performs around the country and returns to Ironworld at Chisholm every year or so.

I used to go up to Ft. Frances with the team. We'd broadcast back to Hibbing on the telephone line. Those were the years when Buhl had two great basketball teams, and so I covered those teams and went down to Minneapolis to the State Tournament with them. They won the state title two years in a row, and my broadcasts were sent out statewide.

I used to try and make the games exciting, especially when Hibbing would play Buhl or Chisholm would play Buhl. One time, Ed Crawford, who owned an electric repair shop, stopped me and said he'd buy me a cup of coffee. He said, "You've given me enough business." I went into his shop and he showed me on his shelf how he had 12 or 13 radio sets that people had wrecked or kicked in while listening to the Buhl-

Chisholm district final game. Buhl was defending its state championship, but was trailing Chisholm in the last minute and Chisholm had the ball. Somehow Buhl pulled off a miracle overtime win and went on to its second state title.

ഇരുഇരുഇരു

I didn't have very many clothes of my own. Instead, I got them from my older brother Frank. I had all his cast-off clothes. He had worked for Macy's in New York and for a men's shop in Washington while going to college, and so he had very handsome clothes. It's ironic that throughout my high school days I was usually named the best dressed because of these hand-me-downs.

ഇരുഇരുഇരു

It was during these high school years that I started my bus advertising business.

I'd seen advertising on street cars and in the buses in the big cities. It wasn't an original idea. One day I stopped up to see Bus Andy. I didn't really know him, and I was a student in high school.

Bus Andy's real name was Andy Anderson, and he was one of the pioneers of the bus industry in America. Anderson was one of the founders of the Greyhound Bus Line that had its origins in Hibbing. Those first buses ran from Hibbing to a little town called Alice which later became the new Hibbing.

The day I went there, he was talking to Gus Dahlner. The two of them owned the Conoco Oil distributorship in town. I said, "Mr. Anderson, I'd like to talk with you. I have a proposal."

The Mesaba Transportation Company lined up its modern buses for a photo. My bus sign business earned me about $500 the first year, and eventually I was making as much as $3,000 a year when I was in high school.

Growing Pains

Introducing the Staff of the New Arrowhead Traveler

S. E. TWIGG

S. E. Twigg is a former mayor of the Village of Hibbing, and has [be]en a printer for many years. [H]e also is president of Hibbing-[V]irginia Typographical Union No. [7]. Mr. Twigg's duties in the [ne]w venture undertaken by the [Ar]rowhead Printers, Inc., will be [to] manage the composing room.

CARL M. D'AQUILA

Carl M. D'Aquila assumes the responsibilities of managing editor of The Arrowhead Traveler. He is a member of many civic organizations, and has had considerable experience in newspaper reporting and editing, as well as radio broadcasting.

JACK FREEDY

Jack Freedy will edit the sports, getting back into this work after an absence of nearly a year. Freedy is an ardent sportsman, and is a veteran newspaperman, having worked for Chisholm and Duluth papers during the past.

JULIE NAESETH

Julie Naeseth takes over as society editor of The Traveler. She will continue to broadcast the program, "Hibbing and the Range in the News," heard each weekday over WMFG at 12:30, presented by the Shapiro Drug Store of Hibbing. Mrs. Naeseth is the wife of Franz Naeseth, now serv-

The Arrowhead Traveler

Published every Thursday by

THE ARROWHEAD PRINTERS
INCORPORATED

CARL D'AQUILA, Editor

Entered as second class matter, February 24, 1944, at the post office at Hibbing, Minnesota, under the act of March 3, 1879.

SUBSCRIPTION RATES - $3.00 PER YEAR EVERYWHERE

30

WHO ARE WE?

The ARROWHEAD TRAVELER is going to be your newspaper. Its interests will be your interests. It is not an experiment, for the appeal of news pictures, human interest and brief, well-told stories will become as apparent to you as it has been to millions of readers in other cities during recent years.

The Arrowhead Traveler was born on Feb. 14, 1944, and I was the editor. The photos above from the first issue show some of the first staff on the newspaper. On the left is the masthead from that first issue. We thought we had a going concern, but newsprint shortages and the difficulty of a weekly going against the established dailies were too much. It folded a few months later.

Count the Pickets in the Fence

Local Help Needed for Our Airport

By Carl M. D'Aquila

Editor's Note—Hibbing's Municipal Airport has made one of the most rapid leaps to success in Aviation during the past several years. Yet, no story has ever been adequately written. With the war training program having been suspended here recently, the editor feels that by writing this feature, he will stimulate enough interest on the part of the community so that the program will be brought back here again. The airport issue has been a "hot" one locally and in Washington, and rather than delve into anything of that nature at this time, this story handles the issue in an accurate, unbiased manner. The pictures in conjunction with the story are published for the first time since they have been taken, and the TRAVELER feels proud in being the first to carry them.

This is one of the first news stories I ever wrote for the Traveler. It showed some of my early interest in the airline industry.

He was impressed that this young lad would come to him like that. He said, "Oh, you have a business proposal. Well, please come in." He treated me very nicely.

He had a very luxurious office. Of course, he had been one of the originators of Greyhound buses, but he had a lot of other interests in town. It was a thriving company. He wore these very lovely suits, and was a very inspiring guy.

I explained my idea to him. I told him it would enhance the look of the buses, and I told him I'd be very discreet. I would only pick upstanding businesses to advertise. "It will give me a chance to earn some money, and it will adorn your buses," I said. "I'll take care of it all."

He said, "Well, you realize somebody has tried that before, and it didn't work out. They never paid me." And I said, "Well, I'll pay you in advance." And he said, "Oh, you will, huh? You'll pay me in advance. Well, are we going to have a contract? My attorney is Vic Hulstrand."

I said, "No, I think I can draw it up myself. It won't cost anything." He said, "Well, draw it up and let me take a look at it. How are you going to do this while you're going to school? The buses don't tie up until midnight. How are you going to get these signs in the buses?" I said, "I'll come in at night. I'll come in at 12:30, and it'll take me a couple of hours, but I'll do it."

He said, "Well, you seem older than your years. I'll take a chance. How much are you going to pay me?" So I told him I'd give him a hundred dollars a year, and I said I'd be totally responsible. He said "Okay." At that time I was doing my tourist guiding business, and I had other jobs. I had plenty of money.

I collected all the revenue from the advertising, but I had to get the signs made up. It was quite a business. Some advertisers wanted double cards, some wanted single cards, some wanted them changed more often than others. If one got dirty or mutilated, I'd

29

have to replace it, but I had very little problem with that. I'd charge more for the ones in front near the clicking machine and the driver, and less for the ones in back. Most buses had 24 signs. The first year, I started out charging $24 a sign, and I promised the advertisers that each had the exclusive rights. I wouldn't take a competitor no matter what happened. Each advertiser had the option to renew every year.

That first year, I made $500 or $600. The signs cost me about $70 from the Jackson Sign Co, and so I made $400 or $500 profit. Business really picked up then, and I started to hear from advertising agencies and companies of national prominence like Bell Telephone. Now I had to pay an advertising agency 15 percent, so I increased the charge to $144 per year.

After the second year, my profits soared into the thousands. I would make as much as $3,000 a year. But Bus Andy never charged me more than $100, and he was very happy.

As the years went by, we became such good friends. I learned so much from him. Fifteen years later, I was elected to serve with him on the Board of Directors of Merchants and Miners State Bank in Hibbing. I was able to repay him in small measure years later by inviting him and his wife on an ore boat trip through the Great Lakes.

During those high school years, I had the bus advertising, I was getting $15 a game broadcasting the games, and $15 a game for umpiring Range League baseball. And I was doing some reporting for the *Hibbing Tribune* and the *Duluth News-Tribune*. I'd get paid by the column inch. I was a busy guy.

※※※※

My first newspaper venture was the weekly *Arrowhead Traveler*. We started it in February, 1944, and I was its editor. It folded several months later, the victim of stiff competition and newsprint shortages.

People might be shocked to go back to the 1940s and read some of my early editorials in the *Arrowhead Traveler*. Some of them just ripped the mining industry leadership.

The mining industry leaders in Cleveland and Pittsburgh didn't sit in the board rooms and say, "We're going to hammer it to those people." But they had some local employees who had autonomy and authority. They were really some rough, medieval, somewhat inhuman characters. They really were.

For example, when they had a blast, rocks would go flying up, and they'd land on somebody's roof. The mining officials would just tell the homeowner that it was an accident. It was too bad. Nowadays, they have regulations, and an insurance man and a government agent would be there in minutes.

The name *Arrowhead Traveler* was not my idea. I gave into Ed Twigg, the old gent from the Typographical Union. He was a linotype operator. He had been mayor. He was the one who picked the name. He was a quiet, humble fellow, always very serious.

I was going to call it *The Range Ripsaw*.

I was a little bit wild. Yes, I was, and I don't deny it for one minute, but I thought I could make a difference and make things better.

Growing Pains

Chapter Four

ON THE CAMPAIGN TRAIL

I guess I have had the political bent all of my life. I remember writing speeches in high school for candidates who were running for city council and school board and so forth. I was doing radio work and I was doing newspaper work, and I realized, as many have today from those two arenas, that you're in the public eye. You have a lot of responsibility, but you also have an image and the respect that maybe you don't deserve.

But people had great faith at that time in people in the media. As I wrote for the newspaper and as I worked on the radio, I was attracting a wealth of friends from all walks of life. Nowadays, people in the media and politicians are both very suspect, but in those days, they still had an aura of respect.

I enjoyed it not only for the popularity, but I had a strong desire to run for public office. Even in my Hibbing High School Hematite yearbook some classmate had written, "I'm sure you'll be president some day."

Now it was 1946, and people along the street began to pick up on my political possibilities, and they would urge me to run.

I had gone to Hibbing Junior College for a year and then to Marquette University for part of a year. I had dropped out when I got the chance to come back and run the St. Louis County Independent, a labor newspaper, while its owner, Oscar Widstrand, was in the Legislature. It was a real opportunity for me, so I moved back to Hibbing.

During that time, I had two expert political mentors. John Slattery, the assistant to the superintendent at the high school, was a political genius. I'd say that Slattery and Art Timmerman, a linotype operator at the Hibbing Daily Tribune and former mayor, were on an altar together, just below the Pope, as far as infallibility of political intuition.

Slattery was relentless: "You ought to run, you ought to run." He started with, "You ought to run for the school board," because he always wanted to get a Catholic on the board. When that didn't work, he encouraged me to run against Elmer Peterson for the Legislature. He just kept after me.

I know that John had became very disenchanted with Peterson, the state representative at the time. Peterson, as stubborn as he was, didn't listen to John. What made it worse was that John had encouraged him to get into politics in the first place. John was a king maker, but then later he became one of the destroyers.

A lot of the Chamber people and the merchants on the street had also tried to talk me into running. I particularly remember one gentleman, Bill Feldman, would pester me everyday saying, "Run for this and run for that, and run for the Senate," whatever office was open. He was very persistent. He was a department store owner, a frugal and conservative guy, but he'd back up what he'd say. He'd reach in his pocket and pull out a couple of hundred dollar bills and say, "Here, come on. I mean it. I want you to run for governor."

There were Morris Zimmerman from Micka Electric and Bill Schirmer from the plumbing business, Mike Marinac and Frank Berklich from the bars, Sammy Edelstein and John Fena from the beer business, the entire radio staff, and George Fisher at the Tribune — they were all great supporters.

A vacancy occurred for a local House seat in 1946 when John Blatnik, who was a state senator at that time, decided to move up and run for the United States Congress. Peterson made his move by vacating his state house seat and running

John Slattery was one of the true geniuses of the Iron Range, often working behind the scenes to accomplish great things. He was not only one of my mentors, but two decades later he also was one of Rudy Perpich's closest advisors early in Rudy's political career.

for Blatnik's seat. It was one of those rare political opportunities.

I decided to give it a try.

There was a lot of interest in Peterson's seat, and there were a lot of qualified candidates. This was the 60th legislative district, and the voters elected two House members and one Senator. At that time, there were 135 members in the Minnesota House and 67 in the Senate.

Ironically, the other House seat was occupied by the man who had hired me for the newspaper job, Oscar Widstrand. I had really appreciated the job and the exposure that Widstrand had provided me. We had a very nice relationship. I left him on good terms, and we were very friendly. Because there were two House seats open, I really didn't look at it as running against Oscar. I was just running for one of the two positions.

In fact, I had no visions of ever defeating Widstrand. He had been in for many years. When we started out, he was going his way and I was going my way. It was only later on, when he started feeling the pressure, that he started attacking. He took a pretty severe shot at me, and so we decided to fight back.

I looked back through my papers and I found a letter Widstrand had written earlier saying what a great guy I was and what I had done for his newspaper. So we ran an ad saying. "What's different now than it was then, Mr. Widstrand? What has he done to change your mind except to file against you?"

One of the major attacks against me during the campaign concerned my military record. I had been rejected for military service because of a bladder problem. I had really wanted to get in and serve as a journalist. I wanted to be in camp newspapers and radio, and I'm sure I would have been.

So then I volunteered to go over with the 1391st Air Force as an expediter and possible interpreter. I went to Europe as a civilian and spent about 13 months overseas. I took care of mail, and when we got to Italy I was the one who did all the interpreting. During the

WEDNESDAY, APRIL 24, 1946.

Legislative Post Sought By D'Aquila

Carl M. D'Aquila, Hibbing, is a candidate for election as state representative from the 60th legislative district. He is the son of a well-known pioneer miner. This is his first bid for a political office.

D'Aquila has been affiliated with the newspaper fraternity and is now engaged in advertising and promotion work. In addition, he has been a radio sports broadcaster since 1941. During World War II, he served with the War Department and was in the European Theater of operations for one year.

He is a member of the Knights of Columbus, Elks, Redmen, Hibbing Municipal Athletic Association, and the Minnesota Editorial Association. He is a former secretary of the Junior Chamber of Commerce.

In announcing his candidacy, D'Aquila said, "The young people of today must take an active part in the future legislation of our state, and I enter this race with open mind, vision and courage, and will be guided in my thought and action only by sound and easily understood principles."

The first story in the Hibbing Daily Tribune about my candidacy.

On the Campaign Trail

One of the candidates for the legislative seat in 1946, Mel Clark of Chisholm, was a veteran of World War II, and he attacked my campaign because he thought I was claiming veteran status. I never had, and we ran this advertisement to meet his charges head on. It seemed to work.

House campaign, I never claimed any kind of service connection. I never said a word about it.

Mel Clark, a candidate from over in Chisholm, decided to take a shot at me. He had based his campaign strictly on his military record. We did an ad that was just tremendous. The headline on the ad was "A Humble Apology!" The ad said I didn't have to go, but I went anyway and went through the same dangers as everybody else. And in the process, the ad said, I had waived any rights to any military benefits.

The ad was the idea of Timmerman. He was clever. He called up and laughed and said, "Kid, it's all over. Rest in peace. Mel Clark's done." I said, "Art, how can you say that?" He said, "Carl, I've got veterans all around me here at the paper and in the linotype shop. You should hear them talk. You'd think this guy Clark had won the war all by himself."

It was such a good ad, that after it was published, people surmised I might get 93 percent of the vote.

We had a lot of help in the campaign. We had membership cards with our goals and aims on the back. We sold these memberships all across the Range. We'd sell them for one, two, three, five dollars or whatever -- anyone who wished to contribute. We made a lot of money that way. We also had some substantial contributions. These days you read about all the PACs, but in those days there were only a few and they weren't really legal. There were the beer dealers and the liquor dealers, and Minnesota Power and Light always took an interest and made contributions. There was the mining industry and there were the unions. But I would say that about 80 percent of any candidate's funds came from private contributions in those days.

Kenneth Pederson, the high school principal, used to say that even my high school campaigns were flashier than anybody else's. We probably spent about $5,000 that year in the legislative race. That was a lot of money then. I think the job only paid $2,000 a session. But we had hundreds and hundreds of contributors.

People really took an interest in the campaign. When we had a debate at the Little Theater in the Hibbing Memorial Building, it was jammed. The Range communities were politically vital, and people turned out. I was a pretty good speaker; I guess God gave me that gift.

I had the capability of doing all my own writing, but my friends, supporters and I would get together to talk things over. After those meetings, I wrote all my own speeches. I think you could take those speeches today and not change them very much and get elected on them. They were that good. I spent hundreds and hundreds of hours on them.

But the newspaper ads and all the rest of the planning and the strategy were done by Timmerman. He had one of the most strategic political minds I've ever seen in my life. He was cagey, smart — he could plan a military movement. And I really liked him because he never blew smoke. I'd come to him with concerns and worries, and he'd say, "Forget it," and he'd laugh like heck. He was an amazing, amazing guy. His perception was tremendous.

Aldo Boria was my able campaign manager. He was also a great friend. He was the assistant manager at the Androy Hotel and he was the best man at my wedding. Aldo

The Iron Range had a large Finnish population, and they were very conscientious voters. There were people who even thought D'Aquila, pronounced DAK-a-la by some, was a Finnish name.

On the Campaign Trail

A VOTE FOR D'AQUILA IS A VOTE FOR...

- State Bonus for World War II Veterans.
   - Promotion of New Industries for our District.
- Adequate Housing.
   - A Sound Farm Program.
- Improved and Increased Social Security, Old Age Pensions, Health Insurance.
   - Continued Experimentation of Low-Grade Ores.
- Highway and Road Improvements.
   - Protection of Labor Rights. Better conditions for the working man.
- Extensive Rehabilitation and Conservation Program.
   - Increased Interest in Fish and Game Conditions.
- Better Educational Features for Teachers.
   - More Cooperation Between State, County, Township, City and Villages.
- A Closer Union Between our State Representatives and the People.

This was the back page of the major campaign pamphlet we issued during my first election. I stood for all the right things. It was interesting that we listed experimentation with low-grade ores. It was another decade before a working taconite plant was built on the Range. I was a little ahead of my time on that one.

had been one of the main forces in my decision to run. "Why don't you run? Why don't you run? You're yellow. I'll help you," and so forth.

Helmer Olson from the chamber, Alex Steele from Charleson Mining, Lawrence Pervenanze from Buhl, Andy Babbini from Mt. Iron, and Doctor William Heiam and E.P. Drummond from Cook all helped me a great deal.

Of course, some people thought I was too young. I was 21 years old when the campaign got started, and I didn't turn 22 until August 1946 just before the primary. Despite my youth, all the newspaper and radio work that I'd done, all the chamber work, and my longtime association with older people, gave me and my supporters the confidence that I could do the job. I think the only fear was, and I heard it from friends as well as foes, that once I was elected I might not be able to handle it with all those sharpies. Those veteran legislators would be much older, and they'd either take me on or take me under their wing and so on. Some people admonished me that I was too young, and that I'd never put up with that kind of pressure. Others, who were friends, were just saying, "Please be careful. Because if you embarrass yourself, you're going

> November 16, 1946
>
> Honorable Carl M. D'Aquila,
> Representative 60th District,
> Box 679,
> Hibbing, Minnesota.
>
> Dear Representative D'Aquila:
>
> I want to sincerely congratulate you on your election as Representative.
>
> We will probably be facing one of the most difficult legislative sessions in the history of the state. I am extremely anxious to work with all members of the Legislature cooperatively, for a constructive program of legislation for the benefit of all of our people.
>
> I look forward to meeting each member of the Legislature personally and getting his views.
>
> Sincerely yours,
> Luther W. Youngdahl
>
> LWY:OE

This was one of the first letters I got after my election in 1946. Governor Luther Youngdahl was known as the "Crime Buster."

to embarrass us too, and the whole area."

Part of the problem was that Billy Berlin from Buhl had been in the House as a young man (not as young as I was, but pretty young). He had joined the Conservatives. He was a really flashy guy, always in the papers. Bill Berlin ended up being very successful in the legislature, but one night he ended up in a fight on the Washington Avenue Bridge at the University of Minnesota with Larry Armstrong, the Gopher hockey coach. It wasn't a very politically astute move because of the significance of hockey in the region and the respect for the Gophers. He was just a marked man from that point on. He never politically recovered from that fight.

In addition to the newspaper and radio advertising, I chose to go house to house.

On the Campaign Trail

I door-knocked in Hibbing, Chisholm, Buhl and Mt. Iron. It was interesting because although we didn't plan it that way, I'd be campaigning somewhere and John Blatnik, who was running for Congress, would end up on the same block. Some people assumed that we were running together, and I really profited from it. It helped him, too, with my supporters.

One of the issues at that time was the direction of my political leanings. Some people classified me as a Republican, but I'd never been to a partisan meeting of any group at any time. By law the legislature was then nonpartisan, and a candidate was not allowed to even use party affiliation in advertising. The only acceptable designation was "conservative" or "liberal."

When I ran that first time I felt there was much to be done on the Iron Range particularly in the areas of education, highways, conservation, and, of course, mining taxation. I didn't know there was anything like taconite on the horizon, but I knew there needed to be a definitive tax policy that would be fair in order to attract the type of investment it would take to save the mining industry.

I promised that I would caucus with whatever group was in the majority. The conservatives -- the Republicans -- were greatly favored to organize the House. Many people assumed I was a Republican, and I was labeled that way.

The election was a lot of fun. In the end, I took first place. Widstrand came in second and was also elected. After I won, I went back to thank everybody, to all the fire halls and coffee shops and everywhere.

I felt that for the first time in many, many years there had been a true grassroots election. You might have to go back to when Vic Power and John Gannon used to have fights for the mayoralty of Hibbing. In those days, it was the mining industry versus the public, and they had some great battles.

I felt it was a mandate of an election. I realized that the older people had joined hands with the young people, and everyone had come together. There wasn't anywhere we didn't carry. It was an awesome responsibility.

I was determined not to fail. I was driven to make my mother and dad proud. This opportunity had come to me. It was a gift from God. I didn't do this by myself. Whatever qualities I had came from my birth, from my upbringing, from the people who had worked with my father, from the people who had lived with us, the people I had met in school, people who had worked in the election. I had a tremendous responsibility here to succeed, and much of that came from my mother and dad who kept after me to do well. I'd never think to let them down.

I was very careful not to skip anybody with my thank yous. The pronunciation of my name in those days was nearly always DAK-il-a, and when I went up to Cook to see Mike Sorvari, a department store owner, he said, "Am I a happy man. It's about time we elected a good Finlander."

Chapter Five

THE BEST ROOM IN ST. PAUL

When I first got to St. Paul, I made arrangements to stay at the Ryan Hotel on Sixth and Robert. It was *the* political hotel. There was some activity at the St. Paul Hotel and the Lowry Hotel, but most of the action, when people came in from Rochester, Mankato, Duluth or the Iron Range, was at the Ryan. It had that atmosphere. It was an old, gracious hotel with the high ceilings and beautiful rooms. The Ryan Hotel was right in the heart of the downtown, less than a mile from the Capitol.

I got in about a quarter to five the first day I arrived, and Henry Horowitz, a former legislator who was the owner, said, "Oh, we've been waiting for you. I'll take you to your room." I said, "Oh, that's all right, I can find it for myself."

He said, "No, I'll take you to your room because I have to tell you that you owe this room to my friend, Mr. Quigley." Roy Quigley was the owner of the Androy Hotel in Hibbing.

He took me up to Room 443, just off the elevator. I opened the door. It wasn't a room, it was a suite. The ceilings were about 14 feet high. There was a huge fireplace in the living room. The bedroom came equipped with its own bar. The elegant bathroom had a heated toilet seat and a telephone next to the toilet.

Horowitz said, "It's yours." And I said, "No, wait a minute, I have to pay for this." He said, "Oh, you're going to pay for it, but it will just be the regular price for a room, $140 a month. Listen, we always favor somebody with this room, and there are going to be a lot of Range people down here, and you're going to bring me a lot of business."

41

The Best Room in St. Paul

The Ryan Hotel in St. Paul was one of the grand hotels of the Midwest. Quite a few of the rural legislators stayed here, and it was a hotbed of political activity. Below is the Ryan Hotel lobby, with all its grandeur.

Well, I didn't know it then, but that room became Range headquarters, and headquarters for a few other people as well. There probably was as much legislation passed at the Ryan Hotel at the end of each day as there was at the Capitol during the day.

I hadn't been there very long when Sixth District Judge Mark Nolan walked in to my room. He was a former legislator from Gilbert. He said, "Well, you've got my old haunt here. This is really great. This is where everything takes place. This will be the gathering spot."

Nolan was something, a gigantic guy who smoked a huge cigar and was a prolific orator. Everybody liked Mark Nolan. He represented the district judges in legislative matters, and he was often in St. Paul from his home in Duluth.

Oftentimes, I would come back at the end of the day, and Mark Nolan had gotten the key and was up in my suite. And he'd say, "How are you? I've been waiting."

In those days the joke was that, if legislators were going to get a payoff, it would be delivered in black bag thrown over the transom into the room. Mark Nolan would laugh and say, "I've been here almost three hours and nothing's come in over the transom. It's certainly not like the old days. This Youngdahl bird is putting the brakes on everything." Luther Youngdahl was the crime-busting governor.

That was quite a room. In fact, all the legislators from Southern Minnesota used to think I must be quite a comer to get the favored room.

༄༅༄༅༄༅

The first session opened the fourth of January, 1947. I went down on the train. I guess maybe I was really following the legislative directive that said at the time that, in addition to the salary of $500 a month for each of the four months of the session, the only other benefit was one round trip from your hometown, by rail, to the capital and back. I didn't have a car, and so I took a train down from Hibbing through Duluth to St. Paul.

During the campaign, I had bought an old Stutz. That was our campaign car, but we got rid of it after the election. I wish I had it now because it would really be a vintage collector car.

At the Capitol I usually walked from the Ryan Hotel where I was staying, or I took cabs.

I needed a car after I had been in St. Paul for a while, and some people from Hibbing put me in touch with Glen Atcheson, the executive secretary of the Minnesota Automobile Dealers Association, one of the more prominent lobbying groups. Cars were hard to get in those days.

He brought me a sales brochure, and I looked at it. I picked out a Chevrolet. He said, "Okay, we'll see that you get a good deal." The car was delivered to Hagan's Chevrolet in Hibbing, and I think I paid about five percent more than dealer cost.

The Best Room in St. Paul

There was no skulduggery or anything like that. It was enough that they got me a new car in those days when they were in such short supply.

☙☙☙

In January 1947, Dr. George Young owned WDGY. He came to me and said, "I've talked to the Speaker of the House, Larry Hall, and he said you have a radio background. How would you like to do a radio show called 'Your Legislature?' You can do interviews and do a talk show, and you can do it right from inside the Capitol. You can leave the floor twice a week and go upstairs, and we've a studio there that used to be a janitor's room. We'll just show you how to operate the whole unit. And if you need help, we'll get you an engineer."

This was still the first day of the session, so I said, "Well, why don't we wait a couple of weeks and see how everything works out. Let me see what my committee assignments are. Besides, I want to talk to Mr. Hall about it."

Hall was agreeable to the idea, so that also came my way.

I didn't know where to sit on my first day. I was looking around and looking around. I knew it would be down front because the incumbents got all the seats in the back. They liked to sit where they could watch everything going on. And they could leave the chamber if they wanted to without being noticed.

George Leahy from Maple Plain was the chief clerk and he noticed me standing there. He said, "Are you looking for your seat?" I told him I was. He said, "You sit right there," and he pointed to one of the two seats in the front row. I told him he must be joking. But that's where it was, on the right side, right in front. That was an interesting seat because the rules committee met just outside that door, the retiring room was just to the right, and the bathroom

The Minnesota Capitol in St. Paul

was over to the left. I could see anybody who was going into the retiring room and who was doing what. It was the best seat in the whole chamber.

It was the second or third day when Governor Youngdahl called me down and said, "I've selected you as one of the five new people who I think can give the state a clean, breath of fresh air and who can carry my legislative program. Would you entertain that?"

I told him I thought it would be a privilege.

One of the other freshmen legislators in that group was P.K. Peterson who later was mayor of Minneapolis.

There were also a couple of ministers in that legislative session, and one of them, Rev. Clarence Langley of Red Wing, sat right across from me. I have to thank Rev. Langley because he took an interest in me and warned me about getting into excessive drinking. There were six or seven hours of lobbying and dinners and things like that every night. It went on and on and on. Many times, I didn't come home for weekends.

Several of those people counseled me to be temperate with alcohol. I think I was very fortunate in that respect. There were so many eyes on me that one stumble, and it would have been the end.

It wasn't every freshman representative who had his own radio show in the Twin Cities. I was a little hesitant about starting this, but the House leadership gave me the go ahead.

After the election it turned out that the legislative mix was about two-thirds conservative and one-third liberal. So I caucused that way. I will admit that once I got down to St. Paul, I found that the majority of those conservatives were identified as Republicans. There were people like Roy Dunn, who was a masterful majority leader and a man who got things done. They could use a man like that in Washington today.

He just ran the House like a disciplined ship. Dunn was a big guy, about 6-4, and he weighed about 235 lbs. He commanded a lot of respect and attention. He wasn't a comedian in any sense, just totally professional, honest and ethical.

Nobody from the Range had had much political clout in the legislature for some time. The conservatives at that time wanted to recognize and appreciate what the people had done by sending someone down who would be reasonable. They gave me some very, very good committee assignments. I was in the power structure with a vice-chairmanship of a committee during my very first session.

After a couple of weeks, I got the radio show started on WDGY. I would squeeze into that former janitor's room above the legislative chamber where we had set up the studio. We identified the issues and interviewed legislators. The program was advertised every week in the St. Paul newspaper. Part of the draw for the show was my age. There was a certain amount of glamour that went with the title of "Baby of the Legislature."

I particularly remember one man who took a liking to me. He was the head of the Associated Press Bureau. He checked with me every day before he checked with Roy Dunn or the Speaker of the House. His name was Jack Mackay, the father of Harvey Mackay, who owns the prosperous envelope company and has written all the inspirational books. Harvey's the fellow who tries to save the major league sports in Minneapolis.

Even though I had joined the conservatives, that didn't stop the liberals from trying to bring me into their fold. George Teller and the Steelworker union members came to me and said, "If you'll join the liberals next session, we'll make sure you get re-elected. And we'll run you against Blatnik for Congress. We'll dump John." Now John was a rising star, and I had great faith in John. He went on to have an outstanding career. He was a Godsend for our area.

At that time, though, Blatnik was friendly with a couple of men who were being watched. They were suspected of being "fellow travelers" with the Communist Party. There was a vicious rumor going around the Eighth Congressional District that John was a fellow traveler. It's important to remember that it was the Eighth District that elected John T. Bernard to Congress, and he was an avowed socialist. When the

Congressman John Blatnik was a rising star in national politics when I was in the legislature.

Congress voted on the Spanish Embargo in the late 1930s, the vote was 530 to one, and that one was John T. Bernard.

For a time, Blatnik was being painted with this brush, as were many innocent people in the post-war era. Mesaba Park outside of Hibbing, near where Gus Hall, the head of the American Communist Party, grew up, was considered the communist headquarters on the Range. Well, when John spoke there it was like bringing Franklin Roosevelt and Jesus of Nazareth together on the same night. You couldn't get a parking spot for miles. People made assumptions, but John was no more of a fellow traveler than the man in the moon. John was a total American, an honest and popular war hero.

Anyway, a lot of the union people wanted to abandon him, but I said, "No, I won't do that. I'm not going to change," and I wouldn't go against John. John and I talked about it, and it was wise on both our parts that it never happened. Labor was so powerful in those days that it could have been done, but I just wasn't interested. I wanted to get the job done where I was. I also felt that I didn't want to stay there for a long time. I wanted to get on and do other things. If the state senate job came along, fine, but I didn't have to be there.

It was a great, great experience that first session. Youngdahl was a national craze. He was a purist and his brother was the great minister, Reuben Youngdahl of Mt.

The Androy Hotel was where much of business of Hibbing and Range took place. The Roundtable met for lunch everyday in the dining room. You can see the sign on the side of the building that indicated the studios for WMFG Radio. I spent many hours in those studios. The Androy was the finest hotel north of the Twin Cities for many years and is now a senior housing complex.

47

THE BEST ROOM IN ST. PAUL

Olivet Lutheran Church in Minneapolis. The governor came in on a white horse to clean up crime. He brought about the first mental health program in the nation, and I was part of the team that carried his bills and the bills of the League of Women Voters. I had some very good exposure. By coincidence, the first director of the mental health program in Minnesota was Dr. Ralph Rosen, a Hibbing native.

I never really found my age to be a deficiency in the legislature. I was accorded respect. Several times I was called upon to preside over the House. But all the while, I could feel the undercurrent of the union movement and the movement of the Democratic-Farmer Labor Party and its plans to take over the legislature.

I think the state attracted a better caliber of legislator when it was a citizen legislature. Very few stayed beyond a handful of terms. The average lawmaker would serve two or three terms and then go back to the farm or wherever, and somebody else would serve. You really had a better legislature.

Hall, the Speaker of the House, befriended me. In fact, that's why he gave me that seat right down in front. Every now and then, when the action got hot and heavy, he'd take me aside and ask, "How's it going down there? What do the new guys think?" We became very close.

☙❧☙❧☙❧

The Range people were always big letter writers. My box was often full, and the legislative postmaster would have a big bundle of letters with a rubber band around them and even a few more on the side. It was difficult at that time to answer every letter because the legislature was run so frugally; there were only about 10 women in the stenographers pool for all the House members.

I'd do a lot of memorizing and notes and then do a whole barrage of letters all at one time. But I dictated every one or would write them out longhand while listening to debates on the floor. There was no such thing as mimeographing letters and sending them off to everybody. And I paid my own postage.

☙❧☙❧☙❧

I was the youngest legislator ever elected at that point. The research was done by Jack Mackay. I haven't tracked it since then.

When Dolores and I were married in January of 1949, we went to Chicago for our honeymoon. On our way to Duluth, we had an escort from the State Highway Patrol between Cotton and Duluth. At Duluth, we stayed at the Hotel Duluth, and we got up the next morning at 4 a.m. to go to mass. Our train to Chicago didn't leave until 11 p.m. that night, and so we were pretty tired when we got into Chicago Monday morning.

I really wanted to go down to the radio studio and be part of Tommy Bartlett's "Welcome Travelers" show. They had a sign up sheet to allow guests to write down something interesting about themselves and appear on the show. I put down that I was the youngest legislator in the history of Minnesota.

Well, Dolores couldn't believe this. We'd just come off the train, and we hadn't even had breakfast, and I was hauling her to the radio show. She was ready to take her bags and go back home. She was very, very, very unhappy.

We got on the show, though, and were interviewed by Tommy Bartlett. We were given 12-place settings of Sterling silver tableware and dinner for two at the Shangrila Restaurant.

I haven't checked since that time if anybody has beaten my youth record. To the best of my knowledge, I'll stand by the fact that I was the youngest legislator — and by considerable years.

In order to keep in contact with the folks back home, I conceived the idea that it would be nice to have an office in downtown Hibbing where people could see me, and I could address their problems.

The office was above Teske's Jewelry Store in the Congdon Building. Louie Nides had the New York Life insurnace agency, and he said, "I'd love this. I've got an empty desk in there. You can have that, and when people come in to see you, they can see me too. We'll both benefit."

Down at the end of the hallway was the law firm of Hulstrand, Abate and Wivoda. Vic Hulstrand was a very popular county commissioner, Jimmy Abate was the lawyer for the Public Utilities Commission and the city, and Roland Wivoda was a high school classmate of mine.

We used to have lunch down at the Androy Hotel at the Roundtable, and one day Joe Taveggia, who later became mayor of Hibbing, said to me, "You know, Vic Costanzi came to see me. I do his income tax. He wants a liquor license, so I told him to see you and Hulstrand. I told him it should be a snap with you two guys." Costanzi wanted a license for a small township about 40 miles south of Hibbing called Elmer.

The county board had told Costanzi that it couldn't do anything about a liquor license without a legislative act. As a result, Costanzi came to see me in my Hibbing office. He was wild. "I'm going to do something pretty soon. I'm not going to take it much more. I want a liquor license and nobody can give me a good reason why I shouldn't have one. Somebody's going to get hurt."

I told him that if there was anything I could do, I would do it, "But believe me when I tell you that it's not the prerogative of the legislature, it's the province of the county board. Why don't you go down the hall and see Vic Hulstrand? I just left there a few minutes ago. I know he's there. Go down the hall and see him. Don't let him fool you, he can do it."

So Costanzi went down the hall, and I left. I didn't hear anymore about it. That night, the Golden Gloves were slated at the Memorial Building and I was broadcasting the fights for WMFG. Al Krueger, who ran the J.C. Penney Store, came over and said, "Say, did you hear about Costanzi?"

I said, "No, I haven't heard anything."

He told me that Costanzi had gotten his gun and had shot the entire town board at Elmer. He killed five people and then killed himself.

It was the intermission of the fight, and I turned and Alipio Panichi was sitting behind me. Alipio had no great love for Costanzi, and he also had a grudge against the Town of Stuntz Board for some reason. Stuntz Township surrounded Hibbing.

"Alipio, did you hear what happened to Costanzi?" I asked. He said, "No, what did that son of a bitch do now?" I said, "He shot the whole town board at Elmer this afternoon. He killed the whole town board over this liquor license."

He said, "No. You're telling me the truth? You kidding me?" I said no. Alipio thought about it for a minute, and then he said, "Geez, that's too bad. He shot the wrong board."

Chapter Six

The Politics of Losing

Year after year, our Range lawmakers would come home and say, "Well, we couldn't get it done because of those darn legislators from the Cities," or "We got hurt again by those darn legislators from southern Minnesota." They'd say that people wouldn't help them, and that other legislators were against the Range. That really bothered me.

I felt I was going to have to do what it took, whether that meant joining those people, or using diplomacy or trading issues. I was determined to have a successful time in office.

I have to give tremendous credit to Fred Cina, to Tom Vukelich, to Elmer Peterson, to the Range legislators who were there. These men were on the other side of the fence, but they never had any animosity toward me until the party leaders decided they had to get rid of me a few years later. We worked in harmony. They helped me and I helped them. I can't help but think about today's problems. If the Range had one person on the other side — if we had both sides covered — it would work so well. I don't think there was a delegation anywhere in the state that had the batting average that we in St. Louis County and Itasca County had in those days.

At that time, we had a couple of legislators from the Range who were anti-mining. And, of course, there were a couple from southern Minnesota from the conservative Republican ranks who also opposed the industry. Both factions wanted to raise the mining taxes beyond reason. I was a member of the subcommittee on iron ore taxes. It was a five-member committee and only two of us were from the north, A.B. Anderson of Duluth and I.

House Aide Takes Solon To Committee

D'Aquila Made To Vote To Break Tie

In one of the most unusual incidents in the history of the Minnesota Legislature, a state representative was returned to a House committee room by the sergeant-at-arms today to force him to vote to break a tie deadlock.

The legislator involved is Rep. Carl M. D'Aquila of Hibbing.

A member of the taxes committee, D'Aquila refused to vote to break a 14-14 tie that deadlocked the committee on consideration of a bill to reduce aviation gasoline taxes.

While the committee clerk repeatedly called his name, D'Aquila paced the floor, wiping his forehead with a handkerchief.

"I move that someone get his wife to order him to vote," jokingly advised Rep. A. L. Bergerud of Minneapolis.

(D'Aquila's wife is a telephone messenger in the House. They were married at the beginning of the session.)

Suddenly, D'Aquila left the committee room.

"I move to adjourn," yelled Rep. Edwin Meihofer of St. Paul.

"You're out of order," ruled Rep. Fred Schwanke of Deerwood, committee chairman.

"Get the sergeant-at-arms and have him bring D'Aquila back here," Schwanke then directed.

In a few minutes, C. R. Bjornson of Minneapolis, sergeant-at-arms, returned to the room with D'Aquila in tow.

Again the clerk called D'Aquila's name.

"Aye," voted D'Aquila.

And the meeting adjourned.

REP. CARL M. D'AQUILA

This was one of the more bizarre events of my second session. The vote concerned a tax on aviation gasoline. To vote against it was to support the union position. To vote for it was to favor the airlines. I wanted to support aviation, particularly keeping Northwest Airlines in Minnesota. I also had worked closely with the unions. It was a no-win situation for me, and I asked the committee chair that I be excused. He agreed, and I left the chamber. That didn't solve the problem of the tie vote, though, and they came and got me. I had Fred Schwanke flip a coin to decide which way I would vote. I told him that "heads" and I would vote yes, and "tails" and I would vote no. It came up heads, and I voted yes for the airlines.

(St. Paul Pioneer Press clipping)

I remember that in both sessions I cast the deciding vote to not increase iron ore taxes. The debate on the floor was very, very intense. I argued that we were taxing the mining industry onerously, more than any other industry in the state. We were virtually exterminating them. The other side subscribed to the theory that it was a depleting resource that would soon be gone, and we should get what we can. The southern Minnesota legislators also argued that it was a resource that belonged to everyone in the state, not just the people from the Range.

The leader of the debate in opposition was a Patrick Henry orator who was really a match for me. I had great respect for him. It was Robert Sheran of the Gallagher law firm in Mankato. He later became Chief Justice of the Minnesota Supreme Court. Most of the DFLers on the Range supported no increase. There were a couple from Duluth who were opposed.

Another one of my arguments at the time, and this was long before Dr. E.W. Davis developed taconite, was based on the story I got from various sources that there was a big, big project pending in the Hibbing area. In fact, in my first session, I carried the legislation that exchanged the lands between the Ontario Mining Co., the predecessor of Hibbing Taconite Co., and the State of Minnesota. It made it all possible by giving them the room for tailings ponds. That's how far in advance they were always operating. This was the 1947-49 era, and Dr. Davis didn't make the breakthrough that developed the taconite process until 1950.

Somebody said I looked like Benito Mussolini in this photo, with the wheat shock in my hand. Actually, we were presenting an award to Earl Guentzel as the top farmer in a Veterans Administration program. County Commissioner Vic Hulstrand is at the left. The safari helmet was a nice touch.

The problem with taconite is that it's a very hard rock, unlike the soft natural ore we were used to mining. And it contains considerably less iron than the red ores. It would take a real technological breakthrough to get a usable amount of iron ore out of the flinty taconite.

Dr. Davis of the University of Minnesota made that breakthrough and is remembered as the father of taconite, but Erie Mining Co., Fred DeVancy and others had been working on it for many, many years as well. We all knew the breakthrough was com-

George Fisher, the editor of the Hibbing Daily Tribune, presented me with an award in early 1949 as the Jaycees most outstanding young man. Fisher was president of the senior Chamber of Commerce.

ing. John Blatnik knew it back in 1941 when he passed the original taconite tax which was only five cents a ton. It was an inducement to show the mining industry that it would not be treated as it had been under the iron ore taxes.

Dr. Davis was a kind, softspoken man. He was humble, but he was a genius. Davis didn't enjoy the public part of his role in advancing taconite. Moreover, he was confident that the whole process would succeed if people would just keep the politics out of it.

At the same time, Davis was exciting everyone about what taconite could mean for the Range. The transition between natural ore and taconite, though, was frightening.

My fear was that if iron ore passed out of the picture and the industry moved on to taconite, the legislature would just pass on the same tax obligations to the taconite industry and dwarf it before it had a chance to grow. But we were able to keep the taconite tax at the five cent level during my time in the legislature. The University of Minnesota made four or five replicas of the famous Lynn Pot, historic in the development of steel, and they gave one of them to me in recognition of having contributed greatly to the advent of taconite. Later, the pot was stolen from my desk.

I was very fortunate in both sessions to keep those iron ore taxes down and signal the industry that we really wanted them to develop taconite.

Another major accomplishment was handling the governor's bills on public housing and mental health. I sponsored a bill providing housing for the homeless. Even in the late 40s, there were people on Hennepin and Nicollet Avenues in Minneapolis who were homeless. Of course, it's a problem that's still with us and always will be.

Another accomplishment was the legislation that established the University of

Minnesota Duluth. A.B. Anderson of Duluth and I authored the bill. As it turned out, this may have been the most far-reaching law I authored. UMD is a prestigious university and has developed many great graduates in many fields. I recall how difficult it was to pass this bill. There was serious opposition from the Twin Cities business community, and very intense lobbying and opposition from those within the University of Minnesota and its Board of Regents. If I revealed all we had to go through to get a majority of the lawmakers on our side, it would be a long story indeed.

I also authored a bill that allowed the municipalities in the state to get a share of the liquor and cigarette taxes. I then sponsored legislation that set the closing time for Minnesota bars at 1 a.m., and I was a co-sponsor of the bill that gave a bonus to World War II veterans.

We also made great strides in the highway program. Lee Spanner and Archie Wold of Hibbing were great supporters of good roads. We did much with Range roads, working together with Commissioner Mike Hoffman of the State Highway Department and the Minnesota Good Roads Association.

We did a great deal in the area of conservation. I handled much of the legislation for the teachers. I worked closely with the Range liberals, pulling their bills out of the fire that they might have had difficulty passing since they were on the opposite side of the fence.

The sessions were successful, and looking back today I can say it was because we were operating in the atmosphere of a citizen legislature. I still think that's the answer.

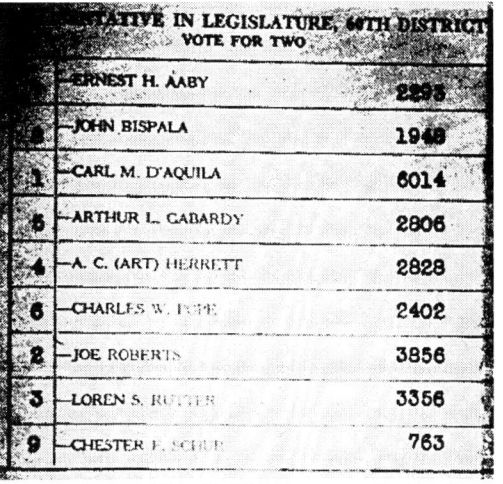

REPRESENTATIVE IN LEGISLATURE, 60TH DISTRICT VOTE FOR TWO	
ERNEST H. AABY	2295
JOHN BISPALA	1948
CARL M. D'AQUILA	6014
ARTHUR L. GABARDY	2806
A. C. (ART) HERRETT	2828
CHARLES W. POPE	2402
JOE ROBERTS	3856
LOREN S. RUTTER	3356
CHESTER F. SCHUR	763

The field was crowded in the election of 1948, but I got through the primary with the highest vote total.

THE POLITICS OF LOSING

THERE IS NO SUBSTITUTE FOR EXPERIENCE

Be Sure to Vote Tomorrow!

★

Polls Open 9 a.m. to 8 p.m.

REP. CARL M. D'AQUILA

LISTEN TO D'AQUILA TONIGHT
AT
8:30 o'clock
WMFG - WHLB
WEVE

Examine the Record and Judge For Yourself!

At top is one of my campaign ads from 1948. As you can see, even though I was still only 24 years old, I was advising voters to choose me because of my experience.

The Hibbing

VOLUME 53
NUMBER 108

Read by Over Thirty Thousand People Daily

HIBBING, MINNESOTA

Enge, D'Aquila, Rutter Elected

Roy Enge appeared today to have clinched an upset victory in the race for county commissioner from the Seventh district according to unofficial returns that gave him a lead of 353 votes with only a small number of unreported

WINNERS

Democrats Take Control Of Congress

WASHINGTON (AP) — crats grabbed control of today. The majority in th approached a landslide.
The voters in a startl set unseated 50 or mo House members and g

I was the top vote getter in the 1948 general election. The union forces were beginning to unite against me, but I still got crucial union endorsements. I was warned not to caucus with the conservatives again.

When those legislative seats became full-time jobs, we ended up with a second Congress in Minnesota which we can ill afford. I blame both sides equally. It's too attractive now, and they can make it a full-time job. It's just grown and grown and grown and deteriorated at the same time, just like the Congress.

In those days, it was just a pleasure working with the quality of people who were there. They were sincere, and there was great camaraderie on both sides. We sat down at a table and there was a Christian atmosphere of consideration. There weren't any angles. It was done beautifully.

We learned about the issues on our own time. There wasn't a week that we didn't meet with or speak to some group. I think at that time there were comparatively few people working in the political system. There was not a high percentage of the total workforce that was working in government. There wasn't that intense interest in politics on a day-to-day basis. It wasn't unusual to pick up a paper during a session and find there were no stories about the legislature. The farmers couldn't wait to get home.

There was a trick some would use to extend the session by a few hours. They'd cover the clock so nobody would know officially that we had passed midnight and gone into a new day. If they covered the clock for a half an hour or an hour at the end of a session, the farmers would erupt and there was hell to pay.

I remember one session that went until about three in the morning after they covered the clock at midnight. The farmers were very upset because they wanted to go home and plant. The only way they cooled down the House was when Lawrence Hall, the Speaker and a prominent attorney from St. Cloud, had a piano brought into the legislative chambers. No one knew he could even play the piano. He sat down and started playing, and pretty soon people were gathered around him singing, waiting for the committee reports to come back and

A clipping from the Hibbing Daily Tribune in January, 1949

end the session. It was 3 a.m. but they could have gone until five or six in the morning because nobody wanted to leave. It was all because of the power of music.

❦

P.K. Peterson and I were sent to Nebraska during the second session to study the unicameral legislature, and came back all excited about the concept. It was all so novel at that time, and when we started sponsoring bills and pushing it, it made a lot of the legislators very nervous — on both sides of the fence. I'm sure there were those who said, "Hey, let's get rid of this cookie. We want to keep our jobs here."

Legislators turned over very quickly from the farming areas. Something would happen on the farm, and they would suddenly bow out, even the very best legislators. They'd just say, "I'm going home."

It was a different time and age, and I think it was because we had so much less money in the game. 1949 was a good example. We had thrown out the slot machines, put in the mental health program, given the most money the University ever had, the most money to the road and bridge fund, the most money to the counties, and the most money to education. The headline that Mike Halloran of the Star-Journal came up with said: "Spendingest Legislature Goes Home." We spent just short of a half billion dollars.

We did not cross the billion dollar threshold until 1966 under Gov. Harold Levander. It took 17 years to double. And then in 1970, Anderson and Perpich went to six billion dollars. And by 1972, it was $10 billion. And now it's $14 billion. So it took 17 years to double, and in the next six years it went up 10 times. And that compounded the problems of power, greed, special interests, and the problem of taxpayers expecting things for nothing.

❦

In my second election in 1948, Joe Roberts from Buhl, Art Herrett of Hibbing, Loren Rutter and Ernie Aabe from Kinney and others ran against me. There were nine people in the race, but I didn't have any difficulty.

In the primary, I polled 6,014 votes and Roberts was second with 3,856. Rutter was third with 3,356 and Herrett edged out Arthur Gabardy of Hibbing with 2,828 votes.

In the general election, I got 10,312 votes and Rutter and Roberts almost tied for the second legislative seat. Rutter had 8,896 and Roberts had 8,863. Rutter won the recount.

It was really a breeze. And that was despite the fact that the union had put me on notice that it would take after me if I joined the Republican side again.

I was still endorsed in that second election by the American Federation of Labor and the Railroad Brotherhood. They were both prominent unions. Loren Rutter was a railroad man and his union endorsed both of us. It was one of the most powerful unions in the state, but it endorsed both Republicans and Democrats, those it felt would vote in the interest of the railroad workers. I was endorsed by the Central Labor Body in Hibbing, the electricians, the painters, all those factions of the AFL.

I didn't get the Steelworker endorsement, of course, but I still got elected without it. The Steelworkers, in order to drag down some of the Republicans, used a report card system to grade the legislators, but they used to delve into some issues that were really not germane to them at all. For instance, they would grade us on whether we thought beauty parlors should be organized. These issues had nothing to do with the Steelworkers, but unless the union blurred the real issues, it would have ended up endorsing a lot of Republicans.

I had been popular, but more than that I had been effective with the legislation I'd passed. As I said, I had a good relationship with all the Range legislators, with Cina, Vukelich, Peterson, and with Vladimar Shipka. We cooperated and met nearly every day or night. They had their side covered and I had my side covered.

Fred Cina and I worked admirably together, and when he had trouble getting some legislation going, I'd get the support from my side.

In fact, I passed all of Vladimar Shipka's bills, or he wouldn't have passed one bill in that session. He had not even been able to get a hearing, and I was able, as vice chairman of Towns and Counties, to get a special committee meeting where we had a Vladimar Shipka Day and passed all his local bills. We had a very good relationship.

೩೦೧೩೮೦೧೩೮೦೧೩

I was doing well on the homefront, too. The Hibbing Jaycees voted me their Most Distinguished Young Man in 1949, and, of course, that was the year I married Dolores.

Yet despite all the positive accomplishments, I could feel the opposition mounting during the second term. One reporter from the St. Paul Pioneer Press, Jack Weinberg, was very liberal and didn't like me from the start. He was a guy who kept dogging me and looking for the flaws. He was on my tail all the time. He made no bones about the fact that he didn't like me. For a newsman, I thought he was not very fair.

I filed for my third term on Aug. 3, 1950, but I knew it was going to be an uphill battle.

Orville Freeman was running for governor in 1950, and the DFL machine felt it had to eradicate "this thing" on the Range. "We can't have this flaw up there." And so they forced everybody into lying. The DFL Party published a newspaper with pictures of Vukelich and Cina and the others. In this newspaper, they didn't run quotes, but the pictures gave the impression that these lawmakers were asking for my defeat when they weren't. One of the headlines said, "These legislators support a liberal legislator from the Range." They all came up and apologized to me later.

The 1950 election was very close, and it was ironic that, after serving with the elder Widstrand, one year before he died, and after working for his newspaper, when I did lose, I lost to his son, Paul Widstrand.

It was his first attempt at seeking office, but he got the Steelworker endorsement, and he used his father's campaign signs. There was nothing illegal about that. It was clever. They just said, "Widstrand, Representative." It would have been unethical had it had said, "Keep Widstrand Representative." I talked to people after the election who told me they thought the father was still alive. The father had been a very quiet guy, and he died very quietly. The father had been defeated several times, but had always come back to win.

I will admit that George Teller came to me from the Steelworkers and said, "If you make your peace with us, we'll support you, and we'll support you next time. We'll elect you to Congress. We'll do anything, but we need you." I said "No," and I'll never forget what George said: "When you leave after this session, you might as well kiss the steps of the Capitol because you'll never see them again as a representative."

Still, I thought that we'd win. I thought we'd carry it because we had such large majorities the first two times. But the opposition did a masterful job on that third one.

One incident that turned voters around was when Sen. Robert Taft came to Minnesota, and I was on the welcoming committee. I should have known they would use it against me.

I was worried about last minute attacks, but I had checked at the radio station, and I didn't see where there would be commercial times left for them to use against me. That year, Hubert Humphrey was running against Joe Ball for U.S. Senate, and he just about had that race won. In the final days, Hubert relinquished his radio time. Suddenly there was an opening for the local DFLers.

They had brought a fellow up named Bob Gannon who was legislative head of the Minnesota CIO. Gannon came on the radio two nights before the election. The gist of his message was: "Meet Mr. Wall Street of the Iron Range, Meet Mr. Taft." It was a masterful job. In fact, my wife turned off the radio after the broadcast and said, "If I wasn't married to you, I'd consider voting against you myself."

It was misleading and unfair. Plus this guy's name was Bob Gannon. Just like people thought Oscar Widstrand was still alive, there were also people in town who thought this Bob Gannon was the same Gannon who was a famous steel company attorney from Hibbing — and a former mayor. So people were getting it wrong both ways. The mining company people thought it was their man, and the labor vote thought it was their man.

It wasn't just that speech, because I made one huge mistake as well. Teller came out with an ad against me about a week before the election. Teller was a shovel runner for U.S. Steel, and he was very popular, a real man's man. Art Timmerman and I thought the best thing would be to take him on because the union people were being misled. So we ran an ad, and the caption said, "You tell them, Mr. Teller." It was really a good ad, and it made such a mockery of him that the ad was posted on the walls of the mining lockerrooms and showers, where the men gathered before and after work. The union people themselves put them up.

When Gannon came into play, we were still getting calls and accolades for the ad. But it was a mistake. We should never have attacked the union. I'll never forget what Louis Rocco, the bartender at the Androy Hotel said: "You know, I've worked at the Ryan Hotel in St. Paul and I tended bar there for a long time. I know something about politics. I know the game. They're going to rally those union people around to the fact that if they vote for you they're breaking their own union." Louie was right.

All indications seemed to say that the public loved our attack on Teller, and as I walked up and down the street, they'd say, "Give it to them," and "Give it to them again."

But Gannon came in and announced that this was a divisive tactic used to break unions. "This is the first step in busting your union," he said on the radio. "If you elect this man and turn down your own guy, you're just bringing about your own death knell." That just reversed the whole tide. I could tell because our ads that had been

A newspaper clipping from November, 1950, tells the sad story of that year's election.

Rutter, Widstrand Make Legislature

Carl D'Aquila, Hibbing, was defeated yesterday in his bid for a third term in the House of Representatives by Paul Widstrand, also of Hibbing, according to unofficial returns compiled by the Hibbing Daily Tribune.

Loren Rutter, Kinney, the other incumbent who was elected for the first time two years ago, topped the four-man field to gain re-election.

Unofficial returns for all of the larger towns and a number of the smaller outlying areas, give this total: Rutter, 8,524; Widstrand, 6,901; D'Aquila, 5,500, and Herbert Heinig, Hibbing, 3,498.

LISTEN
OVER WMFG
SUNDAY NIGHT
from
6:30 – 7:00 p.m.

Subject:
"CARL D'QUILA,
Wall Street Representative"

Reported and paid for by the Iron Range Industrial Union,
Geo. Teller, Pres.

"Wall Street Representative" was part of the union campaign that helped unseat me after two terms.

posted in the changing rooms and other places came down the day before election. I'd run into people on the street, and they were lukewarm. You could see the change.

The attack we made on their man was the catalyst that got them back together. It was a grave error.

In the end, Loren Rutter had 10,458 votes, Paul Widstrand had 8,706, I had 6,806, and Herbert Heinig had 4,028. The top two were the winners.

You've got to believe in divine providence and God's paths, and as it turned out, I was very fortunate that I lost. I kept my influence, I kept my interests, I stayed active, kept up on the issues. I was able to give more time to my family and to my business, and it all worked out. Had I carried that third election, I might very well have ended up as a career politician. I'd have been there like all these other incumbents, opposing term limits and trying to hang onto some committee chairmanship.

I have no illusions. It was a blessing that I lost. But at the time, I felt terrible. I remember walking the streets of Hibbing for two or three days and there weren't that many people who said hello. It was really, really lonely. I felt as if I was on a Western movie set, and someone was going to come out of one the buildings and shoot me.

It was a good four or five months before I realized that life had to go on. I took it hard.

I wrote my congratulations. I appeared on the radio and thanked people. But deep down inside, I was devastated. I got a call from some of the Republicans in the legislature and they said that I had a case for illegal practices during the election. They were in power and they said they could make sure the winner wasn't seated, or that there would be a special election. I thought about it, and I said, "No, I don't want to do that. The people have spoken. And it could be worse the second time. People could say, 'We'll really show you this time.'"

I wasn't angry with the union. I realized it was politics. I realized I'd lost it myself. It was the strategy we chose during the campaign. I'd lost, and it wasn't anything anybody else had done.

Chapter Seven

BACK IN THE REAL WORLD

I absolutely knew I would not run for the legislature again. I had learned in school that I didn't like to lose. I had been class president in the seventh grade, the eighth grade, the ninth grade, the 10th grade, and then I lost in the 11th grade. And then I lost again in the 12th grade. I found out that I don't need to lose.

I had other jobs all the way through the legislature. I still had the bus advertising. I sold advertising for the radio stations. I also sold institutional maintenance supplies for a concern from St. Louis, Consolidated Laboratories. I was selling to schools around the state. I sold to municipalities, companies and restaurants.

For a time during the summer while I was in high school, I had worked in the mines on the track gang. I also went to work on the Great Northern Railroad as a brakeman. I think the reason I did that was because I could get the shift that started at five in the morning. I rode the jitney, and it went the 26 miles to Virginia and back. We were back in Hibbing at the depot at 11:20 a.m. It left me the whole afternoon to pursue advertising and other interests. I did that for a year.

My favorite railroad story happened during the war. A lot of men tried to avoid the draft by working on the railroads, and an employee could get a deferment if he had a critical job. Firpo Maras of Firpo's Tap Room got his notice to report to the draft board, and he went to the superintendent with a certificate that needed to be signed to prove he was essential to the homefront. There was one line on the certificate that asked how long it would take the railroad to replace the employee. The superintendent looked at Firpo and he looked at the certificate.

He wrote down, "15 minutes." Firpo got drafted in the next call.

Back in the Real World

My political career was over when this family picture was taken in 1951. Here we are at the dinner table. From left are my sister-in-law Lucy, nephew Michael, Concetta, brother Mike, Pasquale, me, and son, Tom.

The first job offer I had after the legislature was to work for a radio station in Cheyenne, Wyo. I also had an offer to work for United Press International that could have ended up with a posting as a correspondent in Shanghai, China. I really was seriously thinking about leaving the Range. It may have been that feeling of remorse about having been defeated.

I had no visions of a future in the tire business. My father-in-law was the landlord for the General Tire business in Virginia. He happened to be there one day when Oscar Mathisen asked him, "What's your son-in-law doing?" My father-in-law said, "Oh, he's looking at offers outside of the state."

Oscar said, "Would he be interested in a job with General Tire? They're looking for a special representative to report to them to help develop General in this part of the state."

I wasn't very interested in it when he first brought it up, but people in our families were hoping that we wouldn't leave the area. So I agreed to go for the interview. The O'Neil family who owned General Tire at the time were a very strong Catholic family with a real sense of social responsibility, long before that became

My dad, Pasquale, takes a pipe break on the front steps. One of the main reasons for staying on the Range was to be close to our extended families.

64

fashionable for companies. They were very nice to me. They told me I'd be my own boss on my own time schedule. I could do whatever I wanted. I would be the king of the territory.

I wasn't totally unfamiliar with the tire business. Nobby Valeri's partner Gene LaMothe had asked me if I'd be interested in joining Shell Tire. Lee Spanner was a very good friend of mine, and I saw the dynasty he had built in the tire business.

But there was one consideration that convinced me more than the others. I had friends who were doctors and lawyers who said, "We don't make any money when we go on vacation. Unless we're at the clinic or working on a case, our income stops. And if we die, we don't have anything to sell. Our career dies with us."

So I got to thinking about that. The thought came to me: "Tires wear out." Even when you're sleeping, those wheels are rolling. The tires are wearing out. You can make money even when you're on vacation, or in church or anywhere. Tires are wearing out.

So I gave it whirl and did that for three years. I managed to increase their business over five-fold. Then Uniroyal come along and asked if I'd be interested in taking their dealership. They had two dealers on the Range who weren't doing much, and they were going to cancel the contracts. They had a dog of a product at the time. They didn't have quality. But I accepted the offer.

My father-in-law suggested I should probably do business in Hibbing rather than in Virginia, and he asked me what bank I planned to use. I said, "Let's go to Merchants and Miners." Sig Egge was the president,

After years with Uniroyal, we became a Michelin dealer. Dolores and I spent time one evening with this large fellow.

and I'd known him for a long time. We went to see him.

We had a pretty solid business plan with Uniroyal, and I had proven myself as the successful special representative for General Tire for three years. Egge turned us down flat. He said to Mario, my father-in-law, "You're from Virginia, and this is your son-in-law. I don't know why you're coming to Hibbing." We told him that there would be a branch in Hibbing and a branch in Virginia, and we wanted this to be in Hibbing.

My father-in-law was stunned and embarrassed. As we walked out the door, he said, "What do we do now?" I said, "Let's go down the street and see Barney Koskinen at Security Bank." We told Barney what I needed, and he just got the note. He didn't ask us for financial statements. He didn't ask for a personal guarantee. My father-in-law said, "Do you want me to co-sign?" and Barney replied, "No, I know this young man, and that's good enough for me."

The loan was for $15,000, and we paid it off in about a year and a half.

It was ironic that years later I became a board member at Merchants and Miners State Bank. In fact, Mr. Egge was one of those who pleaded with me to become a director. I told them it was amazing that it was Egge who had turned me down for the

Uniroyal Salutes with Pride
CARL M. D'AQUILA

winner of the 7th annual
LIFE-NTDRA EDUCATIONAL GRANT AWARD
and
1968 ANNUAL UNIROYAL DEALER AWARD

I can thank the people with whom I work for this award, which was the highest award that Uniroyal gave out each year.
My staff nominated me. Steve Zeitler, manager of the Hibbing Chamber of Commerce at the time, produced an incredible scrapbook in support of my getting the award.

loan.

We worked very hard with Uniroyal, and worked with the manufacturer and the development people, helping them to establish a relationship with the mining people. Pretty soon we were at the top of the heap.

Because of my legislative background, I can't deny that those doors were open to me. My degree of success was more outstanding at the immediate outset than it would have for someone who didn't have the recognition and introductions. But even back then, the superintendents were judged on performance. You had to have product. It didn't come that easily, but it came well enough so that I soon became entrenched.

It helped, too, that the two major brands, Goodyear and Firestone, had controlled the market by themselves. They could just sit on the perch and didn't feel vulnerable at all. It wasn't really a miracle to pick them off, but it took a while. It took nearly six or seven years before I really made it. My competitors woke up one morning to find that I had a greater percentage of the market than they did.

For many years, we have been a Michelin dealership. Dolores stands in front of some of the enormous tires that are used in the mining industry.

After leaving the legislature, I was also appointed to the Public Utilities Commission in Hibbing.

For years there had been rumors that there were payoffs on the coal tonnages coming into the PUC plant. It was said that people used to try and buy the appointment, and that the payoff was as much as 50 cents on each ton of coal.

With my interests in the mining companies, I knew I'd be subject to criticism. I took the appointment anyway. I was determined not to do anything unethical or illegal, a temptation some commissioners fell prey to over the years.

Al Hanson was the superintendent of the Public Utilities, and he did a very creditable job. I went out to dinner with him one night, and he said to me, "You know what I'd do if I were you? It's got to come. This place has got to shape up, and my hands are tied. I can't do anything with the commissioners, and they're always adding someone on the payroll. If I didn't love Hibbing, I'd leave this job behind."

I wondered what I could do. Izzy Sher had been on the Public Utilities just before me, and echoed Hanson's sentiments: "You know, that place has got to be shaped up. You've got an opportunity to do it."

So we developed the idea that we would put specifications on the coal bids. We'd command a certain number of BTUs and quality of coal. If the contractors exceeded the standards, they'd get a bonus, and if not, they'd be penalized. As the result of that one move, we were able to give a gigantic increase to the employees, and we lowered rates besides. It also took the opportunity for graft away from the commissioners.

I spent three years on the commission.

I kept active with a lot of legislative friends, but I did not lobby. I wrote speeches for a number of local candidates. I did some freelance newspaper work, and I did some umpiring of city league baseball games.

Two children were born while I was in the legislature, and then we were having one every couple of years. I was getting my family together.

I was president of the Washington School PTA during which we had the new school built. We introduced the idea there of having joint presidents of the school organization, both husband and wife. That way they'd have continuity, and there would be both the mother factor and the father factor. It would be a family-like orientation. That was a lot of fun.

Chapter Eight

BACK INTO THE FRAY

My stint in the legislature was over, and my business was going strong. But I also kept my finger in the political pie. That was only natural for someone who had always been involved in politics, and who was from the Range.

My preoccupation with politics led to the 1960 effort for lieutenant governor. A group of us thought it was time that we had somebody from Northeastern Minnesota on the ticket. Not only that, we wanted it to be a meaningful spot on the ticket.

I met with a group of Republicans from the local area, and I showed them a tabulation I had made of a number of previous state elections showing that the margin of victory was in the Eighth District. I had done quite a bit of research on this. It was evident that if the Republicans could win from 38 to 42 percent of the heavily-DFL Eighth District vote, there was no way they could lose.

Right off the bat, our campaign faced a problem in Duluth, the metropolis at the southern end of St. Louis County. The Range and Duluth were as much separated in politics, in both parties, as North and South Vietnam. Rudy Perpich found that out later.

I told our Range supporters, "If we can infiltrate Duluth with your friends and my friends, and we preach the right message, we might be able to do something."

We went into the St. Louis County convention in Duluth quite late for seeking office. In fact, we'd started all this in motion just before the convention. Jim Hitchcock of the Hibbing Tribune was helping as were Barbara Merklin and John and Kay Boentje. Bob Wallace, the engineer from Chisholm, was very prominent in it. Joanne

Muller of Hibbing was a leader. There were many members of the Hibbing Chamber involved. People fell into it quite rapidly.

Despite our efforts, we ran into the brick wall we had expected with the Duluth crowd, and it was a real struggle. They were very close to the Twin City powers and were very reluctant to go along with my candidacy, but by the time the county convention ended, we came out with the endorsement. However, we didn't have that unanimous vote I felt we needed.

We went to the Eighth District convention, representing all of northeastern Minnesota, and came out of that all right -- with near unanimity. We were able to make a few other conventions in the state, and made enough of a splash so that when we went to the state convention, we were pretty sure we wouldn't win, but that we'd make an intense race of it.

This was the year that Elmer Anderson first sought office. It was still a two-year term for governor at that time, and the governor and lieutenant governor ran separately on the ballot. The candidate Anderson wanted to take with him as lieutenant governor was Art Ogle from Mankato.

We made a very formidable run, and we excited the state convention with the idea that northeastern Minnesota could be such a factor in state elections.

Elmer Anderson wasn't publically involved in our race. Ogle had been nominated by the various district conventions around the state. Outside of the Eighth District, we had some pretty good support, but we did not have any other endorsements. We lost, but there was enough of an impetus built out of that convention to create believers of others.

We were getting support from Duluth, Crookston, down in Rochester and Willmar and St. Paul and St. Cloud. They were interested, and they asked that we get the campaign going earlier next time.

Anderson won the election in 1960, partly because of the help he got from the Range. All the Range mayors were Democrats, but I helped organize them behind Anderson. They felt they'd had enough of the Orville Freeman administration. We were looking at the beginning of taconite, and the Range was having some pretty bad times as the natural ore ran out.

Surprisingly, Art Ogle was not elected. Karl Rolvaag, the DFL candidate, was elected lieutenant governor.

Elmer was called upon by a group from our camp and was told of our intentions to mount a campaign in 1962. We felt that he might realize what he had missed out on. He promised that for the next election he would keep hands off. He encouraged our group to continue.

We proceeded on that basis, and worked quite continually to succeed next time. We didn't work really hard, but every month we went to somewhere in the state. By the time the 1962 convention came around, there was a lot excitement concerning a

Count the Pickets in the Fence

Dolores and I made our way through the convention floor at the 1962 state Republican Convention. I had just been nominated for lieutenant governor. We had done our homework well, but we had also counted on Gov. Elmer Anderson staying neutral. He didn't. I lost on the seventh ballot.

running mate for Anderson. This time we started the campaign in earnest very early.

We came out of the Eighth District with only one or two votes in opposition. We went around the state and made tremendous showings in St. Paul, in the St. Cloud area, and in southern Minnesota.

This was the famous election when A.M "Sandy" Keith decided to run. The DFL Party had endorsed Keith, but Rolvaag decided to run in the primary. Rolvaag eventually emerged as the candidate.

This was also going to be the first four-year term for governor in Minnesota, and we argued with all the people that the northern vote was going to be important to Anderson's chances. It was also the first election where the governor and the lieutenant governor ran as a team.

In the 1960 election, Anderson had gotten a pretty good vote from the Range because of the disharmony in the DFL Party. In 1962, maybe Anderson thought that he already had the Range base, and he didn't have to worry so much.

But we knew at that point that the Democrats had crawled back into their own camp. There had been enough interest in the Keith-Rolvaag situation to make us feel certain that the voting pattern on the Range would return to its usual form.

We campaigned intensely for the lieutenant governor's position, and by the time the convention rolled around, that race had turned into a real ding-dong battle. Our campaign was a real attention getter for the convention. Wheelock Whitney, who later ran for governor and the U.S. Senate, was a very formidable candidate for lieutenant governor as was a young fellow by the name of Donald Clayton. C. Donald Peterson was a third candidate and I was the fourth.

It was an exciting convention. Wheelock Whitney came in with a band and drum majorettes, the whole nine yards. We had a more simple approach. We had tried to make all the contacts on a person to person basis, plus we had some banners and leaflets. The Eighth District was really geared up.

It appeared for a while as though we'd be able to pull this off. The bookies around Minneapolis were betting that we'd win. We had done our homework well.

At the last minute, though, I got a call from Elmer Anderson. He asked if I'd consider being Secretary of State. It was the first indication that maybe he was favoring somebody else. I told him that I wouldn't do that. Joe Donovan, a popular

> **Area Republicans Fete D'Aquila**
>
> Eighth district Republicans Friday night honored Carl D'Aquila, who was a candidate for lieutenant governor last week at the state GOP convention.
>
> Sixty-five delegates and well-wishers from St. Louis, Itasca, Carlton and Cass counties attended the dinner held at the Androy Hotel.
>
> State Republican leaders offered congratulations to D'Aquila for the manner in which his campaign was conducted and the aid it gave to the enthusiasm and morale of the Eighth District Republican organization.
>
> Speakers included District Chairman Harold Olson and County Chairman Harold W. Grams.
>
> Telegrams were received by D'Aquila from B. Kunzig, GOP attorney general candidate; Norbert McCrady, Republican secretary of state nominee; C. Donald Peterson, the successful GOP lieutenant governor nominee; Bob Forsythe, state chairman, and Mrs. T. Dillingham, state chairwoman.
>
> D'Aquila said that C. Donald Peterson, Minneapolis, is "an intelligent, articulate, hard-hitting candidate whom the whole state can be proud of and who should be elected, to serve with Governor Elmer L. Andersen the next four years."
>
> He added that "the Eighth District Republicans have proved themselves an effective and unified group that will elect many candidates to office beginning this fall."

I came home to a nice reception even though our bid to win the lieutenant governorship had failed. This is from the Hibbing Daily Tribune.

DFLer from Duluth, was the incumbent Secretary of State, and even if I could win that race, it wasn't what northern Minnesota needed. It wasn't meaningful enough. The people of northeastern Minnesota had made great contributions to this state. They deserved more. The people up north needed someone who was close to the throne, who might succeed to the office, and, at the same time, make people aware of the significance of the north. Having a northern lieutenant governor could unite the whole state.

I should have been able to read the signals. The position had been offered as an olive branch. We turned it down flat. Gov. Anderson was very amicable, and he said, "Well, we'll see what happens."

The next day was the election for the lieutenant governor position. Our camp hadn't realized that earlier that morning all the delegates had received some written material under their doors at the Hotel Leamington. The message was that Elmer Anderson had established a preference for C. Donald Peterson. That put a considerably different light on things.

It was really too bad. Anderson didn't adhere to his earlier promise. He shouldn't have feared us. He still would have been in command.

That day was really exciting. After each ballot, I'd be surrounded by people from all parts of the state. Early on, it felt like it was snowballing. You could just feel the tempo. I had to remind myself that I was still the same kid from North Hibbing. I had to remind myself what it was all about.

It was a moment where Duluth and the Iron Range finally got together. Dorothy Nelson of Duluth, the St. Louis County Chair, was just like an opera singer. She was bubbling and singing, "We've got it, we've got it."

Clayton disappeared first. On the second or third ballot, Wheelock Whitney dropped by the wayside. Then it became a head to head battle between Peterson and me.

Peterson was a tough opponent, a very smart attorney and a well-known Twin City legislator. His brother, P.K. Peterson, had been mayor of Minneapolis and had served in the Legislature with me.

It went to a seventh ballot, and Peterson began to pull ahead. I realized that we were going to lose. I felt we had achieved a great deal of popularity and acceptance. Because we didn't want to jeopardize these relations, I took the stage and made the motion that the nomination be made unanimous for Peterson.

We took it as real sports. We turned around and gave our blessing to Peterson. We lost, but we became the darlings and favorites of the convention.

We found that our political base and our importance did not diminish with the loss. We had established ourselves as a very formidable group, and we were in a position to get a lot done. Even though we had lost, we were a pretty happy lot.

In the general election, though, it was evident that our loss hurt Anderson. The

Eighth District Republicans and some Democrats were very disappointed that I wasn't on the ballot, and, as a result, Anderson dropped significantly in the vote tabulations in the district, particularly on the Iron Range. The newspapers, particularly the Hibbing newspaper, had made it appear as though I was going to get the nomination. There had to be several thousand people from the Range who were disappointed in that what was expected didn't happen.

Anderson lost the election by 91 votes in a recount to Rolvaag. I have little doubt that if Anderson had a running mate from the Eighth District, whether it was me or any number of other people, it would have been enough to put him over. In fact, you could pick any town on the Iron Range and say, "This is where Elmer Anderson lost."

I was disillusioned by what Anderson had done in supporting Peterson, but I never really got bitter about it. I was unhappy, but I didn't profess that to him or any of his people. In the end, I felt sorry for him. He was a bigger loser than I.

The whole thing may have cost Elmer Anderson a chance at a much larger political career. He might have gone on to the Senate, and I heard later from Nelson Rockefeller that if Anderson had been elected in that 1962 election, he would have been a possible running mate for Rockefeller in 1964 when he sought the Republican presidential nomination. Anderson lost more than just that election.

And, it was within the realm of possibility that if Anderson had been elected, he might have succeeded Hubert Humphrey, who ran as vice president with Lyndon Johnson in 1964, as a U.S. Senator. It was a time when sitting governors still could become senators and nobody thought much about it. I could have become governor.

I regretted the fact that I never had a chance to try for statewide office. I felt that if it had happened, I doubt that I would have wanted a second term. I just wanted to get things done, whether they were popular or unpopular. You could do great things if you didn't have your eye on the White House or some other office.

Outside of the piece of my inner soul that was left unsatisfied, I must admit that the good Lord, as usual, guided me in the right direction.

Chapter Nine

FIGHTING FOR TACONITE

One of my favorite photographs of my father shows him in 1932 with a horse-drawn cart loaded with ore taken from Scranton Mine in 1932. That was the entire production from that mine and all other Pickands Mather mines that year as the depression hit the Iron Range hard.

The story nobody knows about that cart was that those sacks of ore were eventually studied by the Erie Mining Company research lab. Scientists were looking at a way to use the low-grade taconite in a commercial process.

It was no secret taconite was the future of the Range, and people had known that for years. By the early 1960s, there were only a few pockets of the high-grade natural ore left scattered across the Range, but there were endless acres of taconite.

The thought behind the Taconite Amendment, a constitutional act that would protect an industry from undue taxation and encourage investment in taconite plants, goes back at least as far as when I was first elected to the Legislature in the late 1940s.

As I mentioned earlier, the Ontario Mining Co., which was the predecessor of Hibbing Taconite, was exchanging lands with the state to get ready for the development of Hibbing Taconite. I carried that legislation for the mining companies. Dr. E.W. Davis was engaged in the early 1950s in his research work at the University of Minnesota. Along with the research being done by Erie Mining and Reserve Mining Co., Davis' experimentation was a key to the development of the taconite process.

In conjunction with these leases and land exchanges for Ontario Mining Co. north of Hibbing, I took to the floor of the House and proposed the passage of a declaration by the legislature that would not be legally binding, but would be morally binding. It

Fighting for Taconite

Scranton Mine, —1932— "A One Horse Operation."

My father, Pasquale D'Aquila, at right, poses on a rail flatcar with the only ore taken from the Scranton Mine in 1932 as the Depression hit the Iron Range. In fact, this was the only ore shipped by all the Pickands Mather open pit mines that year. Contrast that to 1942, when World War II was beginning, when PM shipped over 10.5 million tons. Those few sacks of Depression-era ore, however, were studied by researchers attempting to find a way to extract iron from the low grade taconite ore. The taconite era began in the 1950s as the high grade Mesabi ore played out. Marko Pribic is holding the horse. They had to rent the horse because the company didn't have one locomotive working that year.

was designed to be a fair tax, limiting the tax to less than that levied against the direct shipping ores. I was, in a sense, trying to continue the five cents a ton that John Blatnik had passed on taconite in the developmental stages before my time.

Having been on the subcommittee for iron ore taxes, having been from this area, and having come from a family that was steeped in mining, I became very involved when Gov. Elmer Anderson espoused the idea of a taconite amendment.

Anderson was not able to put it across, though. The Democrats were determined not to let Anderson have any credit. The passage had become a partisan issue despite the fact that it was a worthy issue whose time had come. Karl Rolvaag was elected governor, and the machinations to get the amendment passed were started again in 1963. Rolvaag appointed me at that time as a member of Dr. Charles Mayo's citizens' committee for the taconite amendment. I probably became Charlie Mayo's main stalwart in that whole endeavor.

Rolvaag called me in and was most cooperative and most receptive. In fact, he did everything he possibly could to diminish the opposition of Sen. Jack Davies and a number of the other Democratic legislators who were opposed to the referendum and to my involvement.

There was a group of seven or eight legislators including Rudy Perpich who actually voted against the Taconite Amendment, even though it was to be put to a vote of

Old natural ore mines like the Susquehanna were very picturesque, much like the Grand Canyon, but by the 1950s most of the old mines had played themselves out. The only hope for the Iron Range was processing the low-grade taconite ores.

the people before it became law.

I can frankly say that we got more help from the DFL governor than we could have ever expected from a Republican governor. And so while we lost the 1962 election, we gained something very significant to the well-being of the Iron Range. Had Anderson been re-elected, the amendment probably would have prevailed, but I'm not sure it would have happened in 1964. The Democratic opposition may have been too strong.

There was a time, for a period of about 11 months, when there wasn't a weekend when I didn't leave my business. I traveled across the state to nearly every county, taking nearly a whole year for this effort. Many days, as when we were campaigning for the lieutenant governor job, we would take off at about 4 in the afternoon to go somewhere in the state. We would make a presentation and speak. We'd return by about midnight or in the wee hours of the morning. Sometimes we'd stay overnight.

During that 11 months, I made it to 81 of the 87 counties in the state. It gave me a great deal of exposure that became a political asset later on. It was probably the Taconite Amendment that made me a prospect for governor and lieutenant governor in 1966.

I spent a lot of time with Dr. Mayo. He was really well respected around the state, but he was

Dr. Charles Mayo of the famous Mayo Clinic was the honorary chairman of the effort to pass the Taconite Amendment. Here Dr. Mayo and I show off the Taconite Stamps that helped fund the statewide effort to help the industry.

The Taconite Stamps funded an informational video that was shown all over the state showing the history of the iron mining industry and the need for a Constitutional Amendment to protect the fledgling taconite industry from over-taxation. The stamp was featured in a story in *The National Observer*.

something of a figurehead for this project. He was a real party lover, and there were many very late evenings. It was difficult at times making sure that Dr. Mayo showed up for an event and was his usual diplomatic self. He was magic if he got there and got there early enough. It was more worry managing Mayo than it was getting converts for the Taconite Amendment.

The newspaper fraternity in the state was fabulous. I can't think of one newspaper in the state that didn't reach out and give us the space and support.

We designed the Taconite stamp which, to a large measure, funded the television documentary that was shown on all TV stations in the state. It showed the history of the iron ore industry from its inception, the depletion of the natural ores, and the need for a taconite industry. It showed the broad support the amendment had across Minnesota and the Range.

I served on the taconite group's finance committee with Algot Johnson and Dwayne Andreas. It was a very cherished experience. The three of us were the whole committee.

One of the regrets I still have about the Taconite Amendment was that I was unable to convince key people to put into the amendment a fair tax policy as it related to the local production taxes. I was unable to get the point across to Fred Cina, who was in the legislature and wrote most of the mining tax laws. He just refused to go along with it. I figured if the state was giving the mining companies this blank check promising them favorable tax policies for 25 years, the Range politicians might just say, "Well that gives us a lot more to levy in the Range towns." And that's exactly what happened with the production tax. And that's exactly why we lost some of the plants to Michigan and Canada.

Surprisingly, there was a great deal of initial opposition to the amendment in the north itself. When it first started out, it was questionable whether it would carry because there was so much opposition to it up here. There was that historic anti-mining feeling, and some of the politicians also didn't like the 25-year guarantee. The opposition was led by Bill Ojala, a legislator from Aurora. The towns thought they would be shorted on the revenue from the taconite taxes.

But despite that core of opposition, the Taconite Amendment built a euphoria in this area that was absolutely dramatic. I would parallel it to the end of the World War II. It was a public celebration. At the time, all of us envisioned 12 months a year of work, steady employment, all the things that the Range was lacking. We would be able to retain our young here. It would be more of a technical business, and people could become engineers and stay here. It might increase the educational opportunities in the area.

Little by little, what opposition there was got broken down. In the end, less that 17 percent of people of the state voted against it. Even then, the biggest percentage of the "no" votes were still cast on the Iron Range.

MINING IS EVERYONE'S FUTURE

The battle to keep the mining industry healthy and prosperous on the Range didn't end with the passage of the Taconite Amendment. In 1974, we formed a committee to remind people that we needed to stick together to ensure a bright future. The co-chairs of the Protect Jobs Committee are shown, at left, putting our "Mining is in Everyone's Future" bumper sticker on a car. From left are me; Peter Benzoni, director of District 33 of the United Steelworkers of America; Bob Nickoloff, vice president of Hibbing's First Federal Savings and Loan; and Joe Gustin, staff representative for the Steelworkers. It was Bob's father, C.A. Nickoloff, who sold my father the house I grew up in in North Hibbing.

The Taconite Amendment was one of the highlights of my life. It brought me in touch with many thousands of people. There were farmers, educators, business people. Everywhere we went, we found a great reception.

The Taconite Amendment did more than just establish a fair tax policy; it molded the people of the state together into one effort for the benefit of the Iron Range. I can't think of any other time in Minnesota when people were more happy and more in agreement. They were all working together for the same purpose.

Chapter Ten
JUST THE GUY THEY WERE LOOKING FOR

As the next governor's race approached in 1966, people kept saying, "I'd wish you'd come back. I wish you'd try it again." We received a couple hundred letters a year saying, "Let's start it up again. Let's give it one more shot."

Jarle Leirfallom, who held several statewide jobs in Minnesota government, wrote me, "I keep looking for the D'Aquila name."

For my part, though, I had no intention of getting back into state politics even though it was an interesting political year.

It appeared that Gov. Karl Rolvaag was in trouble. It may have been because of Rolvaag himself and some of his difficulties, or maybe it was a case where Minnesotans were used to voting for a governor every two years, and now four years had gone by. Whatever it was, it looked like Rolvaag was in a good position to be defeated.

The Republicans were beginning to battle to see who would run against him.

The Harold Stassen law firm in the Twin Cities had always been strong in politics, producing Stassen, Dave Durenberger, Arthur Gillen and many others. Harold Levander was the senior partner in the firm and was lead attorney for many groups in the state. He was a tremendous public speaker and had probably spoken to more high school graduations than any other person in Minnesota. Levander also had an outstanding family, his wife, Iantha, his son, Hap, and his daughter, Jean Levander King.

John Pillsbury of the Pillsbury flour-milling fame was another candidate. Elmer Anderson decided to cast his lot as the compromise candidate — as the darkhorse.

Just the Guy They Were Looking for

My name had been mentioned for lieutenant governor in some of the conventions across the state, in the counties and the districts, but we didn't attend any of the conventions. Elmer Anderson had contacted me at one point and said, "Why don't we take a poll together and share the cost to see how you stack up as a person running with me?"

I never had harbored any ill feeling toward Anderson because he had not chosen me in the 1962 election. I had been hurt by it, but I can truthfully say I didn't feel any ill will. He had also been hurt by that decision. I can say, though, that as capable as this man was, and as much as he turned out to be one of the great Minnesotans of all time, I found that we all have frailties, and we all have weaknesses. If Elmer had a weakness, it's that he was really stubborn. It didn't matter how much you argued your position, he wouldn't budge once he'd made up his mind.

We took the poll using Mid-Continent Surveys, a Shenandoah, Iowa, company. The poll showed that I had tremendous strength among the Democrats and independents, and less strength among the Republicans of the Eighth District. It would have made me a perfect candidate. Anderson was very interested, and if he had come through that convention, he would have wanted me to run with him.

I wasn't even a delegate to that convention as late as the end of June. We had gone on a family trip to California, the first family trip we had ever taken. We had driven out through Colorado and New Mexico and had been to see the Mondavis, the family that makes the California wine, who are dear friends of my wife.

When Dolores' grandmother went through a prolonged illness, Rosa Mondavi, virtually was like a mother to Dolores' mother, Helen Casagrande. Rosa later started the Mondavi wine empire with her husband Caesar and their two sons Peter and Robert. We always kept in close contact with the Mondavis. They had moved to California and purchased the Charles Krug Winery. They got the vineyards, the land, the buildings, everything for $75,000.

Years later, we were having dinner with Rosa Mondavi. It was at the time when Robert Mondavi was splitting apart from the family to start what would become one of the most famous wineries in the world. I'll never forget when Rosa said in Italian, "Things were better when things were worse." She remembered the early days when the family worked together, ate together, played together, worshiped together. Now, a few fortunes later, the family was splitting up. It brought home the reality of how important family unity is in a lonesome world, and that success and wealth is not happiness.

I digressed. We had our car driven home, and we flew back when our vacation was over. We got back to Minneapolis the Saturday morning of the convention, and the car was already waiting for us. Dolores said to me, "Why don't you enjoy yourself and go to the convention, and I'll take the kids on home?" So I went over to the convention at the Leamington Hotel in downtown Minneapolis.

When I got into the hall, the candidates and the delegates had been up all night, and they had been unable to reach an endorsement. It was deadlocked between Anderson, Pillsbury and Levander. They needed 60 percent to endorse and nobody was coming close, although Levander was leading.

As I walked in, Val Bjornson, the state treasurer, came up to me and said, "Hey, you're just the guy we're looking for. I'm going to propose your name on the next ballot as a compromise candidate for governor. These people are really at their wits' end. Something has to happen."

I told him, "I'm not even a delegate." He said it didn't matter.

Somebody else came up to me and said, "You're wanted up in the Bloomington delegation." Jim King was the mayor of Bloomington, and he was married to one of Dolores' high school classmates. Shirley Frederickson King had grown up in Virginia and was one of the most active Republicans in the state.

I went up to the room, and it was jam-packed.

St. Paul Pioneer Press – June 26, 1966

22 Votes For... Dracula? Tequila?

By ROBERT J. O'KEEFE
Staff Writer

Twenty-two of the most surprising votes at the Republican state convention sprang suddenly out of the Bloomington section of the Hennepin county delegation.

The 11th ballot in the contest for governor was droning along in routine fashion until State Rep. Lyall Schwarzkopf, Hennepin county chairman, announced:

"... and 22 votes for D'Aquila."

Dr. Harry Weisbecker of St. Paul, convention co-chairman, wasn't quite sure what he had heard, and as he repeated the vote for the benefit of delegates, his pronunciation landed somewhere between "Dracula" and a Mexican drink.

But in the end the 22 votes were racked up for Carl D'Aquila, Hibbing.

D'Aquila has long been a member of the GOP on the Iron Range and formerly served in the Minnesota Legislature. And for a Republican to be elected to the legislature from the strongly DFL range is no easy chore.

The Hibbingite is interested in running for lieutenant governor, and he figures that friends in the Bloomington delegation wanted to give him exposure.

D'Aquila said he was walking out of the Leamington hotel at 2 a.m. Saturday when he was called by a Bloomington delegate and asked how he'd like to have 25 votes for governor.

He said he protested against the idea, but 22 votes were recorded for him anyhow.

The Bloomington delegates went back to their normal voting on the 12th ballot.

A story in the St. Paul Pioneer Press told of my improbable venture into the governor's race in 1966. I was able to work with the candidates to bend the rules and get someone nominated.

Just the Guy They Were Looking for

Someone said, "Yes, we're going to put you up." I argued against it. I told them it was ridiculous, but they said, "Nope, we're going to do it. We're not getting anywhere with this convention." So they voted to go downstairs and to support me on the next ballot.

When Val Bjornson nominated me, the hall shook with the excitement of a possible solution because the other three candidates were so closely tied. It was beginning to look as if no one would ever come through with the nomination. The delegates were getting very short-tempered. It was a beautiful warm day, and people wanted to go home.

I assured people that I had nothing to do with this, but on the next ballot, we picked up a great deal of the Bloomington delegation and some votes from Rochester and Willmar. Some of the candidates began losing votes. For a while, it began to look like the convention could be shaken loose, and, if not me, some compromise candidate could come out of this thing.

Instead, it just stalemated again. We began to sense that this convention could go on for a month of Sundays. Levander was still in front with Pillsbury close behind. Anderson's support had begun to wane.

I talked to the Levander and Pillsbury camps. I told them that I had no idea this was going on until I walked into the convention, and I suggested that they change the rules. I suggested that they go to 58 percent needed to endorse on the next ballot and 56 percent on the following ballot and so forth. They did that. They went upstairs and made an agreement between the candidates to bend the rules.

It took a couple of more ballots and Levander won.

Art Gillen, with whom I'd served in the legislature and who was a very good friend, came to me at that point and said, "Do you want to run for lieutenant governor?" Gillen was a law partner of Levander's, and I guess Harold wasn't keen on Jim Goetz.

Goetz had been active at the district conventions. He was popular, good looking, dynamic and a radio station owner. He was very colorful, and had his eyes on national office. He was leading the pack. In fact, he was the only one out there. I didn't realize at the time, however, how strongly Levander felt about not wanting Goetz as his running mate.

The ironic thing was that even though we had not made any effort during that year, we had enough support left over from past years that we were a very formidable second throughout the state at most of the conventions.

I asked Gillen how much time I had to think it over, and he said the convention was going to reconvene in about 45 minutes.

It was an interesting situation. We'd tried for it in 1960 and again in 1962. Destiny being what it is, Dolores had suggested to me out of the blue that I stop at the convention. There was no preconceived plan, but I was there. It's at that point that you start wanting to believe what you want to believe. You start to say to yourself, "Well, maybe God wants this to happen. Maybe it's my turn now."

I talked briefly to some of my old supporters, including Gus Ekola from Hibbing. Gus said, "Let's do this. Let's go." I asked where we were going, and he said we were going up to the North Star Hotel to George Steiner's room to make a call. Steiner was head of the Steiner family that owned American Linen.

They were very enthusiastic about it, but I told them I couldn't do it without asking Dolores. "I'd like to," I said, "Very frankly, I wasn't expecting this and now that it's come, I'm very excited about it."

We went over to Steiner's suite in the North Star Hotel and I called Dolores. She'd already heard on the radio. She'd heard that I'd been proposed as a candidate for governor. I told her I had to make a fast decision on whether to get into the lieutenant governor's race.

"Well you know darn well that I've been with you for the last 21 days on vacation, and I'd never even made a call back here," I said to Dolores. "I had nothing to do with this."

She said, "Would you like to do this?"

I said, "Yeah."

She said, "Well, if you want to do this, go ahead and do it. At the same time, they have very good divorce attorneys in Minneapolis, and you can do both things at once."

She said, "I don't want any part of it. We have six children. We have a business. You'd better take care of those things first."

So I went back and told them I wasn't going to run.

The funniest part about this whole thing came later. I was very close to the Levander administration. During his time in office, they reorganized the executive branch of state government. It was a year-long study of all the top levels of government. Levander appointed me as chairman of the Natural Resources Division. That committee handled conservation and minerals and all the rest. It was a big job, all year, plus I served on the main committee. Dave Durenberger became the chief administrative officer for Levander.

I remember one day when Levander called me in, just after he'd had hip surgery. He was a wonderful man. I think history will judge him as one of the more sincere, apolitical governors in the history of the state. He just had a lot of integrity.

Harold said to me, "Too bad you didn't run with me. I'm not going to run again. Had you gone with me, I'd probably be considering resigning right now and letting you fill out the term. You could be the incumbent.

"But I won't do that for Jim Goetz. I just don't think he can do it. I'm not that fond of him. My candidate in 1970 is going to be Doug Head, the attorney general."

It was becoming clear to most people in the know that Head would be the

Republican candidate and Wendy Anderson would be the Democratic candidate for governor. Dave Graven and Nick Coleman and seven or eight other Democrats were seeking the governorship, but Wendy Anderson had the inside pole. He was glamorous, he was a hockey star, he had the name, he was just built for the job.

I said to the governor, "Doug is an astute, honest, bright guy, but this is going to be the first election that's really a television election. He won't beat Wendy."

That's exactly what happened. Head picked Ben Boo, the mayor of Duluth, as his running mate, and Boo ran very well against Rudy Perpich, the DFL lieutenant gubernatorial candidate, but Head didn't fare very well against Anderson, the golden boy. Anderson and Perpich won.

As I look back on those days, I guess I can say that somewhere deep in my soul, I wish things had been different in 1966. When I was first in the legislature, I didn't think I'd ever want to run for governor. Along the way, I thought of Washington, diplomatic jobs, Federal Communication Commission appointments, newspapers, radio, television, but I don't think I ever had my eye set on the governor's job. I don't think that ever came into my mind.

But through other people, and the chance to run for the lieutenant governorship, it could have happened. I sometimes wonder what would have ensued if we had been successful. I'm sure we would have paid attention to northern Minnesota. I'm sure the state would have recognized the contributions of the northern part of the state. I'm sure we would have done every bit as much, if not more than Rudy Perpich later did.

In fact, if I carry this fantasy a little further, I can't help but wonder if I had been elected if Rudy Perpich would have ever been elected. In fact, Nonnie McKanna, one of Perpich stalwarts who served well on the state's Public Utilities Commission, once told me, "Carl, with your broad support, if you had been a Democrat, you would have been elected governor."

Even in 1970, there were people who wanted me to pursue the lieutenant governorship nomination. By that time, there wouldn't have been any problem statewide with getting the nomination. If I'd wanted it, it would have been almost automatic. But as I saw Rudy Perpich get into the fray on the Democratic side, I could see there would be bloodshed, and the area didn't need that.

I'd had my chances. I knew I was through. I didn't want to play the game anymore. It had been a chapter in my life, and it was over.

I may have been luckier in a sense because over the years I witnessed many people who had aspirations that didn't work out. They became more effective out of office than had they won.

Chapter Eleven
My Good Friend Rudy

The Perpich name has always been very prominent in Hibbing, but I was unaware while growing up that Rudy Perpich even existed. I first heard the name Perpich in the late 1930s when Hibbing had the fantastic football teams. In fact, that 1938 team had a front line as good as any front four the Vikings ever fielded. When Hibbing played Virginia in a crucial game late in October, the scouts were here from all over the country to watch some of the great players including George Perpich, a distant cousin of Rudy's.

My brother was going to Georgetown University in Washington D.C. at that time, and it had some tremendous football teams. The Georgetown staff asked Frank if he could line up some of the football material from the Range. My brother got scholarships at Georgetown for George Perpich, Bernard Munter and Bob Gelein. Gelein was the son of the prominent Hibbing athletic director, Hud Gelein.

George was a great, great guy. He spent a lot of time in our home. He went to Georgetown and paid attention to his studies and athletics and became a tremendous football player. He was honorable mention on the all-American team, and played in the Orange Bowl game. Later, he became Hibbing's hockey coach and led the Bluejackets to two state hockey championships.

That was the Perpich I knew.

Rudy was about four years behind me in school. I didn't really get to know him then, and I didn't get to know him well until he got into politics.

John Slattery was the assistant to the superintendent for the Hibbing schools. John was always very suave and intelligent, and a brilliant student of history and politics. John had been a neighbor of ours in North Hibbing, and had been a close friend. I knew he was very politically intuitive. There's no doubt that John, as he had with me, began to advise Rudy, who was on the Hibbing School Board, as to what he should do and the opportunities he might have in the political arena.

I had no relationship with Rudy until he decided to run for the State Senate. The incumbent was Elmer Peterson, chief electrician in the school district, who had served in the Legislature for many years. He was a prominent DFLer, and had been mentioned as a candidate for lieutenant governor. He had an outstanding record in the Senate.

At the time, I was the chairman of the legislative affairs committee of the Hibbing Chamber of Commerce. We were active, and would meet with the legislators on Saturdays and try to develop a legislative program. Elmer had been around a long time, and he had become a little calloused. I don't know if he was ill, or what was going on, but he really showed a temper and impatience in meeting with the chamber group. I thought that was completely uncalled for. One time, he said, "I've got better things to do then to come back every Saturday and talk to you people."

Perpich was running his campaign, and one Saturday evening Lionel Birkeland and Jack DeLuca came to my home to urge me to help Rudy. They were both good friends, and they made a strong case. I had served with Elmer Peterson, but it had become clear to me that we needed some new blood.

I entertained thoughts of helping Rudy's people, maybe sharing some of the experiences I'd had. But the thing that bothered me was that I never really knew Rudy and what he stood for. I guessed that his political ideologies would be completely DFL and probably would be anti-mining.

I've always felt that unless we keep our backbone, the mining industry, flourishing as much as possible, the Range will be in real trouble. There were many legislators in the southern part of the state who were jealous of our natural resources. We had enough problems fighting the elements from the south, let alone our own DFLers from the Range.

I told Rudy's people that I'd take it under advisement. I sent word back that I'd consider helping Rudy if he'd agree to at least be fair-minded with regard to mining taxation. I didn't expect he'd caucus with the conservatives.

Hugh Harrison was on the Hibbing School Board with Rudy. He was president of Pacific Isle Mining Co., and was well-respected in the industry. I consulted with Hugh about my worries that Rudy would be really bad for the industry.

"Well, I think you're wrong," Hugh said. "I've been with him on the school board, and I'm very impressed with him. I'd trust him, and I think he's going to be

A clipping from the Dec. 14, 1966, Hibbing Daily Tribune shows Sen. Rudy Perpich and the other district legislators. I moderated the Chamber of Commerce meeting.

LEGISLATORS REPORT — Legislators of the 63rd District reported on prospect for new legislation in the coming session at the meeting of the Hibbing Chamber of Commerce Tuesday noon. In the picture, from the left, are Sen. Rudy Perpich, Rep. Loren Rutter, Ca D'Aquila who presided at the meeting, and Rep. Jack Fena.

okay."

So I agreed.

I had used a number of strategies when I was elected. One of them was to go to the printer and have a letter made. It was done with very high quality, and it looked like a hand-written letter, addressed to every motor vehicle owner in the legislative district. It had been tremendously effective for me. It was one of greatest tactics that I ever used.

Elmer Peterson was very strong in the country, and I knew that Rudy wouldn't have time to go house to house. The district included Hibbing, Chisholm, Buhl and Mt. Iron and a rural area of about 5,000 square miles.

I suggested to the Perpich group that this kind of letter could really help them win. At the time, I contracted with the R.L. Polk Company to get the vehicle lists and to have all the envelopes typed. I remember paying that bill, and it was a substantial bill because of all the hand typing.

The letters were very impressive with the constituent's name typed on the envelope. The letter said that Rudy was a member of the school board, and that he was seeking the senate position. It said that Rudy could provide new leadership and new ideas and vitality to the area. Rudy said in the letter that he owed a great deal to the area for his education, that his family was from the area, and they had worked hard in the mines. It dealt with education, highways, and something for everyone. We tried to touch every group.

Rudy did very well. He went into Peterson's strongholds and held his own, and he was able to squeak out a victory by a couple of hundred votes.

My Good Friend Rudy

This is a real confession on my part. Outside of my wife, I don't think there are a half dozen people in the whole state who know about my contribution to Rudy's first state election. And they only know about it because in later years when Rudy was lieutenant governor or governor and I was frustrated by his actions, I'd sometimes tell people that I was partially responsible for bringing him into political existence.

§

Rudy called me one day after he was elected to the State Senate, and he said, "Do you need your teeth fixed?" I said it was getting about time to have a check up. He said, "Come on up, and we'll talk as I check your teeth."

He said as he poked around in my mouth, "You're really a sharp guy. You've made some mistakes, but you've got a tremendous future ahead of you. You ought to think about going back into politics. I think you ought to run for something."

I said, "I can see why so many dentists have become governors or other public officials. They stuff the cotton in your mouth and then they start asking questions. All you can do is nod. Pretty soon they think everybody's agreeing with them."

"What office do you think I should run for?" I asked.

He said, "I think you should start out with Stuntz Township supervisor." That was about the lowest position that existed in local politics.

Anyway, he did pretty good work on my teeth.

§

The Perpich era clearly had all the earmarks of a Kennedy-like dynasty. The three brothers, Tony, George and Rudy were all in the Minnesota Senate, and they had their eyes clearly set on higher offices.

The main one in the early 70s was John Blatnik's Congressional seat from the Eighth District in northeastern Minnesota. There was no doubt that Rudy had no love for John, and was ready to take him on at some point. As time went on, though, Rudy shifted his interest to the governor's office.

Instead, the Congressional pursuit would be taken up by brother Tony. The manifestation of this occurred in the Democratic District Convention held that year in Grand Rapids. The Perpich forces packed the early caucuses and were able to upset Jim Oberstar of Chisholm, Blatnik's longtime assistant and handpicked successor.

Many in the public were shocked that the Perpiches were able to maneuver the endorsement for Tony. Oberstar was a brilliant scholar and had made very valuable connections in the Congress and around Washington during Blatnik's final years. Some said that he was the de facto Congressman during those years. It was just assumed by many of the politicos that Oberstar would simply replace his boss in

Washington.

On the Monday following the Grand Rapids convention, Oberstar's uncle, Heine Grillo of Hibbing, came into my office and sought my advice as to whether Jim should run in the Democratic primary against Tony Perpich. He wondered whether a petition shouldn't be initiated to encourage Oberstar to continue in the race. I said, "By all means. Oberstar will win because he can benefit the district better because of his tenure and experience. Tony Perpich is a newcomer."

The campaign began to draft Oberstar. It gained tremendous momentum, using the slogan "Let the People Decide," and Oberstar defeated Perpich in the primary. He went on to win the general election.

Oberstar has become one of the most influential members of the House of Representatives. He is the ranking Democrat on the Transportation Committee, and if he is re-elected, which he surely will be, he will be one of the top ten ranking Democrats in the Congress. If the Democrats ever capture the House, he will be chairman of the Transportation Committee.

Jim Oberstar challenged the Perpich machine and he is still serving in the U.S. Congress.

I've always had the greatest respect for Jim Oberstar. He's returned the sentiment by introducing me at times as "Mr. Taconite" or "Mr. Iron Ore."

If Jim Oberstar had not run in that DFL primary election, who knows what would have happened in the next couple of decades. The Perpiches were angry at the Oberstar challenge, but Rudy later followed the same path by challenging the DFL-endorsed candidate for governor, Attorney General Warren Spannaus, and winning. In fact, it's become something of a pattern in the Democratic Farmer Labor Party for the endorsed candidate to be defeated by a strong challenger in the DFL primaries.

In the aftermath of losing my legislative race in 1950, and in the competitive spirit of "I'll show them," I started to devise the plan by which I would study state elections. I studied them county by county, precinct by precinct.

The Eighth Congressional District was always key to state elections. I figured out that if the Republicans didn't get just 18 or 20 or 22 percent, but instead could get 36 or 38 or 40 percent, there's no way they could lose a state election. In 80 percent of past state elections, the pluralities had been made up of Range votes. Stassen, Levander and Elmer Anderson won by that route.

There are some who claim that John F. Kennedy was elected President because of the plurality he received on the Iron Range. Minnesota was the deciding state in that election.

One day after Rudy Perpich became lieutenant governor, he called me to have lunch with him at the Crystal Lounge of the Androy Hotel. I think it was the day after the election.

The Androy had the noon buffet with the baron of beef. He had reserved a table right near the front. He was very cordial as we sat down. "I want to thank you for helping me," he said. "I want to see that you get some recognition for this. I just want you know that I followed your recipe with the importance of the Eighth District."

He said, "But I was a little smarter than you, because I didn't swim against the tide. I did it with the predominant party from the area."

Rudy said, "I'd like to get a four-year college for this area. Towards that end, I'd like to see someone appointed to the University of Minnesota Board of Regents. Would you consider an appointment to the Board of Regents if I can manage it?"

I told Rudy I thought it be difficult to get a four-year college on the Range since we were only 78 miles from Duluth, the site of a University of Minnesota campus. I told him of my legislative involvement in establishing UMD. "All of us have had this dream to keep our kids on the Range," I told Rudy.

At the time, each district caucused and picked its own regent. It was unusual for the governor not to go along with that recommendation. Rudy said, "If you can go down to the southern part of the Eighth District and a get a letter from those people supporting you, I'll see that you get in."

I went down to Paul and Muriel's, a cafe in Pine City, and called all these people together and gave them this story. I came back with the resolution.

"Hey, this looks really good," Rudy said. "I think we've got a real shot at this."

Lo and behold, I heard later that Rudy went to the conservative element in Duluth and talked with those people, and they were very reluctant to support any competition with UMD. And they were strongly against the removal of the regent position from Duluth to the Range.

My name had not been mentioned in the newspapers up to that point, and I asked Rudy that it not be mentioned unless there was a chance that this was for real. I didn't want to make it a political contest.

I got a call one day and learned that there was a darkhorse in the race for regent. It was Bill Montague who was the lead attorney for the mining companies and their chief lobbyist in the Legislature. He was a renowned and honest man, respected by every single legislator. He had been there for years.

So, once Montague got in the race, I started getting calls saying, "Carl, will you please bow out?" There wasn't any question, and I did that immediately.

It was very clever that Perpich came to me and sold me on the idea, and then after

I had accomplished what he had asked me to do, he went to the Duluth people and set up this other scenario.

※※※

Jeno Paulucci was always a big factor in the Perpich administration. I will always remember when Jeno and Rudy passed the big taconite tax, the largest increase. They had a hearing in the Senate Office Building and there were several hundred people there.

After Perpich and Paulucci had made their presentations, I told the hearing, "Look. Usually before you levy a tax, you justify the need. First you set a budget. What do you need all this for? This will bring in a lot more than the communities up there need right now."

Paulucci got up and said, in true Jeno fashion, "Forget that. Just pass the tax, and we'll figure out how to spend it."

※※※

The D'Aquila and Perpich children were always close friends. Mary Sue Perpich and my son, Jim, were on the prom committee together at Hibbing High School. Later on, when Jim was with Drexel-Burnham in New York, Mary Sue was hired by the same company. The Perpiches are very nice people. Outside of politics, he was a very personable and impressive guy.

He always talked about his heritage, growing up in Carson Lake and how he didn't have a tie. He talked of his hardship, and how his father suffered at the hands of the mining company. His father was treated no differently than all of the European immigrants working in the mines.

I can't help but wonder how comfortable Rudy felt in the homes of the rich and famous once he became governor. Irwin Jacobs, Carl Pohlad, Curt Carlson, Marilyn Nelson — you name them, Rudy was in a constant and close relationship with all of them. He spent a lot of time with them, socially and otherwise.

※※※

Rudy was the kind of a guy who if you told him he couldn't do something, he'd go out and do it.

Bringing the Super Bowl to Minnesota, bringing in Soviet President Gorbachev, choice in schools — Rudy had a lot of dynamic ideas. I feel sorry that his own career that could have been more illustrious was nipped in the bud by the chip he held on his shoulder.

My Good Friend Rudy

Capitol Corridors ran for many years and always had a good audience and a lot of controversy. Here I'm interviewing Warren Spannaus, who was Minnesota's Attorney General and a candidate for governor. The co-host at that time was Marcia Fleur from KSTP-TV in the Twin Cities. She later became a member of the University of Minnesota top staff.

**WATCH!
CAPITOL CORRIDORS
SUNDAY MORNING
MARCH 4
AT 11:30 A.M.**
(After 'Issues and Answers')
**OVER CHANNELS
WDIO-10 or WIRT-13**
Featuring
Nancy Brataas, Senator
and Host Carl M. D'Aquila

How many people can say, "I was a member of the school board, the state Senate, I was lt. governor, I was governor." He very well could have gone on to be U.S. Senator, maybe even vice president or president of the United States. From Hibbing, Minnesota, that's a long, long road.

He will have to go down in the annals as an unbelievable figure.

୨୦୧୨୦୧୨୦୧

Rudy was very brilliant in appointing those who had press backgrounds to critical administrative positions. He was a tremendously intuitive, smart politician who knew the value of media experience. He picked former news people for about 80 percent of his key people when he first took over. A press pass was like a passport in the Perpich administration.

୨୦୧୨୦୧୨୦୧

Count the Pickets in the Fence

I had been doing "Capitol Corridors" since 1968. WDIO in Duluth had called and said they wanted to do a legislative program, and asked if I would be interested. I had been doing election-night analysis for many years both on radio and on television. This was an outgrowth of that.

It was interesting that after a few years, KSTP in the Twin Cities called and said they wanted the program. Once we got down there, the program had something of a statewide significance.

Every week I would fly down to do the show. The connection from the airlines left no margin for error, as the taping schedule was absolute. On the other hand, I wanted to have a rental car because I usually had other business to do in the Twin Cities.

I would rent a car and hire a cab at the same time. I would give the cabbie the location of the KSTP studio, and then I would follow him to the studio. That may have been a little crazy, but I got to the studio on time.

~~~

Capitol Corridors ran live on Monday nights at 6:30 p.m. A legislative staffer actually would transcribe the show, and on Tuesday mornings there was a copy of the transcription on every lawmaker's desk.

We were getting a lot of mail, maybe two or three hundred letters a week.

Rudy was very unhappy with the Capitol Corridors program because his activities provided so much of the material for discussion. He was that active. He was that much of a target.

I used to take a lot of pot shots at him, but I would say that in all those years, I never made it personal. I addressed the issues. It was strictly my feeling that he was anti-mining, and that he had broken a promise to me when he was about to become a member of the Senate. I just felt he was leading the area down a path that we'd been many, many years before with anti-mining sentiment. With the Taconite Amendment in place, I thought we should be moving on. If one looks back in the records, one would find that during those years when we were all pushing so hard for the Taconite Amendment, it was Rudy Perpich who was one of six or seven people in the Legislature who voted against taking it to a vote of the people.

Rudy was always giving grief to WDIO Television's Fran Befera about the tenor of the program. I'm sure he was behind the letters to the FCC saying the show was bent in one direction. The more popular the program got, the more intensely Rudy's followers opposed it, and the more letters were sent to the FCC.

I have one letter in my files that was sent to the station from George Perpich. It said in no uncertain terms, "Get this guy off."

George wrote: "I recommend that KSTP either give the DFL equal time in countering D'Aquila's opinionated facts, or that your replace this particular commentator with a genuinely fair moderator." KSTP wrote back and invited George to appear on the show, but he never accepted the offer.

They wanted me off the program so badly that Rudy called Befera, who at that time was the chairman of the Metropolitan Airports Commission. He was up for reappointment. He told Fran that he'd make sure he got reappointed if he took the program off the air, but Fran wouldn't do it. I was absolutely amazed because Fran really liked that job, and he really wanted it, but Fran did not give in. He told me, "I won't sacrifice the program, and I won't sacrifice a friend."

Perpich was true to his word, and Befera didn't get reappointed. Instead, the governor appointed Ray Glumack of Eveleth whom Befera had hired as his deputy. It's ironic that the drive into the airport is now called Glumack Drive. It should have been called Befera Drive in recognition of what Fran Befera did for Minnesota air service across the state.

※※※

As a former House member, I had a right to be on the floor of the Legislature. I also had the credentials of a newsman. One day when Rudy was lieutenant governor, I walked into the Senate and was setting up a taping session with Sen. Jerry Blatz of Bloomington. I went down the aisle to Sen. Blatz's desk and handed him a note that I wanted to see him at the back or outside the chambers. Rudy saw me hand him that note from the podium. He ordered the sergeant-at-arms to remove me from the chambers and charge me with lobbying while the Senate was in session.

He also charged that I wasn't a registered lobbyist. Well, of course, I wasn't a lobbyist at all. The whole incident was bandied about in the newspapers, and they had committee hearings. I was absolved of any such charge. When they checked it all out, my credentials were as valid as anybody from the Minneapolis Tribune or any other media representative.

※※※

I suppose I became somewhat famous as Rudy's arch nemesis when he verbally attacked me one day on a radio show. I was appearing on WMFG's call-in program with Dave Cook, who later became one of Rudy's press people.

Rudy called in, and we had quite a debate on the telephone. He ended up calling me "the worst liar in the state."

It made the front pages of all the newspapers in Minnesota. It was really a prelude to the debate that happened on television somewhat later.

We invited Rudy to participate on Capitol Corridors a number of times. At that time I had been sharing the program with Veda Ponikvar, the newspaper editor from Chisholm. We were trying to give the show a better political balance, and she was a very astute newsperson, an outstanding leader and a DFLer from the Range. Her presence alone achieved our goal. The ratings had always been high, and whatever we talked about was always the subject of conversation in the coffee shops. It got people thinking. Whether they agreed on it or not, they liked to talk about it.

Finally, Perpich did come up and do a debate with us at WDIO. I'll never forget that occasion.

We had invited the statewide press to be there, and Fran Befera had cooked an Italian dinner, personally provided wine, and had all the places set downstairs at the television station. It was getting time to tape it, and no one was showing up. So we called the media in the Twin Cities who informed us that, "Oh, we're not coming up any more. We had a call from the governor's office this morning that it was a private taping."

Yes, I always have looked up to Rudy if not his politics. This photo was made in the Governor's Reception Room at the Capitol in 1987. I had introduced the Twins stamps to honor the world champions. Carl Pohlad was on hand to present the World Series trophy.

So here was Fran with all his ravioli and all his spaghetti, and no one came to eat it.

We had our debate, and it was as lively one as one might expect. The governor flew right back to St. Paul. The next morning we picked up the newspapers, and read that the governor had said he had smashed me in the debate. The governor did not disclose that he had lost his cool in that program very badly. It was in the first few minutes of the program.

So I waited a couple of weeks and went down to do the regular show. Without saying anything to the station management, instead of having the regular program, I

My Good Friend Rudy

told the viewers that were going to see the tape of the famous debate. We showed it to the Twin City area.

We had hundreds and hundreds of letters the next week. They were about 90 percent in our favor after they saw Rudy's demeanor. It was that fall, then, after the debate, that he was defeated by Gov. Albert Quie.

☙❧☙❧☙❧

Prior to that historic debate, Rudy appeared on the show one other time. He had a second home over at Lake Eshquagama on the east end of the Range. I lived in Hibbing in the other direction. Rudy would not let me drive down that day, and so we arranged to meet at the Lantern, a restaurant about halfway between us. We would then commute together to Duluth for the debate.

We drove down, and it was a beautiful day, and the conversation was very congenial. We completed our debate and came out of the station, and, all of a sudden, the sky turned black. It started lightning and cracking and the car was vibrating. The wind was blowing hard. Rudy said, "What's going on?" I replied, "Rudy, God is just paying you back for all those lies on that program."

He laughed, and as we drove home, he said, "Carl I know you're the friend of the mining companies, but they've screwed everybody -- their friends and everybody else through the ages. Why do you think I have the feeling I have after what they did to my father and everybody else?"

At this point, he pulled a dime out of his pocket and gave it to me. "When they get through screwing you, call me. You can at least admit that they did it."

We've had that dime for years taped to a cabinet door in our kitchen. The trouble is, if I ever felt the need to use it, a call now costs 35 cents and Rudy didn't leave a forwarding number.

☙❧☙❧☙❧

It's hard to figure out where Rudy went wrong. Was he driven by a desire to redeem his father and to redeem all the people on the Iron Range?

Was he driven by a desire to represent all those people he claimed were abused by the mines. Was he saying, "I'm going to show them"? Did it get out of hand?

I think Rudy's difficulty was that he was surrounded by a lot of yes people. They stroked him and said, "Hey, boss, you're wonderful. Keep it up." They never said, "Hey, you'd better take inventory like so many who have gone before you."

Rudy either took bad advice, or what he himself had determined was inappropriate, and nobody dared tell him.

He had an ego a mile high, and he'd get tremendously upset if there was a critical editorial about him in the Minneapolis Tribune or St. Paul Pioneer Press. He'd call the media and take them to task right away. He would become absolutely wild when he or his actions was challenged.

He once told me, "The secret to politics is that you've got to move. You've got to know when not to stay in one place too long." I think he may not have followed his own advice. He stayed with the power and didn't take the risk. He stayed too long.

☙☙☙

Through it all, I was never jealous of him because he had achieved a political office I had dreams of attaining. I never challenged him personally, but he was often critical of me and my relationship with the mining companies.

I may have taken shots at Rudy's politics, but I also took shots at the conservative leadership when it was merited. Rudy may have felt it was a vendetta against him, but it wasn't. He always maintained that since I was in the business of selling to the mines, I was a tool of the industry. This isn't true, and there were many times I opposed what the industry was trying to do, and I publicly stated it.

One of my pet projects was fair taxation. In fact, when the industry sometimes wanted taxes lower than what they should be, I opposed it. But then I also opposed Perpich when he was talking about a hundred or two hundred percent increases.

Nothing I ever did was done with any malice or animosity. It was always issue-oriented. His replies, though, were always personal darts.

As the years went by, making personal attacks continued to be his trouble with other people also, and was partly to blame for some of the defeats he suffered.

It makes me realize how frail public life is. I've often said, and people have scoffed at me, that with a couple of different breaks, Rudy Perpich, instead of Bill Clinton, could have been sitting in the White House. They both came the same route. They were both chairmen of the council of governors. They were both chairmen of the education conference of the governors. They both had the same political philosophy. They both worked hard to get where they got.

Rudy Perpich was a very astute politician. He probably was as astute as Hubert Humphrey, although not as good an orator. Rudy knew the game. He had instinct and he knew what to do. Even in his shots at me, he'd laugh. I wondered if under the surface he might be thinking, "Well, Carl, I really don't feel this way, but you're good fodder. It works."

Rudy was driven. He was driven so much, he had to be a frustrated individual. He felt the elections he lost were unfair, particularly the Quie election. Rudy was pro-choice at the time, and when the anti-abortion people put a leaflet under everybody's windshield wiper at church that Sunday morning before election day, he felt that was a dirty hand.

When Arne Carlson was governor, Dolores and I were often invited to stay overnight at the mansion. On the first such occasion, it was a warm moonlit night and Dolores and I couldn't sleep. We went down to the lawn and sat visiting.

I reminded Dolores that on several occasions there had been the possibility that we might have ended up living in that house. We finally went back to bed near midnight.

The next morning, Gov. Carlson said, "What were you two doing walking around all night?" I replied, "I thought Rudy Perpich's ghost was in the house."

One last thing about Rudy. Behind every smart politician, there's somebody. It might be his wife or somebody else. In Rudy's case it might have been his wife, Lola, or his brother, George, or other family members.

But I'd be willing to wager that from the time Rudy sat on the Hibbing School Board, the genius behind Rudy was John Slattery. John planted the seed in Rudy to run for the school board, to run for the Senate, to seek the lieutenant governorship, and on and on and on.

I'll bet there wasn't a day they weren't in contact.

And when it came time for Rudy to be inaugurated, he came back to the Hibbing High School Board Room. It was not only a tribute to his school and his town and to education, but it was a tribute to John Slattery.

We were in Italy when Rudy died. I got a call in Rome from the office, and I was shocked when they said Rudy Perpich had died. I said, "How can this be?" I asked if it was some sort of accident because he had such good living habits. They said, no, it was colon cancer.

We cut our trip short by a few days and headed back for the funeral. I thought deeply about whether I should go and about what people were going to say. I know how cynical people are, and I knew there would be some who would question my motives. But in the end, I was glad I went.

My son, Jim, and I went over to the Basilica in Minneapolis. I was impressed with the arrangements. The family could have stacked the deck and had a section for the luminaries, but they didn't. There was no pecking order, no protocol, you just sat wherever you found a seat.

It was a packed church and it was all very impressive. When a powerful politician dies in America, there's a sense of shock and loss much more than when somebody else dies. It might be because we think of politicians as invulnerable. Their death brings the reality of life back to us.

I heard from people at the funeral that even six weeks earlier, Rudy had been making plans for another try at running for governor. These people wondered if it was just wishful thinking on his part.

I don't think so. I think Rudy was sincere, even knowing his health condition. I believe that Rudy thought he could overcome his cancer. He had overcome so much in his life. He was such a fighter.

My Good Friend Rudy

Chapter Twelve

Trying to Preserve Reserve

The Reserve Mining Case really blossomed into public recognition around 1968. The litigation over the disposal of the taconite tailings into Lake Superior lasted nearly a decade, and wasn't resolved until April 8, 1977, when the Minnesota Supreme Court approved an on-land tailings disposal system.

In the end, the court's decision cost Reserve $400 million to construct a tailings disposal basin at Milepost Seven on the railroad between Silver Bay, on the North Shore of Lake Superior, and Babbitt, a small town on the eastern edge of the Iron Range where Reserve's mine was located.

Wendell Anderson was governor and Rudy Perpich was lieutenant governor during the critical years.

It was a difficult situation for me to keep in proper perspective because I was in the mining tire business. I was doing a fair amount of business with Reserve, about a one-quarter to one-third share. My family and I knew many of the people involved at Reserve.

The company never tried to influence me in any way to do anything unethical. They waged a fair and honest campaign. People forget that the company, since 1957, was operating legally with a permit from the United States Army Corps of Engineers. In dumping those tons of ground-up rock into the lake, the company was doing exactly what it was permitted to do.

Dr. Cledo Brunetti, my wife's uncle, regarded as one of the leading scientists in the world, had brought a team of researchers to northern Minnesota during the Reserve case. He was the inventor of the proximity fuse for the atomic bomb and had led space research for major American companies. He was from Virginia, Minnesota, and he was concerned about what he saw as a frame against Reserve.

Brunetti's team dove to the bottom of Lake Superior and conducted several studies to find out exactly what was being dumped into the lake.

What they found was that there really were no additives going into the lake. The tailings, the leftover substance after the iron ore was removed, were material that was taken from the bowels of the earth — God-made material. What they were putting in the lake was just the residue of the products that had come from the earth. It wasn't a case of dumping sewage or a chemical or something foreign into the lake.

When Reserve went into business in 1957, no one thought it was a bad thing to dump that material in the water. This was considered a remote location. It was the north shore of Lake Superior. Minneapolis people weren't thinking about it. Iron Range people weren't concerned about it. There was no objection from anyone to dumping rock into the lake.

Dr. Brunetti was shocked that the case could continue without consideration of that elemental fact. But even I could see that we were in a new era, where the environment was a significant part of the balance scale. The job-based factors were overruled by the environmental factors. The American people had changed their philosophy.

In addition, the other companies were not handling their wastes in such a manner. They all had on-land tailings disposal sites. Here was a lake that belonged to everyone, to the world, and anyone could see that the practice could not continue.

Orville Freeman, the Democratic governor, was probably the main proponent of getting a taconite operation started on the North Shore. He worked hard to get Reserve its permits. It's ironic that a liberal Democrat, a man who later become Secretary of Agriculture under Kennedy, was the strongest proponent of Reserve Mining at its inception. Later, it was the liberal wing of the Democrats that took up this fight to drive Reserve out of the water.

My involvement began in 1968 when Alvin Lind of Duluth and his associates began to pound the drums to get the tailings out of the lake. I appealed to the company at that time to find an alternative to dumping their tailings in the lake.

I stated on my television program Capitol Corridors that Reserve should consider and come forth with its own plan to get out of the water. I sat in Ed Furness' sauna — he was the president of Reserve — at 2 a.m. after a late party, pleading with him. I told him he should get out of the water before they hit him with a lawsuit.

The company really used bad judgment in not coming up earlier with its own plan in a constructive manner. When you're dumping 68,000 tons a day of anything into a lake, it's obvious that even if it's pure cane sugar, or milk or anything we think of as pure, it still boggles the mind. People just wouldn't accept it.

Up to that time, Reserve had run a tremendous public relations program under Ed

Schmid. The company always did the right thing everywhere. It was king in the Twin Cities, in Washington, and everywhere else. The company made heavy political contributions to Walter Mondale, to Eugene McCarthy, to Hubert Humphrey and to John Blatnik. It made all the right moves.

But it never took care of Sen. Gaylord Nelson or Sen. William Proxmire across the way in Wisconsin. These two men thought Lake Superior was just as much their lake as it was Blatnik's. Sure enough, the woman who first started the whole effort against Reserve was from the Proxmire-Nelson camp. Mrs. Mize carried a banner in front of the White House for weeks and weeks and weeks. "Get Reserve out of our water — 68,000 tons a day." She never gave up.

Even today, I am unable to reveal many of the details of my involvement in the Reserve case. In any case this important, with so much at stake, there are bound to be intrigues and behind-the-scenes activities. Let me just say that there were some very surprising characters standing in the wings as the Reserve case took center stage.

No one but my wife knew that I had become an intermediary in the Reserve Case, a person who had to try and keep all the sides in balance. My secretary had to know about my dealings, but I would guess that other employees of my company did not.

We had to do many bizarre things. We ran a private telephone line up to our Side Lake cabin because we couldn't trust the party line. It was the first such line that Northwestern Bell ran north of Hibbing. The company said it wasn't in its plans for years, but I got the line installed in one week.

Thinking back on this case, I also remember the words of Norman Borlaug, the University of Minnesota graduate and Nobel Prize winner, that you have to balance the needs of making a living and having a proper, pure environment. He said the pollution of our nation had not just happened in recent years, but over the age of the nation and through many wars and years of industrial output. He acknowledged that the blame cannot be assessed against an organization which occupies an important niche of our society and feel it's that organization's responsibility to clean it up. Borlaug said that one cannot take care of the environment overnight because more harm than good would be done.

And as we watch year by year, there's less concern for the jobs and more concern for the autocratic decisions by environmentalists.

The judge assigned to the case was Miles Lord. He was convinced that the tailings were filled with asbestos, but it was never proven. An endless number of experts were brought in on both sides, nationally known medical research people, and no one was able to prove anything.

There were some people who had been with Reserve for a number of years and were now retired, and there were some asbestos links, but those links could also be identified in the other companies that didn't use the lake for their tailings disposal. In fact, the number of people who had a health link to asbestos at Reserve was lower than at other properties on the Range where the tailings were dumped on land.

Although this case persisted for a decade, I doubt whether Judge Lord, Rudy Perpich or Grant Merritt, also a major figure in the trial, at any time realized that I was a central intermediary in this case.

I was involved in the case for seven very intense years, when I would be occupied for five or six hours a day of time spent handling correspondence, memoranda, phone calls, planning sessions, or just keeping up on what was happening day by day with numbers of people from the company, both at the local level and at Republic Steel in Cleveland, and the legal firms who handled the case.

Only if they read this book will Lord or Merritt or any of the others then know that I was involved to such an extent. It was that meticulously handled. It meant disguising trips to Cleveland as trips I made to call on other customers. I don't know if it ever occurred to anyone that I only needed to go to Cleveland two or three times a year for normal business, but instead I was going every month or six weeks.

Even at the time, it was amazing that I was in such a position with the stakes so great. The company and the attorneys became convinced that I could help. They proceeded very cautiously, but when I made predictions and pointed out certain things to them, they became believers and placed their confidence in me. We became the clearing house for all the activities that were occurring.

> Throw a paper cup out of your car window, and the State will fine you $100.00 for littering.
>
> Dump 67,000 tons of asbestos bearing taconite tailings into Lake Superior, and not only is there no fine, but the company that did the dumping pays less taxes than any other industry.
>
> SUPPORT THE HOUSE POSITION... HELP RESTORE BEAUTIFUL NORTHEASTERN MINNESOTA.   Rudy.

There was no doubt where Rudy Perpich stood on the Reserve Case as lt. governor. By the time the case was settled, he had become governor.

Reserve was looking from week to week for a sense of direction and a plan of action. As I look at the people I was working with, I can't sense any unethical behavior or crime on their parts. What they were trying to do was make sure justice would be rendered, something that would be fair to both sides. These people were not for a status quo, and they absolutely insisted that the company do something. All they wanted was a balance.

Everyone was motivated by the lives of the people who would be affected. As I got close to these people, I spent endless hours in the Silver Bay and Babbitt areas, and I saw the health conditions erode, not because of asbestos, but because of the stress of the ongoing litigation. I saw the heart attacks, the strokes, the divorces, the problems in the families with children. I saw the use of illegal drugs that started. I saw the financial ruination of many people.

It was particularly devastating because of the way Babbitt and Silver Bay were isolated from the rest of the Iron Range, dependent totally on Reserve. Their future was threatened.

It was clear from the beginning that if Reserve was forced to dump its tailings all the way at the other end, back at Babbitt, it would have never been able to survive. As it was, the company not only had to bond for nearly $400 million for the work that was done, but it had to reduce its output.

During the time early on when Judge Lord had ordered the company closed, and it had appealed, I met with Reserve's superintendent Merlyn Woodle whom I had known as superintendent of the Republic Susquehanna Mine. I had always enjoyed Woodle. He had the wit and humor of a Will Rogers.

I said, "Merlyn, I have to have the answers to some questions. I don't think you can win without these answers to eliminate the fears that exist." He said, "What are they?" I told him what they were, and he replied, "Are you crazy? I haven't even given this information to my attorney. I know you wear many hats, but who in the hell are you representing?"

I said, "Merlyn, I don't blame you for your hesitation, but why don't we make a bargain?" I gave him a few predictions, and asked him to give it a little time and see if what I said didn't pan out. Less than a week later, he called me.

"You son of a b-b-b-bitch," he said. He used to stammer a bit. He gave me the answers to my questions.

That started the work of many hours a day, usually seven days a week, for seven years. I was in constant contact with their PR director, their attorney, people in the company, legislators, reporters, television, the works.

A couple of interesting tidbits come to mind.

When they were taking evidence and doing depositions in Miles Lord's court, I was scheduled to appear. I followed Fred Cina who was a legislator and the director of the Range League of Municipalities. Lord was on the bench, and he looked at me and said, "Oh, it's you. I finally have an opportunity to meet you. You've done pretty well for a young guy from Hibbing whose father worked in the mines. You're pretty comfortable now with all these big steel executives, aren't you?

"By the way," he said. "Is Mary Kay your daughter?" I told him she was. He said, "Well, I danced with her on New Year's eve at the Lafayette Country Club. She married the son of the chairman of International Multifoods, didn't she? She did pretty well too." He was really digging in with the poison.

We got into the dialogue. He said, "You're supposed to be an expert." I said, "Well I haven't been reading comic books. I've pretty much stuck to mining and steel and laws and politics. I think I know the Range and northern Minnesota and, for that matter, the state as well as anybody else. I'd be willing to back that up." He said, "Oh, you would? Well, how much do you know about this steel business? You know if I close them up, I'll have a new operator in there in 30 days."

I said, "Your honor, I don't think even the real Lord could do that."

He went wild and slammed the gavel and said, "No more remarks like that from you or I'll hold you in contempt of court. Strike that from the record."

Miles Lord had worked in the mine at Crosby on the Cuyuna Range. He went to law school and ended up marrying Maxine Zontelli, the daughter of Emil Zontelli, who was part owner of the Zontelli Mining Co. It was perhaps the leading mining subcontractor on the Range. It was very successful. So it's ironic, coming out of a family that's deeply involved in mining, that he could turn and be so adamant against the mining companies.

Miles Lord's son, Jim, was the State Treasurer at that time, and he was forced to choose between his father and the governor on the issue. Miles Lord was convinced that Wendell Anderson was interfering with environmental impact studies because he supported Reserve. In the end, Jim Lord sided with his dad who he said he'd have to live with the rest of his life.

Eventually, Miles Lord was removed from the case by the Eighth Circuit Court of Appeals. The court ruled that Lord had exhibited a gross bias against Reserve Mining, and it was clear to see that he'd lost his sense of fairness about the case.

Lord had already set the stage for the demise of Reserve, though, and it would have been very difficult for any federal judge to reverse the procedure, particularly with the environmental attention that was focused on the case.

One other person who was instrumental in bringing Reserve to its knees, Grant Merritt, also had an interesting background. His grandparents were "swindled" by the Rockefellers when the Merritt Brothers were among the original people who founded the Iron Range. You could see where someone could become really biased against big industry.

These vendettas that occur can come from the roots of dissension and the disgust of just a few individuals. It shows what just a few people can do.

The case went on through the years, and I remember when we were bringing it to a head. Rudy Perpich was now governor, and the time had come when we felt it was necessary that, as long as Reserve had agreed to go to Milepost Seven, a statement should be made that the war should end and a blessing should be given. We felt it should be the governor who made such a statement.

Perpich didn't know I was involved at all. At the time, Warren Spannaus was the attorney general, so we went across the hall at the Capitol Building and quietly went to work on Warren. The governor never saw us go into the office. I pleaded with Warren to urge the governor to make a press announcement. Warren wasn't really the kind of man who would do really risky, courageous things. But in this case, he agreed with the theory, and he did go into Perpich and talk with him. He told Rudy that if he didn't do it, he'd do it himself as attorney general.

Lo and behold, Perpich finally did it later that afternoon.

I thought the decision would bring stability and continuity to the company. I thought it would ensure the prosperity of the North Shore. Little did I realize what would happen later on. Reserve was the most modern of all the plants, but it had to go through bankruptcy. In the end, during the 1980s with the shrinkage that came to the industry, the additional cost of building Milepost Seven put the company under.

It was a real calamity. There were the employees who devoted their lives to the company and worked so hard. Some of those men even cut the trees and blazed the path through the woods to build Reserve, and they ended up losing their pension. They finally got only partially what they deserved.

Reserve had completed the on-land tailings disposal and air quality improvement facilities in 1980 at a cost of $370 million. The bankruptcy occurred in 1986 and was a direct result of that financial burden.

It was a shame, especially the toll it took on the employees, families, the area, the state and all its ties to many parts of the economy which benefitted from it. Taconite operations create many more jobs than just the ones who work at the plant.

As it came out of bankruptcy in 1990, the company was auctioned off and Cypress Mining from Colorado defeated Cleveland Cliffs to get possession. Cypress had never mined iron ore, but it was a large and very successful company, mining coal, copper and other minerals. It reopened the mine with a $40 million renovation and without a union. It became very successful. Only a handful of employees were hired from the old work force and most of the former employees became victims of the changeover.

A few years later, Cypress surprisingly decided to sell the property. Cleveland Cliffs, the losing bidder on the first go-round, purchased it in 1994 and is operating it as Northshore Mining. It produces 4.7 million tons of pellets a year.

After the decision was reached, Merlyn Woodle called all his employees to a dinner one night at Lutsen ski resort on the North Shore. All the administrative and management employees were there and Woodle told them he was going to retire. He was replaced by Matt Banovetz, a popular Ely native who was a smart replacement choice. "Before I do, though, I want you know that there's a man sitting in this room to whom you people are responsible for your jobs and for the fact we're still in business." He paid his respects to Dolores and me and asked that the company keep us in serious consideration, bearing in mind that we had to be competitive. It was only then that we started to get 50 or 60 percent of Reserve's tire business, but it was very short lived.

During all those years of our involvement, we had no more than a fair share of the business from them because they didn't dare increase my business because of the hand I was playing.

Now, as I reflect back over all those years, I feel proud of my efforts to save the property. Had we not saved it, Cleveland Cliffs would not be able to operate the property today, there would not be the jobs, and the communities of Silver Bay and and Babbitt would be devastated. The state and the Range would have lost big revenue and the economic impact would have been apparent in many lives.

It's ironic, though, that I became one of the last victims of the whole odyssey. I lost my business there, and Northshore doesn't buy anything from us.

∞⋄∞⋄∞⋄

One short postscript to the Reserve story:

John Farley was the vice president of LTV, Reserve's owner at the end. He was an intellectual. I knew him well. He'd taken trips with us to California and to mining congresses.

He called me the afternoon before Reserve was going to close. There had been rumors of its demise, but nobody knew for sure. Certainly, none of the vendors knew. Nobody who worked at Reserve even knew it was going to happen.

We talked about families and so forth, and then he casually said, "I'm going to read you a poem." He read it to me, and said, "What do you think?"

I admitted that it didn't mean anything to me.

He said, "You didn't listen." And he read it again.

He quizzed me again on what it meant and realized I still didn't get it.

"Machiavelli," he said, "you're not paying attention. I'm going to read it one last time. Pay particular attention to the last two lines."

He read,

"For strike tonight,
For tomorrow is too late."

Finally I got it. Something bad was going to happen at Reserve. I had 12 tires up there worth about $75,000, and none of them had been put on mining trucks despite the fact they had been there for several months. Nor had I been paid for them.

The only reason the tires had not been installed was that Nobby Valeri and the

Goodyear tire people had convinced Reserve not to put them on the trucks. They were experimental tires.

I called Dick Nelson in the Purchasing Department at Reserve and told him I wanted those tires. By now it was about 20 minutes to four in the afternoon. He said he'd open the gate.

I sent two trucks up to get the tires, and we brought them back. At midnight, the company announced bankruptcy, and the place was shut up tight.

Two days later, I was in the Old Howard Restaurant when Valeri, the Goodyear dealer, came in. He pointed his finger at me and said, "You. You. You're the only one. You got your stuff out of there. You're the only one. They favored you. You're on the inside." He was madder than heck.

I said, "Nobby, I only have you to thank." He said, "Why?" I told him that the only reason the tires hadn't been put on the trucks was because Goodyear had convinced the Reserve people to delay.

As it turned out, people only got three or four cents on the dollar for bills they had with Reserve. We got stuck on other things, but at least we got those tires out.

Trying to Preserve Reserve

Chapter Thirteen
STAYING RATIONAL WITH NATIONAL

During the 1990s, another drama unfolded on the Iron Range that involved some of the same characters as the Reserve Case.

I had been involved with National Steel Pellet Company since 1964 when construction of the plant was announced. My work with the Taconite Amendment and my close relationship with Hanna Mining Co., which managed the National plant, helped me become acquainted with the parent company in Pittsburgh.

In the late 1970s, I began visiting the national headquarters of many of the steel companies on a regular basis, and in 1978 I began an annual dinner meeting in Washington D.C., which brought together leading senators from both parties and the chairmen and presidents of the steel and iron ore companies. Together, the two sides could discuss the problems facing the steel industry, in particular the import and dumping of foreign steel and iron ore in the United States. These meetings lasted for a period of about 10 years and were very successful.

Hanna managed a number of mines through the years, including Butler Taconite at Nashwauk and National Steel at Keewatin. Butler was probably the quality property on the Iron Range as far as ore reserves. It was owned by Hanna, Inland and Wheeling Steel.

It was named after the Butler Family — a tremendous Minnesota family and a national power. They really respected and took care of their employees, and there was probably a greater loyalty and camaraderie at Butler Mining than there was at any other mining operation. To this day, former Hanna employees, particularly those who worked at Butler, still get together socially with their wives.

The public never really realized that Butler was in danger. Despite its quality ore, and despite the quality of its workforce, it was in grave danger because of the structure of its ownership. Wheeling Steel had fallen upon hard times. Inland Steel, which was once the most solid financially of any of the companies, started to close down various parts of its empire as things tightened up. Inland had another mine on the Range, the Minorca in Virginia, and it started to think about how it could get out of having to take a certain tonnage from Butler Taconite.

Inland and Wheeling began to put the squeeze on Hanna, and this went on for a number of years. Bob Anderson was running Hanna at the time, and he was able to keep the property open for a number of years despite the great pressure from the other two owners.

I'll never forget the jolt when it all came down in 1985. Bob Anderson called me one night, and he was in shock. They had served papers on him, ordering him to close the property. Inland and Wheeling were calling the shots.

The Range was devastated.

This was the first indication that the Range was in peril. If this could happen to Butler, which was such a sound property, what was going to happen to the rest of the taconite operations? The huge recession in the steel industry had started in October of 1981, and Butler was the first casualty.

I did business with Butler, in fact it was one of my best accounts. We were the leading supplier of tires. It was a real blow to us and a real danger to the future of our business.

Had Butler been able to hang on for another year, until things started looking up for the steel industry in the fall of 1986, I question whether that property would have ever been closed. In future years, especially considering the high quality ore reserves it had, the plant would have been a prime candidate to be converted to a direct reduced iron plant. It could have been high-level operation, and there are still those who are trying to make that happen.

A recent plan by Minnesota Iron and Steel would have the ore shipped to Eveleth Taconite for processing and then brought back to the Butler site to be directly reduced into iron. It was a big plan, but all the pieces were starting to fit together. There has been some legislative funding. In the end, though, Eveleth Taconite turned down the offer to sell the company.

LTV shocked the Range in 2000 by announcing it would permanently shut down in 2001. That's 1,400 jobs. There are some who predict LTV won't be alone in closing down. Energy costs, the problems with capital formation, and the state of the American steel industry indicate that not all of the taconite plants will survive.

Directly reduced iron, or pig iron, is definitely the solution to Iron Range permanency. A value-added product is the answer. There have been some proposals for pri-

The grinding mills at National Steel Pellet Company in Keewatin. These plants take the low-grade taconite, a very hard rock, and grind it down to face powder consistency. The iron is then removed magnetically. National had some cost problems that were being worked on when the labor dispute shut the plant down on August 1, 1993.

vate funding. Ford has apparently agreed to take some of the product in the Minnesota Iron and Steel project. But, still the chances of it happening are less than 50/50.

Cleveland Cliffs, the operating partner of LTV, had planned a DRI plant at Northshore Mining, formerly Reserve, but now the plan has been postponed for another year.

Larry Lehtinen's return to the Iron Range leads me to believe that something may be up with getting a DRI or slab steel plant to replace the LTV taconite plant. I think that's a real possibility, not only because of the urgency of the matter, but because of the tremendous reserves of ore at the Northshore mines at Hoyt Lakes and Babbitt, also owned by Cleveland Cliffs. The project will require more than one half billion dollars. It's still an iffy proposition because of the present weak state of the steel industry.

Anyway, Hanna wanted to get out of the Butler site entirely in the 1980s and sell what it could. Once the decision was made to dismantle the plant, I got involved in the process. I was associated with Hoover Construction and Mining Services as we dismantled the buildings and sold the equipment. I'll tell you, though, if those buildings had been left, I think that plant would have been reopened at some later point.

Many of the Butler employees who were not eligible for retirement transferred over to National Steel. This plant had no real ownership problem as 15 percent was owned by Hanna and 85 percent by the National Steel Corp. In 1984, National Steel was purchased by the huge Japanese steel company NKK.

Years later, who would have ever thought that this other gem of a plant, National, could close? It came about because of a rift between labor and management. There had already been signs of a problem there during a wildcat strike in 1972. National had a very good workforce, but there were a few dissidents who caused problems.

Some of the same people with whom I had worked on the Reserve Case called me. Together, we had helped to put the National picture back together during the wildcat strike in 1972.

In the early 1990s, there were problems with the cost of the mine. When it became apparent that costs were out of line, National formed a survival team and Emil Draskovich was put in charge as project manager. George Kotonias was the general manager of the property. He had worked his way up the ladder and was considered bright, effective and well-liked by the owners and the people who worked for him. Kotonias gave Draskovich, one of several heirs apparent to the throne, the job of calling in suppliers to extract from them the necessary reductions to put the operation in a profitable position. He did an excellent job at this.

During this time, I was called upon by Kotonias and others to try to get the royalties they were paying to the state of Minnesota decreased. There was a piece of property owned by the state, and National could have mined around it and left it as an island so it would have been worth nothing to the state. It was a yearlong battle to get those royalties reduced. We really had to fine tune the piano to do this, and there were a lot of actors in the play. I worked closely with Dr. William Brice, the minerals director of the state, and I don't think even he knew what I had gone through to put together all the pieces and get the governor's support. The goal was to save the mining company some $50 million and ensure the property stayed viable. It would also generate considerable revenue for the state over the period of the 10-year agreement, and would greatly enrich the University of Minnesota Permanent Trust Fund. And, of course, there were the taxes the company paid and the jobs that supported the economy of the area.

The royalty cutting, though, only solved part of National's high-cost per ton problem. In the spring of 1993, National's headquarters in Indiana announced that if costs were not cut $6 to $8 per ton, the plant would be closed permanently. The company was paying $42 a ton for taconite from its own plant, but it could go on the spot market and buy ore for $36 a ton. The contract was due to expire on Aug. 1, and negotiations went very poorly through the summer months.

When the contract expired, the employees walked out. It was a breakdown of relations in the worst way. Clarence Kuusi was the president of the union and Kotonias was the manager of the mine, but there were strong influences above this level in both the union and the company.

It was a great shock to the area when the strike occurred. Everyone wondered if it would end up in another closing like Butler. It looked like it would.

I became involved again at the behest of some prominent people, and I notified the company that I would be participating. Once again, it was a daily commitment of hours and hours, face-to-face meetings, telephone calls, and other communications. As with Reserve, it took time away from my family and from my business.

In September, the employees decided to accept the latest contract offer by the company, but the National people said the offer had been withdrawn. Later, the union agreed to go back to work without a contract, and at that point the strike became a lockout. I remember vividly the television shot of Kotonias at the plant gate denying the workers entrance. Because of that, Kotonias became the fall guy, but he was operating strictly according to corporate headquarters directives. In October, the company said it had idled the plant indefinitely, and it began to buy ore from the other taconite companies.

It was a terrible situation, and there didn't seem to be much hope. There were few employees who thought it could be resolved, and many of National's key people left and found other jobs. They gave up all their seniority.

It was suggested that I write a letter and take it to the mayors of Hibbing, Keewatin and Nashwauk and have them sign it. It asked that the sides get back together and negotiate. It asked that a proposal be made, and that the union employees be allowed to vote on it.

We had no problem getting Keewatin Mayor Dan Kelly and Hibbing Mayor Jim Collins to sign it. However, a driver brought it over to Nashwauk Mayor Bob Fragnito and several hours went by, and there was no response. We were getting quite nervous about it. I asked Mayor Kelly what was going on, and he said Mayor Fragnito wasn't sure if he should sign it. He finally did.

It was in all the Range newspapers, and it created quite a controversy within the union. The public liked the idea. Everybody wanted to save those jobs.

In addition, a National staff employee named Ray Jensen, who was pumping gas in order to survive the strike, created an advertisement asking the union to allow members to vote on a contract.

Jensen's proposal and our proposal never materialized, but they did seem to cause a movement in the union by a number of the younger men — those who had some time

117

to go before retirement — to seek a resolution. The union was controlled by men who were mainly eligible for retirement, and they seemed to care little about whether the property closed. The younger men realized that they'd probably have to overthrow their leaders if they wanted to save the plant. There were tremendous hardships for everybody during the whole period of the strike.

One day, as the strike wore on, I got a call from George Kotonias. He asked me to go down to the Twin Cities and see George Pillsbury, chairman of Sargent Management Co., and see if his company was willing to also reduce royalties. I asked, "When?" George said, "Right now." An hour later I was on the plane, and an hour after that I was having lunch with George Pillsbury. He was a long-time political friend.

After some tough negotiations, the Pillsburys agreed to reduce the royalties. That was another step in making the company viable. Dave Meineke, the Hibbing representative for the Pillsbury interests, was a great help in convincing the Pillsburys to reduce the royalties.

Meineke has done much for the survival of the Range, and was a key player in initiating the planning to bring a direct-reduced iron plan to the old Butler site. Later, when I was vice chairman of the Governor's Task Force on Mining and Minerals, Meineke always drove me to Duluth for the meetings. We had many fruitful hours together talking about what could be done to help the industry. There has always been a great mutual respect between us.

Another major task we had was to negotiate a reduction in electric power rates. This was achieved only with some very fine tuning. I supported the appointment of Marshall Johnson from the Iron Range to the Minnesota Public Utilities Commission, and Gov. Carlson made the appointment. Nonnie McKanna, a close friend, had resigned from the commission. I was also able to help the negotiations through my friends on the board of directors of Minnesota Power.

When Kotonias suffered a heart attack and had surgery at the Mayo Clinic, he was out of the picture for a while. I was told to keep in touch with Jerry Drong, Don Healy, Dennis Johnson, and Dennis Murr. I was in nearly daily contact with them. With Kotonias' illness and age it became apparent that Draskovich would be seriously considered as his replacement. Later, as it developed, Draskovich played a key role in getting the matter resolved and in reshaping the mine.

While I have to admit that Rep. Tom Rukavina from Virginia is not one of my favorite legislators, I must give him credit for a key move during the strike. The company at one point was beginning to dismantle the plant. It was being put in mothballs, and Rukavina passed legislation that stopped them. I thought it was ill-advised at the time, and I thought the bill would never stand up in the courts. You can't force a company to continue to lose money. What the bill did, though, was to use public relations to put the brakes on. It allowed all the machinations that were going on behind the scenes to succeed.

In fact, you have to pay homage to all the legislators and the union men who made the bold move of going over to Japan to talk to NKK Steel, the Japanese industrial giant that now owned National Steel. They tried to show the Japanese managers that the plant could be very viable and cost-effective.

When they returned, they thought they'd really pulled off the victory. What they didn't know was that Fran Befera and I were on the phone every week to Walter Mondale who was Ambassador to Japan at this time. We learned the time differences, and we knew just when we could get through to him. We tried to keep him advised on what what going on here so that he could keep in touch with the NKK ownership. We were trying to make sure that nothing drastic was done without due deliberation and due diligence.

Even people in my office kept telling me that I was crazy to devote this much time to the strike. They told me again and again that it was hopeless.

There was a real human side to the strike that people tend to forget. There wasn't a day that went by that I didn't get calls from employees asking my advice on whether they should leave. I advised people to stick it out, but some left. What choice did they have? People that were used to making a good living were pumping gas to survive. Those employees went through hell. What could they do with their mortgages, their kids' educations, the car payments? They really didn't know if there was a tomorrow. In a span of 10 or 15 years, the Iron Range lost 8,000 jobs in the iron ore industry.

Meanwhile, the strike dragged on. It had become a real challenge.

Denny Grcevich, one of the union members, came in one day and said, "I've got to see you." He said, "Do you want to resolve this thing?" I said, "We sure do."

"Well, I'll tell you what we want. If you do what we want, when we have our election, we'll overthrow the leadership. We'll put it together, and that mine will be back in business."

I said, "What do you want?"

"There's a bill in the legislature to award the men unemployment compensation. We understand the governor won't sign it. We want you to get to the governor. If you can do that, the strike will be over."

I said, "Are you crazy? Do you know the precedent this would set in the rest of the state? Every time somebody went on strike, they'd want to collect unemployment benefits."

He said, "Well, that's what it's going to take, and I know you can do it."

I met with Gov. Carlson, made the proposal and reminded him of his commitment to the Range. Carlson was totally committed to helping the Range. He supported the mining industry, and he supported the jobs that were created. He was well aware that the whole infrastructure of the Range, the schools, the cities — it all depended on the mining industry. Carlson had already played the key role in encouraging Bill Brice to yield to National's request for a reduction of state royalties.

Carlson supported the plan in the end. The union leadership did its part. In April, 1994, the union held an election, overthrew Kuusi, and elected Dennis Enroth. At almost the same time, National cleaned house of its top level management, and the new people came in with a determination to get things moving.

Ray Jensen, who had earlier created the controversial newspaper ad, was working at this time with Great Lakes Steel to garnish customer support for the reopening of National Steel Pellet Co. In an early morning meeting that was held to introduce John Goodwin and his new National Steel management team, Jensen paved the way for the reopening meeting that was held with Kotonias, Murr and Johnson.

The sides met, the differences were worked out, and one year to the day after the mine closed, this impossible situation was resolved. August 1 also happens to be my birthday.

I have in my possession two letters that were written in the months after the strike that are among my prized possessions. One is a letter that was jointly written by Clarence Kuusi and Emil Draskovich. "The National Steel Pellet Company Task Force thanks you for your support of our effort to achieve a royalty agreement with the State of Minnesota," they wrote. "Your communications with Governor Arne Carlson and others regarding this issue were instrumental in encouraging the Department of Natural Resources to engage in meaningful negotiations."

The other letter was from J.N. Howell, then vice president of National Steel Corporation. "I wish to personally thank you for your intervention with Minnesota's Governor Arne Carlson, his administration, and others on our behalf. Thanks to your efforts, both National Steel and the State of Minnesota will benefit. Thank you again, Carl, for your invaluable assistance to this company, this industry, and your community."

※※※※※

Since the strike, the situation has turned around completely. A property that was near demise, in the ashes, not only survived, but it has broken world's records in productivity.

Productivity in a taconite plant can be measured by how many long tons of pellets are produced per hour of employee time. In 1995, just a year after the plant reopened, productivity at National was 5.93 long tons an hour. The next closest was the super-modern Hibbing Taconite plant at 4.5 tons per hour. The cost per ton has dropped not just to the original $36 goal, but all the way down to $26.45 per ton.

They've done all this by being visionary and innovative and forming an alliance with the union, making the union a meaningful part of the decision-making process. A lot of people looked at this with a jaundiced eye and thought it would come back to bite the company. They wondered if it would work. It has.

National Steel and its employees have done a miraculous job in reducing costs and improving the product. National will survive. It is no longer on the endangered list. That spirit of cooperation lives on even through a change of union leadership with Rudy Aho as the current president. Even now it's becoming one of National Steel's main profit centers. Aho is realistic to the changes that must be made.

I was totally shocked in 1999 when an internal audit of National revealed some financial irregularities, and Draskovich was removed as general manager. Since his dismissal, he and his wife have been indicted and sentenced, and restitution has been demanded. I've had such a long relationship with the company, I'm amazed that I didn't have an inkling of this impropriety. I knew less than any employee of the company.

Thomas Peluso, a veteran of 23 years with the company and a man well-liked by the labor force, has become the new vice-president and general manager. He started out as a laborer, and rose through the ranks to the top job. The son of an iron miner, he has never forgotten his humble beginnings, and he has a great respect for the Iron Range and its people. A star hockey player in high school at Greenway of Coleraine, he later was an All-American hockey player at Colorado. He still has that "team" approach that requires the combined effort of all the players to win.

Peluso is the perfect choice for the leaner years the steel industry is facing with steel imports at a record level. As he put it in a recent magazine article, "Give us a level playing field, and we'll compete against anyone in the world."

Peluso will face challenges, but he has the talent to do well in the long run. He is ably assisted by Robert Buescher, who has worked his way up through the ranks to become human resources director. Buescher's grandfather ran a shovel for 42 years at Butler, and his father was a concentrator superintendent and operating superintendent at National.

One of the best things that has come from getting to know Bob Buescher has been the opportunity for Dolores and I to get to know and love his wife, Jodi. She has faced tremendous personal challenges in her life, but her entire focus is toward other people. Jodi has a magnetic personality and a smile that weaves its way into every heart. In recent times, there has been a mutual sharing of love, faith and hope that has sustained both families.

It's come to the point where other companies on the Range have taken a lesson from National and are beginning to include their people in the decision making.

When the next downturn comes, we probably will lose a couple of mining operations in North America, but I don't think National will be one of them. It is a magnificent miracle.

Staying Rational with National

With the decline of the American steel industry, some steel companies, in order to maintain liquidity, have been forced to put their taconite plants up for sale. National's parent company is exploring a sale as is Bethlehem Steel Co., the owner of Hibbing Taconite. Both plants will definitely continue operating. You can be certain that National Steel Pellet Company and Hibbing Taconite will survive these tough times in the industry.

Chapter Fourteen
Hundreds of Ways to Lose Money

There were so many things I was involved with over the years, and I have to admit I lost money in many of them. I won't say I didn't get involved with them to make money. But that wasn't the primary motive. Naturally, you wouldn't want to get into something that didn't make money.

It was the challenge, and probably the intrigue of becoming involved in other areas of the country geographically. There's the romance of being linked with something that could go national.

Remember those geodesic domes? I sold those when they were first invented.

I was involved with a guy from Duluth in a dog food project. He tried to crack the big supermarkets. He started in Chicago. It was a really good dog food, too. It was called, "Right." "If you're not feeding your dog this, you're not feeding your dog Right."

And then there was the Leaning Tower. That was really something.

This was before Sammy's and Pizza Hut and all those other pizza restaurants got started. Dolores and I were talking about it and I said, "Why couldn't we start a restaurant that featured a replica of the leaning tower of Pisa and call it the 'Leaning Tower of Pizza?'" The buildings would be full-scale models of the Leaning Tower.

You could have the ground floor be a pizza take-out place, and then have steps or an elevator go up to the top floor where you'd have a supper club. You could build them in places where you'd have beautiful scenery.

Jerry Jyring, a Hibbing architect, drew up all the plans. I got these Twin City lawyers to search for the patent and the trademark. I was put in touch with Max Winter and Ben Berger, two of the biggest businessmen in the Twin Cities, and they agreed they'd put up the money if I gave them 51 percent. I balked at that.

We went through this whole process, and everybody was enthused about it. We were totally wrapped up in it, and at the height of the excitement we got a letter from the attorney. He wrote, "You've got to be crazy to go ahead with this because there's some little Italian out in Boston that had a big replica made of plywood of the leaning tower. He had nailed it on the front of his building, and he's selling pizza." The lawyer said, "Unless you make a deal with that guy, he could sue the hell out of you."

That was a quick $25,000.

ଈେ୪ଈେ୪ଈେ୪

And then there was the cake project. There were these guys who had won the top cake awards in the United States for a cheese cake and a carrot cake. They had won the award three or four years in a row. The product was going really hot down in Florida in one store. So we said, "Why don't you let us take this, and we'll franchise it for you and go national?"

So we made an agreement with them — on a napkin in a restaurant. In the agreement, I would take over the state of Florida and build a minimum of five places in five years. In return for that, we would get 20 percent of the national rights. We figured it would take off, because all the people visiting in Florida would say, "Gee, I want one of these in Oregon," or somewhere else.

I went so far as to rent a building with the freezers and coolers and everything they'd need to make the product. We drew up a business plan. We were so enthusiastic and went out to Boston to talk to them and visit their original location and headquarters. Well, the owners then hired an attorney in Boston, and when he saw how excited we were, he became like an agent for a sports celebrity. He started changing all the rules. When they finally gave us the contract to sign, there was no resemblance to what we had written on the napkin.

By that time I had invested some $50,000 in renting the building and everything. I was doing almost all this by telephone, and it turned out they had put the building in their name and not in the name of the company we had incorporated: "Southcakes, Inc." What the new contract said was that in 10 years, all the rights to the enterprise would revert back to them.

That cake fell flat.

ଈେ୪ଈେ୪ଈେ୪

Then we had a piece of National Telephone. It was the first independent phone outfit of its kind in the country, and it started in Atlanta. The company would go into hotels and other businesses and set up a switchboard that would connect to their main terminal. They would handle all the long distance calls and would then return back a certain percentage of the profit to the business each month.

That really started to take off. I learned, though, that without a majority interest, one is compromised. In fact, I had cut a couple of Hibbing people into it. At dinner I asked them if they'd like to double their money in a short time. Well, they did better than that in six months. It was bought out a couple of times, though.

❧⊰❧⊰❧⊰

And then there was the Jack Frost Shield deal. I had developed it with Monsanto. It was piece of styrofoam-like material with static electricity in it. You put it on your windshield, and it would keep your windshield from icing up.

We thought we could sell it to one national company, like Amoco, and it would have advertising on it. The world would have to buy it through this one distributor.

It worked pretty well depending on the weather. The windshield could still ice up underneath, so you'd have some scraping to do. The problem was that it wasn't a reusable item. You'd have to have a roll, like a roll of wax paper, where you'd keep pulling off new sheets.

But to show you how short-sighted I really was, I thought only of a frost shield because we live in this climate. I should have realized that a better idea would have been a sun screen to keep cars from getting too hot. Later, a fellow from Israel developed that kind of car shield, and now there are all kinds of them out.

❧⊰❧⊰❧⊰

We almost bought Sheik's Supper Club in Minneapolis. It was owned by a law partner of my son's, and he had oil wells in Texas, and he had pledged the oil wells as collateral to go into Sheik's. Every businessman, for some reason, has a tremendous urge to own a supper club at some point in time.

For not too great a sum of money, he was going to lose the oil wells. We were in my son's office one day, and he asked if we'd be interested in the deal. It was a time when Rudy Perpich was governor, and we thought it would be a great place where Range people could gather in the Twin Cities. It could be Range headquarters.

Dolores was against schemes like this, but she asked me, "What are you going to do?" I said, "I'll be the PR guy and greet the people, and you can run the kitchen." She thought that was great. She was amenable to it.

But she suggested that before we did anything, we go there for a few nights incognito and check the place out. Well, at the time there were all these glamorous couples and Porsches pulling up to the place. It was a hot spot in Minneapolis. We went on a

Friday and Saturday night and were planning to complete the papers Sunday.

Both nights, they were taking cover charges. My wife said, "Now watch this." The place was really packed, three or four deep at the bar. Every third or fourth cover charge this guy was putting in his pocket. And then pretty soon we noticed that the bartender wasn't ringing up all the drinks. He left the drawer open.

So we could see what was going on, and why the place wasn't successful. So at the scheduled signing, Dolores walked out and that ended that.

ஐଔஐଔஐଔ

And then there was the time that we, along with a number of Hibbing people — Bob Nickoloff, John Dougherty, Vince Paciotti — had the world-wide patents to something I still think is the greatest idea since sliced bread. There were also several Twin City businessmen involved.

It was the Preko Manhole Cover, and boy did we invest in that one. The manhole cover cost more, but it was adjustable. When a city did blacktopping, it could just adjust the bolts and raise it up to the right level. You'd pay more at the beginning, but you'd never have to buy another manhole cover.

We didn't have anybody to manufacture it, though, so we had to go to the top competitor in the world, the Neenah Foundry in Wisconsin. They agreed to put it in their book, and they sold them all around the country, and we got royalties. I think maybe we ended up breaking even.

We were so enthusiastic about it that we spent many thousands of dollars in legal fees to get patents all over the world. We thought it would go everywhere. Finally, the 17 years of the patents ran out, though, and now it's a lost cause. Neenah can continue making and selling them, and they'll realize the benefits from them, but we won't.

ஐଔஐଔஐଔ

In Ocala, Florida, Fran Befera and some other investors and I invested in a television station. A man had a chance to get this license, and he wasn't sure if he wanted to do it. He was a neighbor of Fran's brother, Orfeo, in Baraboo, Wisconsin. Fran happened to mention it to me one day, and I said, "Gosh, Fran, that area's just exploding down there. Why don't we go down and take a look?"

We went down and met these people, Norm and Don Sauey, a father and son. They had a business making vinyl closet enclosures. They were very successful. We talked them into starting this television station.

They were enamored of Fran because of his engineering ability and his expertise in getting the station off the ground. They tried to sell a certain percentage to Fran and cut me out. They didn't know me. Fran told them he wouldn't go in unless I did. We

An interesting project was working with Carl Pohlad to create the baseball stamps after the Minnesota Twins won the World Series in 1987 and 1991. It was a labor of love to provide the stamps for people to treasure these historic sports events for Minnesota. Holding the framed copy was our first grandchild, Thomas Scott Phillips, Mary Kay and Scott's son. The presentation was in the Governor's Reception Room.

each got a five percent interest in the station.

There were many other investors, including some Hollywood actor, but these people from Wisconsin kept 51 percent of the business.

In its first year of operation, it was still losing money but George Steinbrenner of the Yankees offered to buy it for $17 million with no money down with 10 payments, one each year for 10 years plus 10 percent interest.

It would have given us about 15 times the amount we had invested in the station

Hundreds of Ways to Lose Money

Fran Befera, the former owner of ABC-TV affiliate in Duluth and on the Iron Range, has been one of my closest friends for many decades. Together we found some pretty interesting ways to invest our money. We had a chance to sell a Florida TV station to George Steinbrenner one time for about a 1500 percent profit, but we couldn't convince the station's majority owner of Steinbrenner's reliability.

because we had leveraged the investment, and the interest would have been staggering.

Fran and I could not convince these majority people to sell it. We pleaded and pleaded and pleaded. Up to this point, they had followed our advice to the letter. They were concerned because there was nothing down, and they wanted some cash. I told them, "Hey, this is George Steinbrenner. His signature is as good as gold, and it will still be in ten years."

In the end, they didn't sell it to him, and a couple of years later, while the station still wasn't making any money, they sold it to Mrs. Howell who owned the Indianapolis Speedway. She bought it for $6 million, or about one-third the price Steinbrenner was willing to pay. We barely broke even on the deal.

Now, of course, it's going bonkers and rendering about a 20 percent return. And I still get calls constantly from television brokers telling me that such and such a station is for sale.

ஒ௸ஒ௸ஒ௸

I ran into a financial advisor on an airplane in the late 70s. I told him I was looking for investments. He called back later and said, "I've got a guy right up your alley, but you've got to go to Melbourne, Florida." I did.

It turns out that this particular party was designing a project with Disney where Disney was going to try and capitalize on the time and money that people spent at Disneyworld. Disney would have a tram that would take guests to the ocean. And they would own facilities on the beach so they could extend the two or three days the tourists might spend at Disneyworld.

His name was Earl Smalley. He was Joe Robbie's partner and they owned the Miami Dolphins together. His wife was very glamorous, and he called her Cat.

Now imagine. My wife and I had never met them, and he's taking us around. He wants us involved in this project, so the first thing he does is take us to the beach to show us all the land he had under control with options. Then he showed us some fancy quarters and said, "This is where you'll be living." We hadn't even discussed any particulars.

Then he took us into an office near his, and there was a nameplate on the desk with my name on it already. This was crazy.

We elected not to go there, but as you read about these deals in the Wall Street Journal, these magical deals, you wonder how much real thinking or scrutiny goes into these projects. He didn't know me and I didn't know him. He wanted to go ahead and sign papers that day. It was just based on his financial advisor telling him he had found the right partner.

That project never developed.

༺☙༻☙༺☙༻

And through all that wheeling and dealing, I found out one thing. You can only live in one house at a time. You can only drive one car at a time. You can only sleep in one bed, live with one woman, eat one steak. Your security blanket is really your own business, where you live and where you stay and where you spend your time.

There's no substitute for your own efforts and your own initiative and being on the firing line yourself to make sure that you don't fail.

So much for that.

Chapter Fifteen
POLITICAL CONNECTIONS

We were up at the duck camp in October of 1977 with the Hanna Mining and National Steel people. Bob Anderson, the president of National, said to me, "We've got a real dilemma in the steel industry. The imports are just flooding into the country. We can't get anything done. Can't you do something with your friend Mondale?"

I said, "Well, maybe."

On Monday, Bob was back in Cleveland and he called me. "Can you arrange a meeting between George Stinson and Mondale?" Stinson was the chairman of National and also headed up the industry's trade association, the American Iron and Steel Institute.

So I called Fritz, who was Vice President at the time, and he sounded willing to meet with Stinson but his schedule was very tight because the Chinese ambassador was visiting. I said, "Well, I think Stinson's got a tighter schedule than you do. He can only meet with you between 3 and 5 p.m. on this certain day because he's on his way to Geneva, Switzerland." Fritz said, "Gosh, that's really restraining me. It's going to really jumble up my schedule." He was rather hesitant.

I told Fritz, "You'd like this guy. He's a Democrat. He's Congressman Wilbur Mills' drinking buddy. He's from Arkansas. He's just a good guy and you'll like him." So, Fritz finally agreed, and they met.

Fritz called me the next morning and said, "Wow, what a guy. I really thank you for sending him to me, and we're going to get something done." And you talk about getting something done. Within 10 days following that meeting, Anthony Solomon of the Treasury Department had written the trigger pricing mechanism against Japanese steel, and the steel industry and the Iron Range took advantage of the protection over the next four years and went bonkers.

I have a letter from George Stinson that says: "I expressed to you before my feeling that the meeting which you arranged for me with the Vice President was a key point in the establishment of a helpful governmental program."

It all started with a conversation at our Squaw Lake hunting lodge, and a suggestion from a friend. The upshot was that the Iron Range and the steel industry had its four biggest years from 1978 through 1981.

And then the industry's best friend, Ronald Reagan, came into office with a free trade agenda and the problem became serious again. After rocky times in the 80s, the steel industry and the

A typical crew at the duck camp. We got a lot of ducks, but there was always a lot more going on.

Iron Range got a respite of relative prosperity in the 90s. Now, as we enter the new century, the problem is becoming steadily worse once again, and nothing is being done by the federal government. The steel industry faces demise, and the defense of the nation could be imperiled.

I first got to know Walter Mondale when I was in the legislature and he was at law school. He would come over to the legislature, and we got to know and like each other.

He was new and I was new. We had mutual friends on the Iron Range.

It wasn't too long after I met Fritz that Fran Befera met him. Fran started taking him fishing and hunting up north. Bob Nickoloff, another Hibbing businessman, had known Mondale, and they were very close friends. Bob was an assistant attorney general when Fritz was Minnesota's attorney general. Nickoloff and Befera were key supporters when Mondale ran for President.

When Mondale was in the Senate, and about the time he was being considered for seeking the presidency, Fran Befera came up to the duck camp with him. It was about 6 in the morning, and pretty late in the season. They had a quick cup of coffee and went out to the blind. It was still dark.

There were three of us in the boat. Fran dropped the two of us off on an island along with my two dogs. He said, "I want you to hunt with Fritz today." My hunting dogs were both golden retrievers. The mother was a fantastic dog by the name of Scooter, and the other was Avanti, the smallest of the litter. Everybody said Avanti would never be a hunter, but she became a tremendous hunting dog. They were also well-loved family pets.

Fritz began dropping ducks, and he said, "Are you going to send those dogs out for those ducks I shot?"

I said, "I can't see any ducks out there." It wasn't quite daylight yet, and it was very foggy. He said, "They're there. They're there. I shot them." So I started sending the dogs out, and when we did the tally, the two dogs had brought back nine ducks.

I said, "Gee, we're over the limit now."

It was at about this point that he realized I hadn't been shooting, and he said, "Let me look at your gun, is there something the matter with it?" So he looked over the gun and said, "You don't have any shells in here. Where are your shells?"

I said, "I didn't bring any shells. Hey, I can hunt anytime, but if you think I'm going to take a chance of having an accident out here with a Republican shooting a potential Democrat President — I'd be in jail for life."

Well, the funniest part of the whole story came as we were considering what to do with the nine ducks. I said to him, "Well, at least you've got your license don't you?" And he said, "No, we didn't get

Fritz Mondale and I at the duck camp in later years. We've been friends for over 50 years.

a chance to pick one up. When I flew into Duluth last night, the places were all closed."

He got one the next morning when Bud Anderson opened his store at Max, Minnesota.

❧☙❧☙❧☙

The Squaw Lake Duck Camp was the scene of many great hunts, parties and associations that led to the solution of many of Range's problems, and, in our minds, many of the problems of the world.

I co-owned the camp first with Bob Anderson and later with Ed Matonich. Now I'm left as the sole owner. Many people flowed through in 32 years. Regulars from the beginning were my children, sons-in-law, Gaylord Chapin, Dr. Vince Paciotti, Dr. Bill Larson, Tom Sonaglia, Tom Dougherty, Joe DeLoia, Fran Befera, Ed Pajunen, Ed Matonich and Tom Hayes. Some have passed away and some have quit hunting, and others have taken their places. With its 16-bed capacity, if you count my family and friends and Anderson's friends and Matonich's friends, hundreds of people have been there at one time or another.

❧☙❧☙❧☙

I always wanted to give Mondale one of the better bedrooms at the duck camp, but he wouldn't have any of that. He always wanted to sleep out on the porch with the boys. It used to get cold on that porch with the slate floors. Inside, I used to keep the fireplace roaring, but the guys on the porch would just keep the door cracked a little bit for circulation. They called it Befera's freezer.

Fritz didn't sleep in a sleeping bag. He just had the one blanket, and he always had one foot sticking out. I'd stay up and keep stoking the fire, and I'd keep pulling the blanket over that exposed foot he had. Finally, he kicked and said, "Hey, leave that out there. That's my thermostat."

❧☙❧☙❧☙

I remember the time when Mondale was coming up to fish with Fran Befera, and I met him in the Minneapolis airport. He had a book in his hand which he had written. He said, "Let's sit together on the plane." That was the day he told me that he didn't have the fire in the belly for the presidential campaign. He said, "Don't say anything about that announcement to anyone until I'm able to release it. I'm going to hold it until I'm coming back out of Canada on Sunday night. I'm going to have a press conference and tell everyone that I'm going to drop out." And that's exactly what he did.

The book that he had written was called, "The Abuse of Power." It referred to the Nixon years. Later, Mondale did run against Ronald Reagan for President.

※※※※

Mondale once told me, "The only difference between being an alderman in the city of Minneapolis and being President of the United States is being in two right places at two right times."

※※※※

At the Carter-Mondale inauguration, Dolores and I had come to Washington from Florida and Fritz sent the vice-presidential limousine to pick us up. It brought us to the swearing-in ceremony. Afterwards, we got back into the limo, and it took us -- Bob and Anne Nickoloff and Dolores and me -- to the head of the reception line.

The limo pulled into the parking lot at the same time as a big bus of Minnesota people and parked a few feet away. People started getting out of the bus, and they see the Nickoloffs and the D'Aquilas getting out of the limo. Wally Jones, a wealthy contractor from the city of Virginia, who had given thousands of dollars to the Mondale and Carter campaign, looked and he saw me and said, "What's that Republican son of a bitch doing in that limo?"

He said, "And he's with Nickoloff, that big Democrat! Just look at that." He was just as bitter as could be, and when I got back to Minnesota I heard about it.

※※※※

George Wallace was a very interesting guy.

When he was running for President, and we had the television program in Duluth, he came up to be interviewed. He came, of course, with the protection of the Secret Service. He was in the wheelchair where he was destined to spend the rest of his life after the assassination attempt.

It was a pretty impressive situation. We found him to be very, very fascinating. He was neither a wild-eyed liberal nor a conservative. He was very moderate, very sensible. Everybody who met him was impressed by him. He was feared by many, but mainly he was a very outspoken guy. He never said anything for political advantage. He really looks better to the historians as time goes on.

The neatest thing about it was that sometime later, when he was being re-inaugurated as governor, he called us. He asked us if we would like to come down to Alabama and be his house guests.

Political Connections

We didn't go down, and it's one of the regrets I have.

ಸಿಂಚಿಸಿಂಚಿ

Once when Al Quie was governor of Minnesota, we were headed over to the KSTP studios in his limo to do the program. We had sandwiches in the car which we ate hurriedly on the way over.

I asked him, "Are you enjoying the office?" And Al, the All-American boy that he is, with his horseback riding and his farm, his genuine 4-H smile, and his sincerity, spirituality and honesty, said, "Oh, no, I'd really rather be back on the farm. But Gretchen's taken up with it, and she enjoys it, and enjoys all the women's activities and the glamour."

Gretchen was a very nice lady. Quie told me, though, "I said to Gretchen, 'Don't get so enamored with the job because we're only custodians here. We're only here for a period of time. One day the janitor will come and tell us we have to clean out the desk so a new governor can move in.'"

He said he never, ever became attached to the office. He was an outstanding governor, and he made the best appointments ever to the Minnesota Supreme Court. He put in some great judges, the likes of whom we may not see again.

ಸಿಂಚಿಸಿಂಚಿ

Luther Youngdahl was one of Minnesota's great leaders and great governors. He had selected me to carry two of his major bills through Legislature when I was serving, but I had opposed him on some other issue. He kind of took off after me and the other young fellows who had departed from the flock. Youngdahl wrote an open letter about this particular issue, whatever it was, and he was critical of me.

Dick Galob, the Hibbing attorney, decided to write the governor. He told him: "You don't treat our people that way, because if you treat him that way, you're treating us that way. He's our representative."

Following that, I went down to visit with the governor. When I was ushered into his office about quarter to four that day, Hubert Humphrey, who was a U.S. Senator at that time, was coming out of the governor's office. Humphrey had a big smile on his face.

In our meeting, I found Youngdahl very receptive, just totally forgiving, understanding. He said, "I know that there are politics involved, and you have to do these things." I thought that was really something.

Later that night, I turned on the news and found out that Youngdahl was leaving the governorship, and Humphrey had managed to get him appointed as a federal judge.

That's the way they got rid of Youngdahl in Minnesota. They wouldn't have beaten him for a hundred years. Everybody was wondering how they were going to get rid of Youngdahl, and Humphrey did it.

~~~

Bill Simon, who was Secretary of the Treasury under Nixon, came into KSTP-television in St. Paul one time while I was taping the program. I was asked to interview him.

Simon had written a couple of outstanding books on politics and economics. I think he pretty much hit the nail on the head very early in the game when he talked about the fact that there were things that had the potential to bankrupt the American system of government. One was the entitlements, particularly Social Security, as our population gets older.

While then in the private sector, Simon was being considered a presidential prospect. He was one of these men whose knowledge of finances was so great that he was able to make millions of dollars in the beginning without investing much of his own — simply on the basis of his name, experience and reputation. Just on his reputation he was able to leverage great loans. He was extremely intelligent and shrewd.

There are some people who, try hard as they might, still have a tough time making ends meet in life, but we still have an ongoing situation where some influential people can just lend their name to a venture and make millions.

I never considered that one day my son, Jim, would be working as a partner of Simon's out in California. It was kind of thrilling when Jim got married out in Santa Barbara that Bill Simon and his son came to the wedding. By that time, Simon was a revered individual.

He stayed to the very end of the evening, and I enjoyed talking and reminiscing with him about

> **THE BOARD** of directors of the Hibbing and Chisholm Chambers of Commerce and of the Buhl Businessmen's Association will hold a joint meeting today.
>
> This is the first meeting of this kind, John Gornick, president of the Chisholm Chamber said.
>
> The meeting will be held at 6:30 p.m. at Valentini's Supper Club — that's the place where they have all that good Italian food.
>
> Gornick said that the joint meetings "were the suggestion of Carl D'Aquila, president of the Hibbing Chamber of Commerce."
>
> The idea behind the joint meetings are to consolidate ideas from the three Range communities into somewhat of a long-range plan.
>
> Gornick said that such planning can be evidenced by "the Chisholm - Hibbing Airport Commission and the Carey Lake (Dupont) Commission."

I was always active in Chisholm, and that's how I got to know Veda Ponikvar, that city's newspaper editor and prime mover. This clipping is from the Hibbing Daily Tribune on February 27, 1968.

when he had visited Minnesota.

✄✃✄✃✄✃

I had always had an interest in aviation. My very first story in the *Arrowhead Traveler* was on the importance of a rural airport. U.S. Rep. John Blatnik, North Central Airlines Chairman Hal Carr and I had worked together to help found the Hibbing Airport, and I was an advisor for North Central Airlines as far back as 1957. In the legislature, I had been vice-chair of the Aviation Committee. Blatnik and I were on the very first Wisconsin Central flight to come into Hibbing. Wisconsin Central was the predecessor to North Central.

An airport and quality aviation service are so important to rural communities. I could see that from the beginning, and there hasn't been a time since the 1940s when I haven't been involved in aviation in one way or another.

I was a presidential advisor for North Central and Republic from 1968 until the airline merged with Northwest in the late 80s. I worked closely with Gov. Arne Carlson to try and preserve the Chisholm-Hibbing Airport and other rural airports in Minnesota. And, for the past five years, I've been a member of the Metropolitan Airports Commission. I was reappointed in 2000 for a second four-year term by Reform Party Gov. Jesse Ventura. Previously, I had been appointed by Republican Gov. Arne Carlson. I fill the slot as a representative of a key outstate airport.

When Northwest was in big financial trouble in the early 90s, I did what I could behind the scenes to encourage the legislature to approve the loan package for the airline.

In fact, I told Northwest's Chairman Alfred Checci that the loan package would pass by four votes. He later wrote me a letter. Part of it said, "I can see why your advice has been sought out by so many politicians from both parties. You called it -- a four vote margin. That's some handicapping.

"As you know, this whole process has been quite an ordeal for all of us. However, when we break ground up north, it will all be worth it. The economic impact of all this development on the region will be magnificent and immediate."

As part of the loan package, Northwest promised to locate facilities in Duluth and on the Range. Chisholm ended up getting a reservations center that employs over 700 people. Al Checci was exactly right about its economic impact on the region.

✄✃✄✃✄✃

I was asked to pick up Dan Rather at the Chisholm-Hibbing International Airport late one afternoon and drive him to the Coates Hotel in Virginia where he was speaking. There was a large crowd. I think it was the banking fraternity on the Range that had hired Rather to speak.

We often think of these people on TV as phenomenal, but he was just a plain fellow without pretense. He said he was fortunate to be Walter Cronkite's understudy.

I asked him what university he attended, and he said, "I never went to a university. I went to a junior college in West Texas."

I was amazed, but it was easy to see how he had become so successful. He did his own writing. He was a hard, hard worker. And he had the nerve to take on the President of the United States during the Nixon debacle.

Gay Chapin has been a devoted friend and employee of ours for 36 years. He has a son, Tom, who is perhaps the most respected game warden the state has ever had.

When Tom applied for the conservation officer position with the state's Department of Natural Resources, he had the highest test scores of anybody. Yet he was rejected because he was too short -- one inch too short.

I thought this was crazy. For one thing, there was an area DNR supervisor who was shorter than Tom.

When Gay told me about this, I called Gov. Wendell Anderson. I told him I felt so strongly about this, and I would seek legal counsel for Tom Chapin.

Wendell asked, "Where was his medical exam?" I told him it was at the Mesaba Clinic in Hibbing. He said, "You call the clinic and have him measured again, and you tell the nurse to tell Chapin to leave his shoes on this time."

He was hired, and he went on to an outstanding career. He became a supervisor, and then went back into the field to do the work he loved best.

They called the Nu Haven Bar the toll gate.

There was a time in Hibbing when city government was the center of our world. The interest in politics and the political races was intense. City Hall was just the focal point of the town.

The Nu Haven Bar's front door was on Howard Street, the main thoroughfare, but the back door was in perfect alignment with City Hall. Everyone who would go to City Hall, instead of taking the long way around the corner of the block and then back down the alley, would walk through the Nu Haven, from the front to the back. And whether they stopped for a refreshment or not, they all used it as a passageway.

If you went into the Nu Haven at 4 in afternoon to meet friends, in the next hour or hour and a half, you'd see all the important moguls of the community.

Political Connections

❦❧❦❧❦❧

When Vic Power was mayor of Hibbing, there was a city attorney here who later moved out the West Coast and became a very prominent lawyer. He worked for Puget Sound Power. His name was Vic Beno.

One of the tricks common in the heyday of Hibbing, when the mining company tax money was rolling in, was that some city officials would go out to the graveyard and pick names off the gravestones for the village payroll. This went on for a long time. Whoever got the checks, the city clerk or whomever, was in cahoots with the local bankers and the checks got cashed. Someone was getting rich, but not the people who were six feet under.

Vic Beno finally caught on. The Village garage superintendent came in one day and he counted the checks and he looked at Beno and said, "There's a whole bunch of checks missing here, Mr. Beno." And Beno replied, "Oh, I forgot to tell you, they were garnisheed."

The superintendent's mouth dropped open, but there wasn't much he could do or say.

❦❧❦❧❦❧

I was invited to Duluth one time when they were christening a new ore boat, the MV Elton Hoyt. It was one of the largest and most spectacular motor vessels of the Lake Superior fleet.

Muriel Humphrey had been chosen to break the champagne on the bow of the new boat, and I was standing on the platform next to Hubert H. Humphrey. Rep. John Blatnik was on Humphrey's other side.

As the ceremony proceeded, Humphrey said in his remarks, "When I think back over all the years and all we've gone through, I think Carl and Dolores were the smart ones. He had his shot at the Legislature and he left. He went out into the world, raised a great family, and built a great business.

"But, John Blatnik, you and I remained in public life, chasing some elusive target we never quite reached."

❦❧❦❧❦❧

I got to know Veda Ponikvar when I was campaigning for the Legislature. She was the new newspaper publisher in Chisholm.

I had a lot of supporters and close friends in Chisholm. Even back then, Veda was becoming the vital link in that city. Everything was checked through and channeled through her. I don't think anybody did anything without her. She had a sincere and intense interest in developing Chisholm into a better community, and her efforts reached out to the entire Iron Range. She has devoted her life to it.

Veda has had an amazing life. She was a WAVE during World War II, and she worked for the office of Naval Intelligence in Washington D.C. She came home and started the Chisholm Free Press. She was instrumental in convincing the city council and the people of Chisholm to help restructure what was called the Hibbing Airport in the late 1940s. It's been called the Chisholm-Hibbing Airport ever since.

She has been an advisor to North Central Airlines, and she is the civilian aide to the Secretary of the Army for the State of Minnesota.

Few people have accomplished as much or had as much influence on the Iron Range as Chisholm Newspaper Editor and Publisher Veda Ponikvar. This photo was taken earlier in her career when Eleanor Roosevelt paid a visit to Veda's newspaper office.

She not only had the power of the press, but she influenced all aspects of the community, the social life, the church life, the weddings, the births, the graduations. She had her attachments and associations with John Blatnik, Hubert Humphrey, Walter Mondale, Eugene McCarthy, and the power structure of the Democratic Party. She was outspoken, capable and became deeply involved in military affairs as an advisor.

As time went by, I became involved almost on a daily basis with Veda. She would consult me about things, editorial ideas, and I would consult her about how to get things moving. Together, we solved many Iron Range problems anonymously.

Many people don't understand that real power in this country comes from people who are not in office. Someday, of course, all of us will be gone. But I hate to think of the day Veda Ponikvar will be gone because there will be a horrible void. Nobody is irreplaceable, but some people come very close.

　　　　　　　　　　　　§○§○§○

  I used to go to Washington D.C. a great deal. Senator David Durenburger was one of my great and dear friends, and we would often meet for breakfast. We would take the tram over to the Senate dining room in the morning. Everyone would greet him warmly. He was one of the best-liked elected officials in Washington.

  We were always the first two into the dining room, and then over the next hour in would come Bob Dole, Pat Moynihan, Ted Stevens of Alaska, John Heinz, and they would sit around the table talking about issues. It was always a great deal of fun for me to be sitting there with him. Usually, I was the only one there who wasn't a senator. There weren't even staff members.

  In the process of observing these breakfast debates, the one thing that came across to me was the tremendous respect these other senators had for Dave Durenburger, and the loyalty they felt towards him.

  He introduced me as his friend, and so I was welcomed in as a permanent member of the breakfast club every time I attended. What I gained from that experience was a real sense of what bipartisanship was all about. Pat Moynihan, for instance, was a Democrat, but as I got to know him, I came to really like him and trust him. He was really dedicated to the country.

  Another thing I learned at that time was that when George Bush was vying with Ronald Reagan for the Republican nomination before the 1980 election, one of the two people he was considering as a running mate was Dave Durenburger. The other was Pete Dominici of New Mexico. The word was that Bush was hoping to get a Catholic on the ballot.

  Dave was held in that kind of regard.

  Later when difficult times befell him, I had no doubt about his honesty. What he did was common in Congress. He was simply a victim of the fact that he was not wealthy. One must remember that the Senate is a millionaires' club. It's so hard for a person with average means to make it.

  After his difficulties, he came to our home one night and stayed upstairs on the third floor. When I went up to say good night to him, I found him in front of his bed, devoutly on his knees, praying. After all he'd been through, he never lost that relationship with God.

  Through all these years, I've always felt a tremendous love for him. To this day, he remains the leading authority in the entire country on health issues. His wife, Susan Foote, is an attorney and also an expert in the health field.

  Dave Durenberger continues to divide his time between Washington D.C. and

Minnesota. He is president of Public Policy Partners. In Minnesota, he continues to serve as Senior Fellow at the University of St. Thomas Center for Health and Medical Affairs. He is also chairman of the National Institute of Health Policy, a joint project of the University of Minnesota and St. Thomas.

POLITICAL CONNECTIONS

Chapter Sixteen
Stories about People

I used to stop on my way to work and have coffee with Morris and Abe Zimmerman. One day Abe said to me, "Carl, I'm heartbroken. You need to help me out. You're younger than I am, not much, but you're younger. I've got a problem, and I would respect your opinion and advice."

I said, "What's the problem?"

He said, "My son's raising hell on that university campus, and I don't know what the hell I'm going to do. I'm getting calls."

It was Bobby Dylan, whom I'd never met. Haven't met him to this day. Bobby Zimmerman. I knew his younger brother, David, very well.

Every time I went in there, he was complaining. "I'm going to disown him. I'm going to disown him."

I said, "Abe, don't cut off communications. In the end, all you'll have left is your family. I've seen many cases of families falling apart, but they always come back together. It might be a wedding, or it might be a funeral or some adversity, but they always come together."

But he was really sour. All he could say was, "I'm going to disown him."

Well, some time went by, and one day I went in, and he was smoking a cigar and was all smiles. He said, "Come here." He's got a newspaper clipping and Bobby's made a big hit at Soldier's Field in Chicago with record crowds at his concert. So Abe started to pay attention to him. A father's pride was on the way to being restored.

It wasn't long after that I walked in and Abe said, "Come here." He had a letter in his hand and he opened it for me. "Look at this." The kid had sent him a check for

Stories about People

$10,000.

Not too long after that, he called me in one day. He said, "Come back here." He brought me to the back of the electric store on Fifth Avenue, and in the garage was a pink Cadillac. The kid had bought him a pink Cadillac.

I never heard any more complaints about Bobby.

ಐಞಐಞಐಞ

If you travel a lot, you'll eventually run into a lot of celebrities.

I remember meeting John L. Lewis, the great United Mine Workers leader. He had those deep eyebrows and that incredible hair and was such a bear-like person. I stopped to ask him to autograph a bill, and I pulled out a $10 bill. He said, "I can't do that. They'll put us both in jail." So I took out a dollar and he said, "Well, I suppose I can do this."

One night I was registering at a hotel in Cleveland, and the lady registering in front of me was Cher. In the Ritz-Carlton in Washington one day a lady spoke to me. I ended up spending about a half hour with her as she waited for someone to come for her. It was Zsa Zsa Gabor, and that was interesting.

Another time, I was walking through the Minneapolis airport looking for my wife and daughter, Barbara, and her friend, Cindy Johnson. I must have looked pensive as I was walking down the corridor, and this lady asked, "What are you looking so contemplative about?" And I looked up and here was my very favorite actress. I said, "Oh, you'll never believe this, but you are my idol. You are my favorite." It was Angie Dickinson. She was heading back for a wedding in North Dakota, and she was carrying this huge, heavy piece of luggage. I told her I would take it for her, and so I spent about three-quarters of an hour with her. All I had on me was a $50 bill, and I wanted her to autograph that. She wouldn't do it, and instead autographed one of her own dollars.

Later I found my wife, daughter and Cindy and they said, "Where have you been?" and I told them I had been with Angie Dickinson. And they said, "Oh sure, a likely story." So, I pulled out the bill and showed it to them: "To Carl, with love, Angie."

One time I was coming home from New York and was riding in first class. I was a presidential advisor for Republic Airlines, and so they would upgrade me all the time. This manager came up and said, "Would you please give up your seat. We want to keep this whole group together." It turned out it was a musical group. I didn't know them from Adam, and I played hard to get for a while before I gave up my seat. Later I told the kids that I had given up my seat for some musical group and they asked which one. I told them it was the "Fifth Dimension." They couldn't believe it.

One time in New York, they held up the plane for about 45 minutes. The cameras were there and there was a lot of commotion. I wondered what was going on. Pretty soon, Twiggy showed up. She was at the top of her popularity at that time.

A fellow who was traveling with her asked, "Would you mind giving up your seat for Twiggy? She's in the back in the tourist section, and she had been promised first class seats." I said, "Well, why don't you guys give up your seat for her? Why don't one of you be the gentleman?" But they said no, they were traveling together and that Twiggy was to be featured at Dayton's Department Store in Minneapolis.

I gave up my seat and headed back into the tourist section. I sat down and looked at the lady next to me. It was Abigail Van Buren — Dear Abby. After we talked for a while, she autographed a bill to my children that said, "Your dad gave up his seat for Twiggy."

I've hardly ever been on a plane when I don't find somebody I know. Dolores gets impatient, but I get up and walk around the plane and see who's on it. I've had some great times on the planes.

Jimmy "The Greek" Snyder had been hired to speak at one of our American Mining Congress dinners. It was during the Ford-Carter race in 1976. He would make predictions on just about anything, be it football or politics.

That night he predicted that Ford was going to pull off an upset. Of course, that didn't happen, but it was interesting to watch the guy operate. He sat up until about 2 in the morning in our suite. People were asking him all sorts of sports questions. He was a phenomenon. If people hadn't gone to bed, he would have gone on for two days. As it was, he just shot the breeze with Bob and Ann Nickoloff and Dolores and me.

A few weeks later, I interviewed him on election eve. He was with CBS, and WDIO, the station I worked for, was with ABC. He agreed before the polls had closed to come on, and I interviewed him for about 10 minutes.

I asked him, "What's your network going to think if they find out you're doing this for ABC?" He replied, "I'll tell you, I really am doing something for ABC. ABC — Anybody But Carter."

It's typical of so many people in so many fields who are at the pinnacle. They never envision coming down that ladder. Snyder made the comments on black athletes, and there are few who have stumbled as badly as he did.

After he was fired by the network, I spoke with him a few times on the phone. The man was crushed, totally crushed.

One time I was out hunting near Bemidji, Minnesota, with Max Edelstein and a large Hibbing group, and it had been raining for days. Every time I took a step, I'd sink into the mud up to the top of me ankles. It was unbelievable.

Even the dogs wouldn't go out. Max shot a duck, but there was no way to get at it. We all looked at each other, and finally I said, "Okay, I'll go get it." I went out and got the duck, and then I was trying to orchestrate my way back over this soft stuff. I was taking little bitty steps so I wouldn't sink. Pretty soon, I was in trouble and I really started going down.

Now I'm in up to my armpits. They're reaching and reaching, trying to get me, but I'm just out of their reach. Finally, Max says, "Throw me the duck. Throw me the duck. Let's not make this a complete loss."

I still have a friend, Don Messner, who to this day who greets me by saying, "Throw me the duck."

ഌൡഌൡഌൡ

Bob Anderson grew up in Hibbing. He was a brilliant student, in fact they called him "Pro" in high school. He was a serious guy, a gutsy guy, a venturesome-type guy. He went to the chairmanship of Hanna Mining Co., one of the largest mining concerns in the world. When he first started out in Hibbing, he was working his way up the ladder. The Enterprise Mine superintendency was up in Virginia. Anderson walked into the office and told Russell Fish, his boss, "I want that superintendency." Fish said, "What are you going to do if you don't get it?" Anderson said, "I'll quit." Fish didn't give it to him, and Anderson quit.

He went to work for a construction company in Crosby. Eddie Rostvold, who was a supervisory employee at Butler, one of the Hanna properties, was really bothered by Anderson leaving. He thought Anderson was a great young man, a guy who was going to be leading us. So he kept going to Fish, saying, "You made a big mistake."

So they finally called Anderson back, and what a career he had. He was just a smart, Hibbing-born kid who was determined to make it to the top.

At that time, Perry Harrison was in Cleveland running the ore sales department, but then another fellow took over. Bob was in Cleveland selling ore, and suddenly the new man up and quit. Bob said, "I'll take the job." So he got that job.

He moved up to vice president, then executive vice-president.

One January day I was in Duluth at the AIME convention, and I was with Dick Whitney, the vice president of Hanna Mining. He was a real charger, and we were going from reception room to reception room at the hotel. By this time, it was about three in the morning. Whitney said, "I've got to call on somebody, come with me." We had been going all night.

We went to a room and met Bob Linney who was with Reserve Mining Co. Right then and there, Whitney hired Linney to work at Hanna. At that time Linney was considered the most knowledgeable taconite expert in the industry. Linney said yes, but the deal wasn't announced for months.

Not long after that, I was coming home to the lake late one night. It was probably about quarter to midnight, and everybody was at my cabin. I walked in. They had had dinner and drinks and so forth. Now Bob Anderson could be the most diplomatic guy in the world or he could be the most outspoken. He intimidated a lot of people, but he had the knowledge to back it up. It's just the way he was. He said to all the people at the cabin, "Get out! Get out! It's late enough, and I've got to talk to Carl."

After everyone had left, Bob said to me, "I've got a problem." I said, "What?" He said, "They hired Bob Linney. I have been there all these years, and they put him above me."

I said, "Bob, don't be a fool. Bob Linney is the most knowledgeable taconite person in the world. You don't know much about taconite. You know mining, but you don't know taconite. This man's been at Reserve. He's got an ulcer, he carries a milk bottle with him all the time. He drinks vodka and milk.

"He's not your competitor," I told Bob. "Learn from him. Learn everything he knows. You'll be president or chairman someday."

Bob hung in there. As time went by, the company gave the top job at Hanna Mining to Jim Purse and named Bob to head up the Canadian operations. It was the same thing all over again. He was extremely disappointed. I said, "Bob, now you've had the experience you've gained from Linney, now you'll be in charge of Canada which is very important to the company. You'll learn the foreign aspect of it. You'll have learned the whole thing, you'll have gone the whole mile. You have to end up in the presidency."

Sure enough, they retired Purse very early, and Bob got to be president. Later he became chairman.

Bob Anderson was a hometown boy who went on to successfully operate one of the largest mining companies in the world.

149

Stories about People

One day during those years, I was in Cleveland. This is really crazy. I had decided just as a control upon myself — I could see what was happening to other people — to stop drinking and I had not taken a drink in four and one-half years. Some of my friends tried to get me off the wagon, but I hung in there. Dutch Weber kept trying to bribe Louie Rocco, the bartender at the Crystal Lounge at the Androy Hotel. I had Louie put in Catawba juice, which looks like a mixed drink, and charge me the same as a drink. I'd always just say, "Louie, give me my usual." Well, Dutch knew what was going on, and it bothered him. He tried to trick me a few times, but I always sent the drink back and said "This must be some sort of mistake."

I was in Cleveland trying to get more business out of Hanna. I'd been good to the mining industry, but I had never gotten much out of Hanna. Bob Anderson and Linney and I went out to lunch, and we were there a couple of hours.

"Why do you think you ought to have more of our business?" Bob said. He was playing the perfect part. I explained. Everybody thought I was a guy who applied pressure, but I didn't. I had taken this criticism for years. I told him, "I've got the quality, I've got the price, I got the service." Bob said, "Well, what do you think you ought to have?" and I told him, "Twenty five percent."

He said, "You've got it. But on one condition." I looked at him, and he said, "Will you take a drink?"

I was contemplating this when Linney popped up and said, "Wait a minute, Bob, you know I'm a friend of Carl's too, but let's not be so hasty. This has got to be studied."

Bob said, "We don't have to study anything. If he takes a drink, he's got it."

So I said, "What do you want me to drink, Bob?" He said, "I want you to drink the same as I am. I've got a Manhattan." I said, "Okay." I took a drink. I took a second one. I figured I had been in purgatory long enough.

Bob told me he'd make the arrangements and I left. I caught the flight back to Hibbing and I was back about 8:30 that night. I walked in the house and Dolores said, "How'd it go?" I said, "Terrific. You can't believe what happened. Bob Anderson is going to close the deal tomorrow. He's going to call their Hibbing office and increase our quota of business."

She was looking at me. She said, "Anything else happen that was significant?" I said, "No." She said, "Did you have a drink?" I said, "Yeah, why?" She said, "It's all over Hibbing." I said, "What is?"

She said, "Bob called John Ryan and Lute Mandsager and said, 'I got him, I got him!'" You can't realize how important it was to these people.

෨ෆ෨ෆ෨ෆ

Bob Anderson was just a humble Hibbing kid who got to the top of Hanna Mining because he was smart. I will tell you how smart he was. Everyone was afraid of the Sanibel, Florida, area because it had been wiped out by hurricanes several times. Totally destroyed.

Bob went down there, and it looked like Side Lake to him. He put a little consortium together and bought it for a song. He invited me to be one of the investors, but I was saving money for college educations.

What that group did down there as become a legend. They developed one of the world's quality vacation resort complexes, internationally renowned Mariner Corporation, South Seas Plantation, Captiva Resorts and Robb and Stucky Furniture. I became financially involved later, and it turned out to be one of my best investments. In 1998, it merged with Meri-Star Hospitality, the fourth largest resort hotel company in the world.

༄༅༄༅༄༅

Nine of us boarded an airplane to Chicago in July, 1947, to see the second Tony Zale and Rocky Graziano fight. It is still considered one of the greatest fights of all time. I've never had the desire to see another one, it was so sensational.

The plane had been chartered from Duluth. The saloon keepers had gotten together on this: Alipio Panichi and Sandy McHardy of the Monarch Bar, Mike Marinac from the Nu Haven, Jack Clark of Clark's, and Oscar Dornack from the Tibroc in Chisholm. The only ones who weren't saloon people were Porky Furlong and me.

I was on the liquor committee in the legislature, and I was the popular young legislator about town, so they told me, "We've got one seat open, do you want to come?"

We drove to Duluth, got on the plane, locked the door, and, sure enough, there was some trouble with the plane. Matt Rocchi from the Tibroc and Panichi had never been on a plane and they were getting nervous. They asked me what was wrong and I looked out the window. "There's something wrong with one of the props," I said. "They're trying to fix it."

Rocchi said, "Hey, Panichi, you hear that? What are you going to do?" Panichi said to me, "You're kidding. You're pulling my leg." I said, "No, no, look. We're not taking off." Panichi said, "Well, tell them to open the door, at least get some air in here."

The actual ticket from the Zale-Graziano fight is still in a scrapbook.

So they were getting more nervous by the minute. McHardy and Panichi were business partners, but they never liked each other very much. McHardy turned to Panichi and said, "What's the matter, Dago, you afraid to die?" And Panichi said, "If I die, you'll go with me."

It was getting really nuts. A half hour had gone by now, and we had still not taken off. Finally, Rocchi said, "Get that door open, I can't stand it. Get the door open!" And I said, "If we open the door, what good will that do? Will it get us to Chicago?"

He said, "Well, at least I could go out and kiss the ground goodbye once more."

We finally got to Chicago. McHardy was one of those guys who, if he's going to travel, will only go first class. The reservations were at the Blackstone Hotel. That was the ultimate at the time.

Panichi had gotten the tickets for the fight from Jack Hurley, the promoter, because he and Hurley had promoted many fights together through the years. The day was very hot, and we got to the hotel about about five in the afternoon. Panichi said, "Everybody come in the bar, I'll buy a drink." He was so happy to get there alive. Rocchi was happier than hell, too, and he said, "No, I'll buy the drink."

So we headed into the bar. I was the last one in, and Panichi was right in front of me. I didn't have a tie on. This is in the afternoon, and there was nobody in the place, but the doorman said, "You can't come in. You don't have a tie." Panichi looked at him and said, "What did you say? Do you know who you're talking to? He's a politician. He can close you down. He runs the liquor committee in the legislature." The guy said, "I can't help it, it's the policy."

Panichi said, "You don't understand. He can shut you down." So the doorman finally said, "What committee is he on?" Panichi was exasperated, and he said, "The liquor committee in the Minnesota Legislature!" Now the other guys are just about rolling on the floor, they were laughing so hard. And the guy at the door is just shaking his head. I said, "Don't worry, I'll just go up to my room and get a tie."

So we had some food and then took three cabs on our way to the fight. Traffic is just one big snarl, and soon one of our cab drivers starts yelling at another cab driver. And Panichi thinks this is great. "Hey, you tell him off!" he told the cab driver. Soon the two cab drivers are out of their cabs, and they're starting to fight. Then, we were all out of our cabs and standing around watching this, and Panichi said, "Hey, this is probably better than the fight we're going to see."

Finally we got to the real fight. The seats were ringside, about the 10th row, the best seats you can get in the house. I was checking out the crowd, and I said to Panichi, "Do you know who's in front of us, two seats to the right? That's Darryl Zanuck, the movie producer. And do you see that black guy right in front of us? That's Eddie 'Rochester' Anderson from the Jack Benny program."

Panichi is sitting right behind Rochester. Sandy McHardy said, "100 bucks, Paneech, I'll take the Polack." And Panichi said, "You got it." The fight begins, and

Zale is killing Graziano. He's just killing him. They probably should have stopped the fight, but just when it looked like Graziano was going to die, he got his second wind. The tied turned, and now Graziano is beating up Zale, and Panichi was going crazy. He was pounding Rochester on the back and Rochester started screaming, "Hey, man, leave me alone."

Graziano won the fight, and Panichi said, "We'll, we're going to party tonight. I'm going to take you to one of my old haunts." He took us to Cicero, Illinois, to a bar in the Capone district. We went in the back, and Panichi knew the guy who was serving us drinks. Pretty soon it ended up in a big crap game, and we were all shooting craps. It was wild. It was a time I'll never ever forget. We were up all night.

When I got back to Hibbing, I didn't tell anybody about it. But the late Bert Ackerson, the newspaper editor, used to get around. He'd go in the Garden Lounge, LaNoie's, Firpo's and the Homer Bar. Most of the guys who went on the trip were these liquor dealers, and the story quickly spread around town. Bert called me one day. He said, "Is this true?" and I had to admit that it was.

So he wrote a column about it.

※※※※※

In all the years I was broadcasting games, I never gambled on any of them -- except once.

Hibbing was playing Coleraine in a district basketball final, and it was a huge game. On my way to do the broadcast, I stopped by the Monarch Bar and Alipio Panichi said he only had a couple of chances left on the jackpot. For $100 a chance, I think you won $3,000 at the half and at the end of the game. So I bought one.

In about the last minute of the first half, I remembered my ticket and I pulled it out of my pocket. I saw that if Coleraine made a free throw, I'd win the jackpot for the half. Suddenly my broadcasting emphasis changed.

"There are just a few seconds left in the half," I said on the air. "And if Coleraine could just get one point now it could be critical at the end of the game. Just one point, just one foul by Hibbing, could change the outcome of this game. Sometimes people let their guard down at this point before halftime, and just that one little point could make the difference at the end of the game."

No sooner had I said it, than one of the Coleraine players was fouled. All he had to do was make one free throw, and I'd have $3,000 in my pocket. He put up the first try, and it bounced on the rim and came out.

My broadcasting was taking on a new level of intensity by this time. "Oh, that was close, folks. Now he only has one shot left. This shot could determine the outcome of the game. This is a district tournament. Everybody will remember this for years. This is really a big shot..."

Stories about People

The second shot hit the backboard, went around the hoop several times, balanced on the rim for a split second, and then dropped off.

I was so disappointed I could hardly finish the first half broadcast. I was sitting there thinking I was going to go down to the Coleraine locker room and vent my wrath on the team when I was informed there was a phone call. It was Panichi.

He said, "Hey kid, what you get so excited about? You got bet on the game or something? Don't worry, somebody won it who needed it worse than you."

I asked him who it was. He said, "These two guys don't even have enough money to buy a ticket alone, so they bought it together."

I asked him again who it was. "Oh, these two guys can really use the dough. Don't you worry about it."

"Who was it?" I demanded.

"It was Oscar Dornack and Babe Maturi." They were two of the wealthiest men in Chisholm.

～～～

"Bus Andy" Anderson of Hibbing was one of the originators of the Greyhound Bus line.

He was quite a guy. All of his clothes were tailor-made, and he was an immaculate dresser. Other than that, he was a typical Scandinavian, just a plain guy.

In those days, the ore boats were luxurious boats, and I was asked by Hanna Mining Company if Dolores and I wanted to go on a trip. Dolores was pregnant and couldn't go. She said, "You know I get seasick anyway. You go ahead."

It was in 1953, and Hibbing was having its 60th anniversary. The town was jumping. I was in the Androy and Bus Andy and his wife, Hilda, were there, and I had State Sen. Arthur Gillen and his wife, Lois, with me as guests. I said, "I've got a problem, Andy. We've got to leave Sunday. I've turned it down a thousand times, but now I've obligated myself to take six people on a Hanna boat trip to Buffalo and back." He asked, "Who's going?" I said, "Well, I'm really embarrassed, but only the Gillens and I are going." And he said, "Hilda and I will go!"

We left on Sunday. We had gorgeous weather, and it was a great trip. We went down through the Sault Ste. Marie and all those narrows. Andy used to get a kick out of telling sweet, sexy Swedish stories. Hilda would protest, "Oh, Andy, stop." But then when he was done, she'd laugh and laugh. Everyday, I'd go to Andy's cabin to gather him for dinner with the captain. Everyday, he would be reading his Bible. I'd say, "How can you tell those stories and read your Bible?" but he'd only smile.

As we were approaching Buffalo, we were wondering what we were going to do there. Suddenly, Bus Andy popped up and said, "Don't worry. I'll take care of us when we get to Buffalo. I have two very good friends there: Jerry Edmond, who used to be

Andrew G. 'Bus Andy' Anderson was one of the true visionaries on the Iron Range. Along with a handful of others, he created what later became the Greyhound Bus Lines. Anderson is in the back seat, second from left, in the photo from the 1920s in North Hibbing. Other bus company founders were, from left, Erik Wickstrom, Ralph Bogan and Carl Extrum.

on the Hibbing City Council with me, and Bill McLain, formerly from Hibbing, who is vice president of Buffalo Greyhound."

We docked, Andy made his call, and a big limo pulled up to the ship and picked us up. Bill McLain was in it, and he asked Bus Andy where we wanted to go first.

Bill said to Andy, "Why don't I take you to your old girlfriend's place?" Andy smiled, but Hilda said, "Oh, no."

Andy said, "Yah, let's go see Steena."

We went to a mansion, and Andy rang the doorbell. A voice came over the microphone and said, "Come in, I'll be right down." So we stepped in, and there were chandeliers and glass all over the place. This lady's husband was one of the more prominent sugar brokers on the East Coast. Time passed, and she didn't come down. We were all just standing there. Finally Andy shouted up the stairs, "Steena, what are you doing?" She replied, "I'm dressing." Andy shouted back, "Oh, just come down undressed, it'll be like old times."

She came down, and we went into a room with a bar. It was all crystal and glass.

Stories about People

They told me, "You be bartender."

Then the fun started. They started reminiscing about the good old days in Hibbing. Both Andy Anderson and Jerry Edmond had been on the city council in the 1920s. John Gannon had been mayor, and he and Vic Power were locked in the old political battle. They talked about the skullduggery and the under-the-table money and all the things that had taken place. I thought the classic line was when Andy said to Jerry, "Well it's past seven years now, and we don't have to worry because the authorities can't do anything about it."

But Jerry Edmond had one more surprise for Bus Andy. He said, "Andy, when I was on that Hibbing City Council, I was not legally entitled to be there. I was a public figure, a baseball star, but I shouldn't have been allowed to be on that council."

Andy said, "Why?" Jerry said, "I was a Canadian citizen."

※※※

The Round Table at the Androy Hotel met everyday for lunch. It was comprised of the powers that be in Hibbing, the mayor, the city attorney, other attorneys, Gus Ekola of American Linen, Dr. Bachnik, the top insurance people, Max Edelstein. They would sit at one long table in the corner, and there would be anywhere from 10 to 16 people. There was a side door there, and it was a quick walk from City Hall.

That's where all the big decisions were made. Emily Nelson, the head waitress would come to the table and say, "You guys solve all the problems of the world every day. All this wisdom, it's just so marvelous. Do you think the rest of the world knows about it?"

※※※

Frank Berklich owned the Garden Lounge. He and Mike and Nick Maras at the Homer Bar probably cashed more payroll checks on Friday afternoon than the banks.

I was never a very good curler, but I had been picked up for a time by the Harold Lauber Rink as their lead. These were some of the great curlers in the world, literally. Lauber went on to become the first U.S. champion and has always been regarded as the godfather of American curling. Pete Beasy was on that team, as was Anthony Broad, who they called Funny Broad. I was the odd man out among these great curlers, and I was going to tell them they should find another teammate, one who could pull his weight.

We were in the Garden Lounge one night, and Beasy was in the back room playing bridge. Because Berklich wanted to play a prank, he called me over and had me stand just outside the door where no one could see me. He yelled out to Beasy, "Hey, Pete, why the hell do you keep that D'Aquila on your team?"

COUNT THE PICKETS IN THE FENCE

Beasy didn't bat an eyelash. He said, "Because he buys all the drinks."

I dashed into the room and stood in front of Beasy. I said, "Pete, I quit."

Pete looked up at me and said, "Oh, D'Aq, I was only kidding." We had a good laugh, but it was more than time for me to quit that threesome. When we curled, Pete would yell, "Sweep, sweep, sweep," and I'd be flitting on down the ice. It really wasn't my sport.

❧☙❧☙❧☙

If you go back to North Hibbing, there was one guy who stood out in the sports world. He didn't have many friends, and he didn't know very many people outside of that North Hibbing group.

He was Al Nyberg.

We had a basketball team together — D'Aquila's Bulls, he picked the name — and we had a baseball team together. There were nights where we'd stand around, 15 or 20 fellows, and Nyberg would say, "Ask Carlo, ask Carlo what the batting average of the top guys in the league are." I used to know all those averages. The only reason he could ask the question is that he also knew what the batting averages were. We both were like computers. We knew those averages like we knew the "Our Father."

That's all we did was talk about sports. We never did anything crazy. We never got in trouble. I'd go out and get the sponsors for the jackets and for the bats and balls and the fees to enter the tournaments. We won the state softball championship with our team.

It was a tremendous tribute to him that they named Hibbing's baseball park after him.

❧☙❧☙❧☙

Charlie Cox ran the Hibbing Airport for many years. He would do everything. He would sell the tickets, collect the tickets, go out and load the plane, wave the plane off, and receive the plane when it came back. He was a one-man operation.

He really was very effective. He truly was dedicated.

But Charlie had a little side business. When he got the chance, he was selling wild rice to the passengers as they came through the airport. Over the years, he sold hundreds and hundreds of pounds of wild rice. Businessmen bought it. People who wanted to give it for Christmas gifts bought it.

It got to be such an issue that the vice president of North Central Airlines said to his assistant, "I want you to go up to Hibbing and fire him. He's begging everybody to buy wild rice before they get on the plane. He's forcing these people to buy wild rice.

Stories about People

The guy came to Hibbing, and later that day he flew back to corporate headquarters. The boss said, "Well, did you do it?" The assistant said, "Well, not exactly."

The boss said, "What do you mean by 'Not exactly.'"

The assistant said, "Well, he gave me the franchise for Wisconsin."

༺༻༺༻༺༻

Ron Marinelli was probably the best radio announcer in northern Minnesota when he worked for WMFG in Hibbing. He continued that tradition when he moved his radio career to North Dakota.

The Marinellis were part of that little United Nations that existed on McKinley Street in North Hibbing. There were Italians, Finns, Swedes, Jews, Irish and English in those days. Ron's dad owned the Niagara Bottling Works, the first pop shop on the Iron Range.

Ron did something a lot of Italians talk about, but very few do -- he moved back to the Old Country. Ron taught English to the Italian soldiers and he also taught it to Italian businessmen. He and his elegant wife, Carla, come visiting from Italy every summer, and we always look them up when we are there. We keep in constant contact all year long.

༺༻༺༻༺༻

I've known Carl Pohlad, the banker and owner of the Minnesota Twins, for many years, and we still communicate often and are involved in some proposed business deals. We worked together after the Twins won their World Series titles to create a series of collector stamps that commemorated the championships and raised money for amateur baseball.

I remember talking to Carl one time when he was about to get an honorary degree from Gonzaga University. He mentioned that he had never received his degree from Gonzaga, and I was surprised. Carl is not the kind of man who doesn't follow through on things.

"Well, there were really tough times my senior year at Gonzaga," he said. "I looked around at the job market, and there were thousands of guys looking for jobs. If I waited until I graduated, I'd just be one more guy in the crowd. I decided to get a jump on things, and so I quit college after the football season."

Carl did a get a job, and he never looked back. He also made a billion dollars along the way.

༺༻༺༻༺༻

I was on the Alliance for Free Enterprise for eight years during the Reagan Administration. We had some of our meetings and receptions at the White House.

On one memorable trip, I left my hotel and tried to catch a cab, but I was having no luck. I was getting a little desperate because I didn't want to be late to the White House. Finally, I decided I'd have to get out on the street in the traffic and flag one down.

A Yellow Cab with a passenger in the back seat pulled over. Evidently, the passenger had seen my frantic efforts and told the cabbie to stop and pick me up.

Much to my surprise, it was Sam Donaldson, the ABC White House correspondent. He asked me where I was going and I said, "To the White House." He replied, "So am I."

Then he asked me what kind of identification I was going to use to get in. These were the times when I was doing Capitol Corridors show, and I told him I was going to use my ABC press card. He seemed impressed and asked me where it was from. I told him "Duluth, Minnesota."

I think he's still laughing. Anyway, he wouldn't let me pay for the cab. The truth was I had my invitation to the Alliance meeting, and that's how I got in.

An elegant older couple from Chicago lived in our Florida condominium. Their names were Anna and Antonio Pasin, and they had truly lived the American dream.

Starting with nothing, they had created the original little red wagon, the "Radio Flyer." At first they built a wooden model and later on the steel models that were on every little boy's wish list.

Antonio died, and Anna kept the Florida apartment. I got to know her quite well, and we visited frequently in the exercise room. One day, she invited me to her apartment and told me her whole family history. She had a lot of memorabilia and she gave me a detailed history of the Red Wagon. She also gave me a few miniature souvenir models.

Her sons and grandsons are still running the company, and it is very successful. She knew I was in the tire business, and one day she asked me if I thought we could supply the tires for the Radio Flyers. I'm not sure she quite understood the scale of the tires we sold for the huge mining vehicles -- truly the largest tires in the world -- but she was so sincere and kind in her offer, I didn't know what to say.

Harry Stuhldreher was the quarterback of the Four Horsemen of Notre Dame, maybe the most famous backfield in college football history. He had been invited to be the guest speaker at the Municipal Athletic Banquet in Hibbing, and he ended up staying in our home.

He was a most interesting guy, and he told all the stories about those old days in the Knute Rockne era.

The night he stayed there happened to be our eldest son's birthday. It was pretty hard for Dolores and me to put aside the birthday and tell Tom we'd have to do it some other night.

But we had to do it. When we got home after the banquet, I found out that my very favorite hunting dog was missing. Stuhldreher was just like a member of the family. He said, "Let's go looking for it." So we walked around the neighborhood and then got in the car to drive around the fairgrounds. We spent several hours but couldn't find the dog. It was Stuhldreher who kept urging us on to keep looking, but to no avail.

A couple of days later, someone knocked at the door and told us our dog was lying dead on the boulevard. He had apparently been hit by a truck.

It's one of those examples of the highs and lows of life. We had gone from the enjoyment of having this famous athlete and coach with us to losing our first hunting dog.

ᔆᓍᔆᓍᔆᓍ

John Dougherty was Hibbing's most renowned undertaker before he retired, and maybe the funniest guy in town. He was the emcee at countless banquets and events, and he always had them rolling in the aisle.

And despite his profession of dealing with those who have gone to the other side, he not only saved my life, he also saved Dolores' life.

I had severely injured my right leg in the late 60s, and I wasn't taking very good care of it. I was up at the lake ignoring how swollen and discolored the leg was, and John came by for a visit.

He took one look at my leg and said, "You are going to the clinic tonight, or I'll have you at my place in a couple of days." I was stubborn, but when the best funeral director in town gives you that advice, you listen. I went directly to the emergency room where they immediately lanced the leg. The blood clots came flying out, and they kept coming out for weeks. I had severe blood poisoning, and if one of those clots had worked its way to my heart, it would have been all over. As it was, I was on crutches for weeks.

Another time, I was getting ready for a weekend at the duck camp. Dolores was recovering in the hospital from surgery, but she said she'd be fine and I should go north. She hid her real pain from me. She knew that Fran Befera was bringing up Walter Mondale, and she didn't want me to miss it. She insisted that I go, and I did.

I called first thing in the morning and talked to Mary Chapin, who had spent the night with Dolores. She told me things were not good, and that I should come home right away.

The doctor who had done the surgery had left for vacation right after the operation. The nurses where doing their best, but there was no doctor looking after Dolores. I was sitting with her that morning, and John Dougherty came by to see how Dolores was doing.

He took one look at her and motioned for me to come out into the hallway. He used almost the same words he had used on me a few years earlier. "If you don't do something, I'll have Dolores in 48 hours."

John gave me very specific advice on what I should do, and how another specialist needed to be called in. He was absolutely right. Another surgeon did a second operation, and it saved Dolores' life. Our dear friend, Dr. Vince Paciotti, was instrumental in detecting the trouble.

You can't have a better friend than one who keeps your mortal flame alive. To this day, John and Mary Kay Dougherty, Ed and Judy Matonich, Dave and Lois Naughtin, Bill and Liz Berklich, Curt and Rochelle Rice, Vince Paciotti and his late wife, Jean, the late Dr. Bill Larson and his wife, Marlene, have been the closest of friends and pillars of support in our lives. We've been there for each other through the years during the joys and sorrows, through good health and sickness, through everything that life throws at you. Friends like that are God's gift.

※※※

Father William McNamara, OCD, of the Spiritual Life Institute of America, was a guest many times at our lake home at Side Lake, about 20 miles from Hibbing. He had been commissioned by Pope John to spread ecumenism throughout the U.S., and he also established retreats in Colorado, Nova Scotia and Ireland.

Dolores and I would leave for work early in the morning, and Father McNamara would stay at the lake, take our pontoon out, and spend most of the day meditating, praying and saying his office. When we returned in the evening, he would say mass in the dining room.

We would be tired and still wrought from the day's business problems, and he would admonish us and say, "Take it easy, relax, don't let it bother you." He'd smile and say, "Look at me, look how serene I am." Of course, he'd just gotten off the pontoon.

Finally, one time, Dolores responded, "Yes, father, but when you need money or some special piece of equipment, you always call us."

※※※

Stories about People

Father Theodore Hesburgh was President of Notre Dame, and we were fortunate at one point to be at a special dinner to honor the leading students, and Hesburgh was there. Our son, Jim, was graduating at that time. There were all kind of rumors circulating on campus that Hesburgh was going to retire.

I was walking around taking pictures at this event, and it was a lot of fun. Dolores and I sat with Joe Garagiola and his wife, and that was a picnic. Hesburgh came up to me at one point and said, "You know, I really am intrigued by that camera. That would really be a nice thing for me to have."

I said, "Father, that might a good thing, I'll keep it in mind, and when you retire I'll see that you get one." He replied, "Well, what I was thinking was that it would be really nice to get one so I could take pictures of my last year here."

When I got home, I went down to Aubin's and bought him one and sent it to him.

About a year later, I opened my mouth with a customer and told him I could get him some football tickets to a Notre Dame game. Hesburgh hadn't retired yet, and I called him up. I asked if he could find some football tickets.

He said, "You know, I have the same problem myself. I have a nephew that wants to come, and I'm in the lottery." It was what kind of guy he was. Even if he could have used his influence to get tickets, he wouldn't do it. He was absolutely strict about such things. He not only preached it, he practiced it.

ಸಂಬಂಧಿಸಿದಂತೆ

Dr. Ben Owens has been one of my best friends for 60 years. We were pals in high school, and we've always stayed close. He dedicated his whole life to medicine and helping people, and he was named Minnesota Family Physician of the Year a few years back. In fact, he was so dedicated to the people of the community, he never had time for matrimony.

When he would lose a patient, he would often stop by our home or that of Jack DeLuca or Dr. Vince Paciotti. One time he came in, and he was tired and haggard and needed a shave. Dolores asked him to stay for dinner.

"Carl," he said, "Can I shave first and clean up?"

I said, "Sure, come on up to the third floor and use my bathroom. You can use my shaver and my shower, and I'll get you a towel. It'll be just like the best hotel in town."

Ben replied, "I'd like that very, very much because I really like it here, and I have a great respect for Dolores. She is like our mothers were. She is dedicated. She is a good mother. She takes care of the children. She doesn't need a doctor, she can diagnose things herself. She is a perfect woman. And I'd like to learn everything about this house, and where everything is. Because if something happens to you, I'd like to marry Dolores."

Count the Pickets in the Fence

๛๏๛๏๛๏

I was getting a thorough physical exam at the Mesaba Clinic. They put me on the table, and the nurse had me in the proper position for a proctology exam. All I had on was one of those flimsy gowns.

The nurse told me the doctor, Ben Owens, would be a little late because he was tending to someone in the emergency room. She said I should stay as comfortable as I could, and then she left. As she slammed the door, the procto table partially collapsed. I dropped about a foot instantaneously.

The nurse rushed back in. "Are you all right?" she asked. I said I was a little shaken up, but I was fine. She left again, and as the door shut, the table collapsed completely to the floor. This time the jolt to my back was pretty extreme, and I laid there on the floor moaning, "Oh, my God. Oh, my God."

The nurse rushed back in again. She said, "I can't believe this. This is the third time this has happened, and I've told the maintenance man to fix it."

Suddenly, Dr. Owens appeared. "Are you all right?" he asked, looking down at me laying flat on the floor.

I said, "Just get me the phone. I'm going to call Ed Matonich." Matonich is one of the top personal injury attorneys in the state. "I'm sure he'll take this case."

"Don't be so sure," Owens replied. "In fact, you'd better get someone else because I keep Matonich on a monthly retainer."

Laughter must be the best medicine, because when I was done laughing, it didn't hurt so much.

๛๏๛๏๛๏

One of the most colorful and best physicians in Hibbing was Alexander Levitov. He was Russian-born, and one of the top graduates ever from the University of Moscow Medical School.

Our daughter Mary Kay was visiting us when we were staying at our Grand Rapids cabin one time. I had been uncomfortable for several hours with a pain in my chest, and Mary Kay urged me to go to the hospital. I didn't really want to because I was sure it wasn't my heart. Mary Kay said, "Until you go, I'm not going to leave. And then you'll have to worry about me being out on the highways late at night."

So I went to the emergency room. The doctor took some x-rays and diagnosed my condition as costrochondritis, an inflammation of the chest wall. He got the drug store to open up for me, and I got a prescription filled.

The next day, back in Hibbing, Dolores called me and said I had to get to the clinic right away because my daughter, Patti, a doctor, had arranged an appointment with

Dr. Levitov. I rushed over to the clinic, and the nurse had me take my clothes off and sit on the cold examining table.

A few minutes later, Levitov came in. "So, you are Mr. D'Aquila. Your daughter is very concerned about you. I understand you work very hard," he said in his Russian accent. "But I only have one question for you. Mr. D'Aquila, why are you naked?"

I told him the nurse had told me to disrobe.

"Well, that's very fine," he said. "That says a lot about how they program nurses like a computer. But I don't choose to talk to naked body. Please put your clothes on, and I'll let you know if you need to take them off."

With that settled, he asked me what the emergency room doctor had diagnosed. "What he said you had?" I told him I had costrochondritis.

"And what he said costrochondritis is?" I told him it was a severe inflammation of the rib cage.

"And how did he tell that?" I told him he took an x-ray.

"Well, that's just fine, because you'll never need to work again. If you can tell costrochondritis from an x-ray, you and he can write an article in the New England Journal of Medicine, and you'll both be famous."

He asked me if the doctor had prescribed any medicine. "Did he get you five little pills?" I was surprised. I told him yes.

"Give them to me," he said. "No, I'll need them," I said.

"Give them to me," he repeated, and so I did. He casually dropped them in the waste basket. "Now, do you know where Spies Super Valu is? I want you to go down there and buy a pod of peas. There will be five peas in there, and you should take one every day. They will do you just as much good as that medicine, and you will get well just as fast."

Of course, he was right. I had just over-exerted myself.

Dr. Levitov and I had a great relationship until he left Hibbing. In fact, we became business partners. He was way ahead of his time in knowing that computers could be a great aid in helping doctors correctly test and diagnose for heart disease. We had the program all ready to go, but the medical industry wasn't ready at that time.

༺༻༺༻༺༻

Our cabin in Grand Rapids has really been a big part of our lives. Since we had it built in 1981, we've become very well-acquainted with the people of Grand Rapids. And, amazingly enough, some of our oldest, closest friends lived in the same neighborhood on Lake Pokegama. Dr. Vince Paciotti and his wife, Jean, Ed and Judy Matonich, Eugene and Jean Ryan Rothstein all lived within seven or eight cabins of ours.

The Rothsteins had been our next door neighbors on Side Lake years before. They had many children, but some of the boys never seemed very interested in getting out on the lake for any kind of water sports. It seemed they were always just standing by the lakeshore, looking at the water. Later on, after they had become all-state hockey players, I told Jean I finally figured out what they were doing all those years. "They were waiting for the lake to freeze over."

Grand Rapids over the last couple of decades has had a real spark, the same kind of spark Hibbing had before the mining industry downscaled so dramatically. Part of it is that Grand Rapids is better situated highway-wise, and it got out of mining and became the gateway to recreation and diversification at the right time. It had the entrepreneurial spirit in Grand Rapids, not like Hibbing where mining was king.

I've had a chance to meet so many great people over there. The Wayne Jacobson family owns the Sawmill Inn where so many of the important meetings have been held. I've watched the Judy Garland Museum, and the Reif Center, the Showboat, and many other projects bloom and grow in Grand Rapids. The Jerry Miner family, too, has been one of the driving forces, as has the Claire Wilcox family.

It's 38 miles from Hibbing to our lake home in Grand Rapids, but it's like going to another state or another country.

Stuart Parsons was a good friend who owned a condo near ours in Florida. He invited us to his home in Saddle River, N.J., for an extended weekend one time. His next-door neighbor was Richard Nixon, and he said that he would get Nixon and me together to play golf in a foursome at his country club. He wanted to hear the two of us talk politics. We passed it up to stay at the lake with the family, but it sure would have been fun to talk it over with the former President.

Halsey Hall let me sit in and watch him broadcast Gopher football games when I was a kid. He was the grand old man of sportscasters in Minnesota.

At that time Rudy Sikich from Hibbing played for the Gophers. One time Halsey said on the air, "Well, Minnesota is doing quite well. You know that front line, paced by Rudy Sikich, weighs tons. You know what they say about Rudy. When he makes a hole in the line, you could drive one of those Euclid mining trucks through that hole."

Well, one time when Minnesota was playing Indiana, and Halsey was announcing the game, Bernie Bierman, the Gopher's legendary coach, sent in Sikich with a play.

I can still hear Halsey calling the game: "Well, it's Sikich coming in, and you know he's going to open up those big holes. He's trotting onto the field and is looking up into the audience. He sees a pretty girl and waves to her. He's in the huddle now,

Stories about People

and what's this? Rudy is bent over, and the whole team is gathered around the big lineman's backside."

Sure enough, Bierman didn't trust Rudy to remember the play. He had written it on the seat of Rudy's pants.

ಸಿಆರ್ಸಿಆರ್ಸಿಆರ್

Carl Dahlberg was the owner of the Keewatin Sawmill. He was also a bank director, investor, businessman and an elegant gentleman.

When I went to the Mayo Clinic for an exam one year, I arrived at the Kahler Hotel in Rochester about 4 p.m. in the afternoon. I looked around the lobby and the coffee shop to see if there was anyone I knew. When I looked into the bar, there was Carl Dahlberg sitting on a bar stool and talking with the bartender. He spotted me and excitedly said, "Come on in and have a drink."

I told him I was having medical tests in the early morning, and I had been given strict dietary instructions to follow. He said, "So am I, but don't worry. Are you going to 7 West?" I told him I was. He said, "Then come on, have a drink and I'll take you up to the Pinnacle Room, buy you a steak and we'll have a great night."

I told him I couldn't possibly do that. "Carl," I said, "that would invalidate the tests."

"Look, I know the doctor well," he answered. "I bring him ducks and wild rice every year, and he always gives me a clean bill of health."

ಸಿಆರ್ಸಿಆರ್ಸಿಆರ್

Frank Lomoro was a former prominent Hibbingite and an avid skier. I ran into him one time at the airport in the Twin Cities, and he asked me about skiing on the Iron Range. We used to ski as a family every weekend at Lookout Mountain near Virginia while it was open. It was a great time of family togetherness.

Now I was never much of a skier, and I never learned all that there is to know about skiing, but I was anxious to show Lomoro what an expert I was. He wanted to bring a busload of skiers up from the Twin Cities.

I bragged all about Lookout Mountain and what a great place it was. I told him every detail about it.

Finally Frank asked, "Well, does Lookout Mountain have a T-bar?"

I replied, "No, but they have a very good coffee shop."

ಸಿಆರ್ಸಿಆರ್ಸಿಆರ್

So many Iron Range kids grow up and move away and never come back. Michael

Valentini was one of those who did come home, and the Range is better because of it. For the past 50 years, Dolores and I have been perhaps the best customers of Valentini's Restaurant in Chisholm, one of the finest restaurants in the state.

We have come to know Michael very well, because there's no better way to get to know someone well than to sit down with them over a good meal and a glass of wine. We think of Michael almost like one of our own children. He has shown real leadership on the Range, and his potential is unlimited. Being named to the statewide committee that is trying to save Major League Baseball in Minnesota is just an example.

The day he gave us the news that Valentini's was closing was both happy and sad. I'm glad for the family. Michael's mother, Dionella, and his uncle and aunt, Bruno and Rose Valentini, are some of our closest friends. His father, Nello, who is deceased, was also a close friend. The family will no longer have to work those 16 hour days necessary when one has a family business.

But I'm sad for all of the rest of us who came to love Valentini's for its food, atmosphere and history.

෨෬෨෬෨෬

I went to Golf Digest School in Phoenix, Arizona, at the Troon North course with a couple of Hibbing pals, Dr. Vince Paciotti and Curt Rice. We were instructed in all the essentials of the game for three days.

On the last day, instructor Chuck Cook, who was well-known nationally as a consultant and friend to the pros including Payne Stewart, was having our efforts videotaped so we would have a reference when we got home. Cook later did the eulogy at Payne Stewart's funeral.

I had missed breakfast that morning, and I was starving. Cook kept me out on the course, though, because I wasn't quite as polished as he had hoped. We had to hit three balls out of the sand, hit three pitches to the green, and then hit three long putts. My efforts on getting out of the trap weren't very successful, and I watched all my buddies finish up and head for lunch while I was still stuck in the sand.

Finally, Cook asked me if I had a sand wedge.

I said, "No, but if you'll let me go up to the clubhouse like all the others, I'd be glad to get a sandwich." Cook nearly went hysterical with laughter, and I just stared at him, dead serious. I was really hungry.

Later on, I found out what a sand wedge was. When my family heard the story, they just roared. My daughter, Barbara, even bought me a sand wedge.

෨෬෨෬෨෬

Sometimes, friendships emerge from business dealings. I first knew Stuart Seiler of Security Jewelers in Duluth through some business dealings, but as time went by, we became very close, and for many years we phoned each other almost on a daily basis. We were fortunate to be able to attend the weddings of each other's children, and we also attended bar mitzvahs and other special events. Stuart and his wife, Robin, are among our best friends, and, along with Tom and Jean Dougherty and John and Mary Dwan, we broke bread together many times through the years.

༄༅༄༅༄༅

I have watched many of my friends and co-workers die, and I have started to think about my own mortality. I have even wondered if I should start making plans for my own funeral.

I was driving between Hibbing and Grand Rapids one day, and I was saying the rosary, as I often do. As I drove along, the thought came to me that maybe I should plan my list of pallbearers. Should my children pick those people? Should I pick them? I don't know. Should I put down a list and make it a longer list than need be because some of those might also be gone? It's a very difficult thing.

But then I started to think of it as if I were having a party. If I can only pick six, won't so and so feel slighted? That's one of the yardsticks I used in evaluating my real friends. I come down to a basis of who do I want to show my last respect. It would be my tribute to them as well as it might be their final tribute to me and my family.

That's probably where the use of honorary pall bearers came from. I just can't get it down to six regular pall bearers.

But Dolores put an end to all that speculation. She told me, "All that's going to be in the newspaper is 'Carl D'Aquila, age so and so, died yesterday. He was the father of six children.' That's all that's going to be in there. Period. I'm going to fool everybody. It'll be my chance to do it the way I want to do it," she said.

༄༅༄༅༄༅

I don't know why I'm constituted that way, but it just seems that when I meet people, I have to weave myself into the fabric of their existence. Once I become associated with someone in any way, shape or form, I'm like a worm. I have to make it a more lasting and permanent relationship, and I go all out to do that. My best friend, though, has been Dolores. In fact, I've often said because of her God-given blessings, she's my "breast" friend.

As children get older, graduate from college, and get families of their own, I really don't look upon them solely as children anymore. That becomes secondary, unless there's some illness or some need. I really look upon them as trustworthy best friends.

Chapter Seventeen

FAMILY TIES

Virginia High School was on its way to the state tournament in 1943. In fact, it had such a good team that year, it made it all the way to the state semifinals — losing to Alexandria in an exciting game.

Dolores Casagrande was in school at that time. I was broadcasting one of the regional tournament games in Virginia, and somebody pointed me out to her and asked if she knew me. She told me years later that she replied, "No, I don't, but I'd be interested in meeting him."

These were the days of just radio, no TV. Unless one was at an event being broadcast, one had no idea what the broadcaster looked like. When I had the radio program over WMFG in Hibbing from my high school freshman year on, and I was doing a lot of play-by-play, I always wondered what the network stars looked like. I envisioned how they looked from their voices. I sent for some pictures of these great men and women, and without fail they looked nothing like their voices. That must be what pundits mean when they say, "He's got a great face for radio."

Anyway, I'm sure that's what Dolores' interest in me was when she first saw me at that young age. She just had a normal fan's curiosity.

I didn't know her at all, but I knew the family name because the Casagrandes had a prominent beverage business — beer and liquor and a Pepsi-Cola bottling plant — in Virginia.

Several years later, however, we met through some unusual circumstances.

Jack Fena was one of my best friends, and we saw each other on a daily basis. The Fenas had the identical business in Hibbing that the Casagrandes had in Virginia. In

Family Ties

ENGAGEMENT ANNOUNCED

MISS DOLORES MAE CASAGRANDE

Dolores' engagement announcement in a local newspaper. This photo appeared in every Iron Range newspaper, as well as Duluth and Minneapolis. This was high society.

fact, Mario Casagrande had worked for John Fena, Jack's dad, in earlier years. When Mario ended up with the Grain Belt Beer franchise for the entire Range, he befriended his former employer and gave John the west end of the Range. Just think of what he would have had if he had kept it all for himself. They were both among the top five volume distributors in the state every year.

Since their parents were both in the same business, they got together on weekends at their lake cabins. The Casagrandes had a cabin at Sand Lake, north of Virginia, and the Fenas had a cabin at Sturgeon Lake near Hibbing. It was pretty ritualistic that Italian families would get together on Sundays, and they'd often have three or four other families for a bountiful pot luck, bocce ball, plenty of red wine and fun. Weekends were generally quite festive. Everyone would sing and play cards. There was a real conviviality, and that's something that's really lacking today.

Jack said to me one day, "Why don't you go over and check out my friend in Virginia?" He said her name was Dolores Casagrande.

It was 1948, and I was in the Legislature. After the session, I had helped start the new WEVE Radio station in Eveleth for the Duluth News Ridder family and Cully Bloomquist. I was doing some broadcasting for WEVE and selling some advertising.

In the course of making my calls, I stopped in to sell some ads to the Casagrande Beverage Co. in Virginia.

When I went in to sell, her dad wasn't there, but Dolores was. In typical Casagrande fashion, she said, "Why don't you come back and see my father in the afternoon?" I came back in the afternoon, and her dad gave me an ad.

I had never met him before, but he asked, "Can you stay in town? Would you like to come to dinner tonight?" They were that friendly. So I had dinner that night with

170

Ting Town was one of the major attractions of the Iron Range, located north of Hibbing on the way to Side Lake. It was a frequent destination for Dolores and I when we were dating. It featured a barbeque sandwich that was unbelievably good. To this day, the recipe is kept a guarded secret. In this publicity photo, Ting Town is showing off the amount of bread it went through every day selling its sandwiches. The political entity of Ting Town had two voters, a husband and wife. One voted Democrat and one voted Republican.

Dolores and her dad, mom and sister, Sally Jean. It was a great dinner and a joyful evening.

I came back and reported to Jack that she was really a great, great gal. "She seems like a gift from God," I told him.

He said, "Oh, I don't know if I want to get tied down or anything. My dad would love to see a merger of the families, but I've got a lot to do. There's a lot I want to see."

Because he seemed pretty much disinterested in Dolores, I started to pursue her. I asked her out for a date. I wanted to take her to see Alan Jones at the Hibbing High School Auditorium.

But before our date, I was calling on customers on the east end of the Range, and I was driving back home along Highway 37. It was just about sunset, and there was a cow going across the road near the Hibbing Airport. I swerved and rolled the car over. The worst part was that I totaled the car, and it was a brand new car.

The newspaper story the next morning reported the accident and said that I'd been taken to the hospital and later released. She sent a very lovely card that I still have. Of

Family Ties

> **Stag Party**
> in honor of
> CARL D'AQUILA
> *Wednesday, Dec. 29, 1948*
> Wine, Whiskey and ? ?
> $2.50 TO GET IN

Prospective Bride Feted at Shower Held Last Evening

Approximately fifty guests attended a pre-nuptial party last evening at the women's clubrooms in honor of Miss Dolores Casagrande, daughter of Mr. and Mrs. Mario Casagrande of 827 Fourth Street South. The prospective bride was presented with many lovely gifts from those present and she also received a shoulder corsage of yellow roses.

The evening was spent playing games and prizes were awarded to Mrs. Emil Pettinelli, Mrs. Louis Marchetti, Mrs. John Giorgi, Mrs. Leonard Petrosky, and Mrs. Michael D'Aquila of Hibbing.

Refreshments were served by the following hostesses, Mrs. Anthony Benkusky, Mrs. Leonard Petrosky, and Mrs. Sam Abbanot. The luncheon table was centered with a miniature bride and bridesmaids flanked by tapers set in candelabra.

Miss Casagrande will be married January 8 at Our Lady of Lourdes Catholic Church to Carl D'Aquila, son of Mr. and Mrs. R. D'Aquila of Hibbing.

Before our marriage, we had the customary events. Above is a ticket for my stag party. I can't remember what the "? ?" was. At right is a news clipping from Dolores' bridal shower.

all the people I knew, she was the only one who sent a card.

So when our date night came around, I had no way of getting her from Virginia to Hibbing. She was going to come over on the bus, but, lo and behold, Jack Fena was over there doing some business. So she asked him if she could have a ride over to Hibbing. It was kind of embarrassing for Jack to have to drop her off for a date with me, after he had introduced her to me.

After the show, I was able to borrow my brother's car to take her back home.

We hit it off very well. There was some chemistry right from the beginning. I never had it in mind that I would have somebody of my own faith or nationality, but it really seemed like a proper fit.

She was a very serious gal, personality plus, disciplined, very detailed and very organized. I was so impressed with her maturity even though I was nearly five years older than she. I saw that she had qualities that would complement the ones I had.

That was the fall of 1947. From then on, we spoke by phone each day and dated

Our wedding day on January 8, 1949. Dolores' cousin Kathleen Crispigna was taking pictures. Left to right are Norman MacCormick, Gus Ekola, and the happy couple. Seated is my cousin, Anthony Spensieri.

nearly every weekend. On May 1st, 1948, after having had dinner earlier at the Androy Hotel's Crystal Lounge with Tom and Jeanne Dougherty and John and Jennie Biancini, I began to take Dolores back home to Virginia. En route, we stopped at our favorite hangout, Ting Town. I asked Dolores if she would like a barbequed pork sandwich, and while we were waiting, I presented her with an engagement ring. She was so surprised, she said, "I'm not hungry anymore. Take me home so I can tell my parents."

We married on January 8, 1949.

I moved with a lot more suddenness than you might expect if you knew me then. I don't know if unconsciously I was worried that Jack Fena might reconsider.

We tied the knot while I was still in the legislature. Aldo Boria, the assistant manager at the Androy Hotel, was my best man. He had also been my campaign manager. We were married in Virginia at Our Lady of Lourdes Church. It was a very stormy winter day with lots of ice and snow, and many of the Twin Cities' legislators who tried to come up for the wedding couldn't make it. A group of them got stranded in Moose Lake and had to spend the night at the Moose Lake State Hospital, a mental

173

institution. Some Capitol pundits joked that the hospital should have kept the lawmakers there.

We still had 450 people at the Elks Lodge for the reception. Festivities then continued at the Casagrande residence after that.

Our first child was Tom, and he was born on Nov. 4th, 1949. I'll always remember when Dolores told her mother that we were going to have a baby in late October or early November, her mother started counting on her fingers. Her mom's life was carefully guided.

Patricia was born on Oct. 15, 1951, two years later. Mary Kay was born on June 9, 1953. Barbara Jean was born on Aug. 2, 1955. Margaret was born on Aug. 9, 1957. Jim, the other male bookend, was born June 10, 1960.

We had a happy, close family existence. We lived close to the schools, the church and the library. We had a good quality of life. Except for some volunteer work, all of Dolores' hours were aimed at the children.

We always had nourishing meals. We had bacon and eggs or ham, or pancakes, or French toast and cereal for breakfast. Lunches were soup, sandwiches, or stews. The dinners were always full-course, and we had pasta three times a week.

Dolores set down the rules. We had three or four television sets in the house, but the children were not allowed to watch any TV during the week unless there was some special program. She would check and recheck to make sure they all had their homework done everyday before they could entertain any idea of going out.

※※※

Over the years, Dolores has given me a sense of deep inner security. She's totally capable and was able to step right in and start a household. We went through all the pangs and pains that people of those days did, and we had to take everything very slowly.

From the beginning, Dolores said she wanted a large family. She always said she wanted to have eight children. She knew where she wanted to go. She was beautiful, she was intelligent, she was well-liked. She was religious.

When she graduated from Virginia High School, the inscription next to her picture best described her: "She does lovely things, not dream them."

Yet she had a great sense of humor. I guess I had a more serious, duty-filled compulsion every day. I felt as if the world was not something to be enjoyed, but something you had to conquer. She brought a lot of lightness into my life.

Most of the friendships I had came out of school, sports, church or public life. But the real friendships that endured over the years were more the friendships that came out of her associations with people, and the associations made with parents of our children's friends. Women's friendships are often a great deal more solid.

We ran a home in which there was reverence and order. Every morning we got up and went to mass with the kids when they were in parochial schools. We said our prayers. We said a daily rosary as a family.

Any trips we took, to Minneapolis or anywhere else, were complete family participations. She kept the children neat. She taught me how to save money. She was very budget conscious, and I wasn't. I had an easy time making money, but even though I was conservative with other people's money, I wouldn't have saved anything for our family if not for her prudence.

It was a gift from God that I was able to meet her. But I don't want to imply that life was all easy, of course. There were health problems and what not. I would always fall apart when things would happen, whereas she might suffer inside, but she was always the Florence Nightingale being at somebody's side. She kept a stability and gave everybody an inner confidence that things were going to be all right. I tended to worry and look at everything in the worst light.

She is not one who will hold back if she feels I'm wrong. She is probably my most severe critic. At first that didn't set quite right with me, but then as I matured, I realized that she was perhaps right in a lot of those assessments. She wasn't doing it because she opposed me, but because it was wrong. She was trying to steer me in a different light.

We were the happy, young couple in 1948. We recently had our 50th wedding anniversary.

Family Ties

I probably would have followed my political yearnings and stayed in a great deal longer, but politics was very distasteful to her. She didn't want any part of it. Now, years later, it's ironic that she's become tremendously interested in politics — maybe even more so than I was in my youth. She follows all the news. She served on state commissions and boards.

I'm amazed. I just sit back and watch. Sometimes she'll try to inspire me to get more involved in some of her public concerns. I'll listen and then say, "Well, when I tried to do something about those things many years ago, you were holding me back."

I always tell her, "I could have been the governor or a U.S. senator if it hadn't been for you holding me back." I know that hurts her when I say that, and I realize that's my selfish side. The truth is that in reality, things worked out better the way they did. As I look at the politicians and what has happened to politics, there are very few who have escaped with any degree of happiness, or had good families, or have had the success we've had.

Once, when I could have had the nomination for lieutenant governor, Dolores had said she wouldn't even come to the convention. Then, at the zero hour, somebody informed me that she had arrived at the Leamington Hotel and was letting it be known that she didn't want it to happen. That was one incident that led to some disagreement.

Another one involved her dad. When he retired from his business, I took him in as a partner in my business. We were good partners, and worked well together. He ran the service operation in Virginia and I ran the administrative and sales departments. Suddenly, he indicated he wanted to get out.

I was torn. Dolores' mother would call me and say, "Please don't let him out. I don't want him to quit. I want him to be busy." That was a real family problem. First, he indicated he wanted to gift the business to Dolores. Then he changed his mind and decided he wanted to sell out. It put Dolores in such a compromising position. She could either support her husband, or she could be loyal and follow her parents. It was a no-win situation. It led to arguments, but Dolores stuck with me. Eventually, it was all resolved with complete harmony as though it had never happened.

One other area where Dolores and I have not seen eye to eye is about the children. She feels that I'm overly concerned about their future, that I work harder every year, and that I should enjoy myself more now that the children are on their own.

The children have applied themselves and been successful. There have been reasons.

They had a good home life. There was a system in the home; there was religion, discipline and order. Television time was controlled. There wasn't any monkey business in any manner, shape or form. They could use the home to entertain their friends.

We tried to monitor their friends, but in the end we were very lucky. They selected great ones for the most part.

A gift from God has given them a sense of duty, a sense of conscience, a sense of achievement. They had the gifts with which to succeed. They had to have good friends. They had to have good teachers in both the parochial schools and the public schools. They had the best teachers that one could wish for.

Since their mother was successful and driven, and since I was very driven, there was a competitive spirit that became ingrained. They saw the battles I fought in both politics and in business, and they picked up the example and made up their minds they were going to succeed.

Around the table, it was like the Kennedy family. We discussed the world and we discussed school. We would go around the table and let each one of them bring up what each wanted to discuss that day. There was hardly a problem, subject or personal concern that we didn't discuss.

One of the things I remember is coming home from work, tired, and saying, "Oh, my God, what a horrible day I had." I can't blame the kids, after seeing my reaction, when none of them came back to be in the business. They decided they all wanted to be professionals. They didn't want to be in my kind of rat race where you worked so hard. Now, years later, one of the children may be interested in the business.

A lot of Range people in my generation had children that became very successful. They're all over the United States and successful in any field of endeavor you can think of, but they have not come back to the Range. It's a pity for the Range. This might be a lot better place if some of those people had come back.

Even with the gifts our children had, though, fortunes and misfortunes do occur. They all had an equal opportunity. They all went out in their own chosen field. They're all honest, they're all sincere, they're all trying their best.

They've all brought Dolores and me a great deal of pleasure and pride. I have to give Dolores credit. No matter what was going on in her life, she made it a habit of always being home when they arrived from school that day. And we always had supper together. If I had a situation where I couldn't get home until 7 o'clock, they waited for me. When there were functions where I couldn't be home for dinner, say a Chamber of Commerce, political or business function, I often attended alone because Dolores felt she should be with the children. She did a remarkable job.

☙❧☙❧☙❧

When I married Dolores, the D'Aquilas were a very close family. My father said to me, "Now I know you're going to want to come home on weekends and holidays and Sundays, but your place is with your wife. You stay there." That tore me apart.

But the problem was solved because on many Sundays Dolores' mother would

Family Ties

Pasquale and Patricia in 1955.

Pasquale, Concetta and Margaret in 1958.

say to me, "Have your folks come." Many Italians did that, and it made it very easy. We had great times — conversations, playing games, singing, going to their great dinners at home and at the lake.

In our family, we started taking everyone to the Twin Cities three or four times a year. We would go to a football game, or to Dayton's, or the ice shows. Those were great times.

We stayed at the Curtis Motor Lodge until 1964 when I convinced the Minneapolis Athletic Club to remodel and allow families to stay there. Since then, it became a second home to us.

❧☙❧☙❧☙

We went on a family trip once, our first great family trip in June 1966. I had promised the kids that we would go to Disneyland in California. They thought I was kidding them, but I had made all the reservations.

I had a nine-passenger Chrysler wagon that I had just bought a few weeks before. I was going back to work one day just after lunch, and I came back in the house to show Dolores I really had the tickets. We got talking about it, and pretty soon it was ten after one instead of quarter to one.

I backed out of the driveway and the accelerator stuck, left rubber all over the road, and the car went about 60 miles an hour backwards and took out two or three cars.

There was a defect in the wagon's accelerator, and I called the Chrysler consumer products division. I finally connected with a vice-president, and I told him, "You know, we're scheduled to leave in a week." They brought in an identical wagon two days before the trip and told us it had been checked and rechecked.

178

The D'Aquilas in 1962 at home. From left, back row: Dolores, Patricia, Tom, and Mary Kay. In front: Jim, Barbara, Carl and Margaret.

Think what could have happened if the accelerator had stuck on one of the perilous mountain roads in Colorado.

Incidents like this have made me realize there is a God looking out for us.

They all wanted to see the Grand Canyon, and when we got there they spent about 10 minutes and said, "Let's go." I said, "Why?" and they said, "Well, our mines at home are prettier than this."

I also remember from that trip that we had stuffed Jim way in the back of the station wagon, and there was also a large box of fudge back there. We had only been on the road a few hours when somehow the box had gotten open, and we could hear Jim back there. I stopped the car, and his feet were in the fudge.

LOST or STOLEN BRIEF CASE

On Tuesday night, May 11, from the back seat of my 1975 LTD brown Ford, my black brief attache case with initials C. D. in chrome. No money in it, but papers important only to owner. My car was parked in parking lots at Mesaba Country Club, the Kahler, and Androy Hotel. Will promise in writing not to prosecute. Just want brief case back in its entirety. $200 reward if all contents returned.

Call 263-4940 Between the Hours of 8 a.m. and 5 p.m.

After I lost my briefcase, I put this ad in the Hibbing newspaper. Instead of taking the reward money, the thieves sent the threatening letter on the next page.

One time I was up at the Mississippi Hilton for the fishing opener when I got a call from Dolores. We didn't have a phone there and you had to go next door to take the calls.

A week or so earlier, my briefcase had been stolen. Dolores told me that the thieves had sent a ransom note. While digging through it, they had found a picture of me arm-in-arm with a bathing beauties dressed in hot pants. They wanted $500 or they were going to release the picture.

What they didn't know was that the picture had been taken at the Bull and Bear Restaurant in Boca Raton, Florida. The bathing beauties were waitresses, and we had just taken the picture for a lark. The place was where we usually stopped for breakfast after tennis in the early morning, and Dolores had been there when the photo was taken.

Dolores said they had told her to bring the money and meet them at the bottom of the South Agnew Mine near the small mining location of Leetonia at 3 p.m. on Sunday afternoon.

There wasn't much I could do from the camp. I was the guest of Dave Naughtin, assistant county attorney, and Tom Carey, who was a prominent Virginia attorney and is now a Hennepin County district judge. I didn't even have a car.

I asked Dolores not to go anywhere near that mine, but Dolores said she was going. There was nothing I could do to talk her out of it.

The next afternoon, she was heading down into the mine. She didn't take any money. She was just going to deal with these kids who had stolen my briefcase.

What Dolores didn't know was that the sister of one of the kids had heard them plotting the whole thing the night before and had gone to the police. Just as Dolores was approaching the thieves, Bill Grillo, the chief of police, stepped out. "I'll take care of this," he said.

Those kids probably never knew how lucky they were that they were confronted

My friend,

      I do not know if I have been hearing right out is it true you wish to have your briefcase for $200.00/? If it so important to you, Im sure you would pay $500.00 I have gone completely through all papers and have found out quite a bit about you and your buisness! If you do not want a scandal on your hands(which would be the biggest on the Iron Range)you will pay the price. The police shall not be involved if you wish your name to be safe!!! I shall be watching your every move. You are to bring the money in $10.00 bills to the South Agnew Mine road. This is thru Leetonia and the first right after the rail road tracks. There will be a white arrow pointing to tis turn. Follow this road and keep looking on the left, when you see a big cement block, you are to throw the money INSIDE the block. This is all to be done on Sunday May 16 AT 3.00PM and NO LATER!! There will be a black X on the cement block. Enclosed are some pictures if you believe this is a hoax. After I recieve the money (and it better be without interferance) I will notify you by telephone at your home where your merchandise willbe.

    P.S. YOU DONT CROSS ME , I DONT CROSS YOU

                                          A FRIEND.

The blackmail letter Dolores received while I was away fishing.

Family Ties

The family in 1964 at home. From left are Barbara, Dolores, Jim, Carl, Tom, Margaret, Mary Kay and Patricia.

by Chief Grillo rather than Dolores. Later, we got her a badge that said, "Leetonia Sheriff."

❧☙❧☙❧☙

I miss all the dogs we've had. The best trained was Scooter. I taught her a trick where I would put a piece of meat or something on her nose, but she wasn't allowed to take the treat until I snapped my fingers.

I was showing that trick to somebody one time. I put the meat on Scooter's nose, but then we got to talking, and we went out in the yard. I finally remembered about 45 minutes later. I came back in the house and Scooter hadn't moved a muscle. The meat was still there. I snapped my fingers, and she tossed the meat up in the air, caught it and ate it. That was some trick.

Joe DeLoia had prize hunting dogs that had won many trophies. He owned a kennel in Duluth, and was recognized as perhaps the top hunting dog expert in northern Minnesota. We were hunting on a really bad day one year, and Joe's dog had tried to retrieve a duck that had come down in the lake, but hadn't been able to get through the ice, waves and cold water.

I said I'd send Scooter, but Joe tried to talk me out of it. "Your dog will never come back," he said. "It would be murder."

But Scooter headed out and grabbed the duck. The amazing thing was that she

The family about 1980. From left in back are Tom, Jim, Carl, Dolores, Scott and John. In front are Barb, Margaret, Thomas, Christina, Mary Kay, Jonathon and Patti.

didn't try to come back to the duck blind by going through the ice where she would have had a hard time. Instead, she stayed in the open water and followed it along the shore until she found a spot where she didn't have to break so much ice. She brought us the duck. I was deathly worried. She had been in the ice water for about 15 minutes.

Later, Joe DeLoia brought us one of his dog's trophies. He had replaced the inscription with one of his own. It said, "To Scooter, the Ice Breaker."

Tom was an excellent student and retained everything he read or heard. He never had to study very hard. I remember a nun at the Catholic School calling and saying to Dolores, "Will you please come over to see me? I have a problem with Tom." Dolores was apprehensive, and she wondered what it could be. This was a good kid.

The teacher told Dolores, "You know, he's always getting up during class, four or five times, and going up to sharpen his pencil."

"Is his school work falling behind?" Dolores asked.

"No, he's got straight A's," the nun said. "That isn't the problem. He's just driving me nuts sharpening his pencil."

"Well," Dolores said, "Tom's just got to be doing something. He's bored. Give

Family Ties

him more work. Give him more to do."

Another time, Tom came home from school and he said, "I've got to go right back to school. A big group of kids is waiting, and I've got to fight. Paul Larson called me something, and I've got to fight him. I've got to go, mom. I can't back down."

Paul Larson was one of his best friends. He later became a popular priest in the region as pastor at Coleraine's Mary Immaculate Parish where we often attend mass while at the lake.

Dolores called Sister Adelaide and asked if she should come over. Sister Adelaide told her to stay home. "Tom's right. They've got to have it out."

I don't know who won. I'm sure they both thought they won.

Tom played football and and swam in high school, and he once swam in the state tournament. He was an honor student all through high school, and he also played piano.

All the kids had cherished friendships while growing up. One of Tom's best friends was Andy Micheletti from one of Hibbing's outstanding families. To this day, they are great friends, and Andy has stood by Tom during the tough times.

About six months after Tom was born, we were in South Bend, Indiana. Dolores went into the registrar's office at Notre Dame and said she wanted to apply early for Tom to go to the university. The registrar asked how old Tom was and where he was in school. She told him that Tom wasn't in school, he was in the car, and she came and got me to bring Tom in. They couldn't believe it.

Tom did graduate from Notre Dame, and then went on to receive his law degree from Denver University. He practiced law in Denver and Minneapolis. In 1996 he suffered a disabling stroke. He and his wife, Donna Fleming, have two boys, Carl and Dante.

༄༅༄༅༄༅

Patricia was blonde, as were all four of the girls until their later teens. She was a good student, a very effervescent child. She had a lot of friends. She spent a lot of time in the library. She was a perennial honor student, active in school functions, and she played the piano.

When she was a freshman or sophomore at high school, she came home and announced that all the children were going to this particular dance or party. Dolores didn't like it. It was a school night. Patti said, "Well, Cathy Carey is going." The Careys were a wonderful family.

Patti wasn't happy that she was denied permission, and the talking went on. Finally, Dolores called the Careys, and Mrs. Carey said, "It's funny you should call because our daughter just told us that Patti is going." All the kids had conspired and told their mothers that everybody else was going.

In the end, none of them went. The mothers exercised their discipline.

Patti was active in 4H, winning blue ribbons at the St. Louis County Fair. She also did well in home economics, taking after her mother, and she won an essay contest sponsored by U.S. Steel.

From the ninth grade on, she knew she wanted to be a physician, and instead of working for her dad, she chose to work for Dr. Bill Larson, an optometrist and a great family friend.

She graduated from St. Mary's College at Notre Dame and then from the University of Minnesota Medical School. She married Dr. John Merickel, and they have two boys, Jonathon and Andrew. Patti practices internal medicine at the Willmar, Minnesota, Medical Center, and she also has a television program called, "On Call for Health."

෴෴෴

Mary Kay was third. She really had a fine touch at decorating and was very imaginative. She was also very poetic, and a good writer. She was a fashion bug. She was a good student but was more interested in being artistic and creative.

Like Patti, she did well in home economics, and she also won blue ribbons at the county fair. She loved to sing.

She tried out for many of the plays, and participated in several community college productions including "My Fair Lady." She had a lot of friends, and always had people over to our house.

In school, she had some political interest, and she was the first of the children to evidence that. She was selected as a delegate to Washington D.C. for a youth conference.

She always had that special flair for design, and she's still active in that field. Her creativity still shines through to this day.

Mary Kay graduated from St. Benedict's College at St. Joseph, Minnesota, with a degree in interior design. She is married to Scott Phillips. They have two children, Thomas and Christina, and they lived in Hopkins and Lake Minnetonka in Minnesota, and then in Santa Fe, New Mexico. They have recently returned to the Midwest and reside in Chicago.

෴෴෴

Barbara was our next child, and she was so pretty that her baby picture won first prize in a local contest when she was six months old. When they showed her photo on

Family Ties

TV, she pointed to it and got excited.

At that time I was president of the PTA at the Washington School. We lived at Side Lake, north of Hibbing, during the summers and would usually stay at the lake, if the weather was nice, for the week following Labor Day. The parents would take turns driving the children into school.

On the first day of school, I took Barbara in. The teacher was Lucille Allard. Barbara walked in and was very jovial and was mixing with all the kids. But as I started to leave, she grabbed my hand. She didn't want to stay there. She started to cry.

She had really wanted to go to school, and she was more excited about it than any of the kids had ever been. Miss Allard just said, "Leave her with me." But as I went out the door, Barbara cried more and more. So I hung around the school for another 10 or 15 minutes. Miss Allard had commenced the class.

Finally, I said to Barbara, "You have to stay." And she looked at me. "There's a state law, and if you don't stay in school," I said, "they'll put me in jail." That was when she took off her coat and decided to stay.

From the very beginning, she was a conscientious student, striving for perfection, and always an honor student. She was active in 4H and played flute in the high school band. In junior high, she created a very innovative colored shield, a family crest that we had framed and still display. Like Patti, she won the U.S. Steel Essay Contest.

She graduated from Notre Dame University and the University of Minnesota Law School. Barb lives in St. Paul, and is a partner in the firm of Flynn and Gaskins in Minneapolis. She was recently chosen as one of Minnesota's "Super Lawyers." She is also a certified public accountant.

ଓଷ୍ଠଓଷ୍ଠଓଷ୍ଠ

Margaret was our fifth child. She was a really independent and stubborn child from the time she could walk — very self-sufficient.

The whole family used to go skiing. Margaret was only four, and she'd go up the tow rope with me or with Dolores. One day, she decided to go up by herself. One of the staff stopped her and said, "You can't go by yourself." And she said, "Why can't I, buster, I paid my money. And besides, they let me go last year when I was only three." She went up by herself, and she came down by herself.

That was the way she approached everything. When she was seven, she tried out for a Vern Wenberg-directed play at the community college — "The Sound of Music." She came home one night after tryouts and said, "It's down to two of us for the Gretl part, and I'm going to get it." And she did. You know, it's hard for parents to be unbiased, but I saw that play twice on Broadway, and the Hibbing production was just as good if not better. The production played to a full house in the Hibbing High School Auditorium for an entire week.

We had a lot of stubbornness on my side of the family. But on Dolores' side, the

Brunettis and the Casagrandes — excellent people, kind and considerate, smart and personable — they really had a stubborn streak. I think it's that stubbornness that drove them on to success in many ways. For good or bad, I think Margaret can thank her ancestors for this characteristic.

Margaret, like her siblings, played the piano and was in recitals. She had a flair for her school and extra-curricular work. She was an honor student, and she was on the high school swimming team.

She graduated from Notre Dame with a degree in biology and chemistry. She worked in Washington D.C. in the environmental field, and has since worked in the same area with many private companies.

She is married to Douglas Mader, and they have three children, Nicolas, Meaghan and Charles and live in Lakeside Park, Kentucky.

෴෴෴

Jimmy was the last one to come along. He was a good child. He had serious health problems when he was four or five, and we almost lost him.

You talk about malpractice in medicine. We had a doctor at the time in Hibbing who gave Jim the wrong prescription. Jim, who was just a child, kept going downhill, downhill, downhill. One day when this doctor was out, we went to the clinic and saw another doctor, Dr. Bernard Flynn, who was a friend of the family. I think we owe Jim's life to Dr. Flynn. He asked what medication Jim was on, and he knew immediately it was the drug that was dragging Jim down so low. He had become very anemic.

Dolores and I worked at liquefying, pulverizing, trying to make calf's liver palatable for Jim. We spent time each

Our house in Hibbing where we raised our family.

day trying to build him back up. We fed him calf's liver twice a day for months.

I've been out to eat with him many times, and I've never seen him order liver as an adult.

Jim was a likable child, with a vivid imagination, and he was a good writer. I thought I could see a lot of myself in him.

He loved cars and racing, and he was a good Little League ball player. He once pitched for Coach Al Nyberg, for whom the Hibbing baseball field is named. He was the only one of our children not to play the piano, but he loved music and he loved the opera.

Jim started working as a disc jockey for the teen center at the Armory Youth Center and at Bimbo's Octagon up at Side Lake. He wanted to be a radio announcer, and so he applied at WMFG. He found that at WMFG there was often only one person running the operation. One had to be an engineer in addition to being an announcer. So he was turned down. He came back home and he was very upset. He decided to seek a waiver, and he even went so far as to see an attorney. He went to St. Paul, and he got his waiver. He'd work at WMFG nights as both the engineer and announcer.

Jim attended Marquette University and transferred to Notre Dame where he graduated with honors. He became employed as an investment banker in New York on Wall Street and later moved to California. He worked as director of the Consumer Group with Donaldson, Lufken and Jenerette in Los Angeles. He and his wife, the former Bonnie Manhan, have one daughter, Isabella Rose. They have a home in Vail, Colorado, and they recently moved back to St. Paul. Jim has originated and is the executive managing director of an investment banking firm in Minneapolis, The Mercanti Group.

ഒരുഒരുഒരു

Every time we ate at home, somebody would spill some milk. I knew that I rattled everybody when I got so upset, but with six children and eight people around the table, sometimes guests, when milk is pouring across the table, I'd have to get up and wipe it up -- under the chairs, under the table.

I had gone to a Jesuit religious retreat, and I'd been thinking about this, and how I always reacted. I had absolutely promised myself that no matter what happened, I wasn't going to comment.

I came home from this retreat with this imaginary "halo" on my head. I thought I'd really arrived. But about a half hour into the dinner, Jim spilled his milk. There was silence at the table, and everyone looked at each other. I didn't say a word. I got up and walked around the kitchen table and into the dining room. There's a large mirror there, and I just kept looking at it in total silence.

Finally I could hear Jim's voice from the other room: "Well, at least when he got mad, he'd help me wipe it up."

They're still laughing about that one.

ഇരുഇരുഇരു

We wanted the children to learn to speak Italian. Both Dolores and I spoke Italian at home when we were growing up. Dolores' grandmother taught her how to speak Italian, asked her things in Italian, conversed in Italian at the table.

It was the same for me. My father spoke a little English, and it got more acceptable as time went by. But because my mom only knew a few words of English, it was all Italian at our table.

We decided to do the same, and only speak Italian at the table. Everything went well for two or three days, but then it collapsed.

I'd be speaking in a dialect that's prevalent south of Rome, the area closer to south central or southern Italy. Dolores' folks come from the other part of Italy where they speak grammatically perfect Italian. She'd start correcting me.

I'd say, "Does it make any difference? I got by with my mom and my dad. Look how I've spoken all my life with Italians and they're satisfied."

That was the end of our experiment. Later on, when the kids got older, they told us that they really regretted not being able to speak Italian. Several of them have learned the language through adult study.

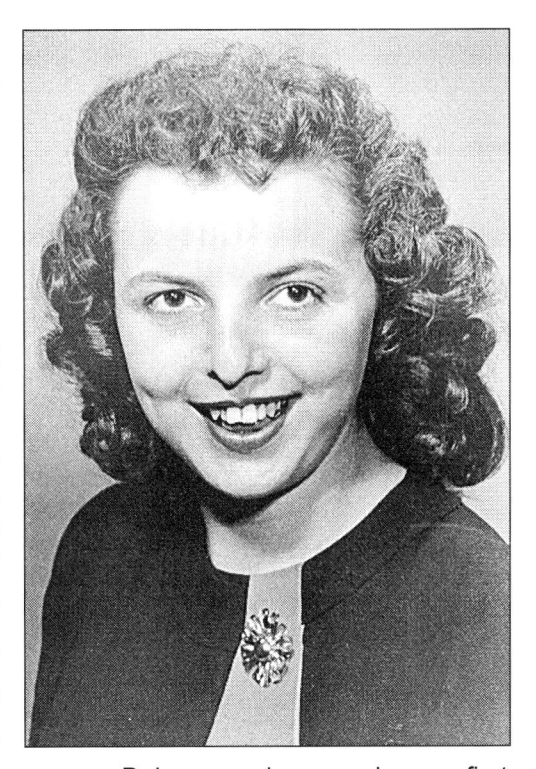

Dolores as she was when we first got married. She's still just as beautiful.

ഇരുഇരുഇരു

One time, Dolores, Tom and I were shopping at Dayton's in downtown Minneapolis. We decided to have lunch at the Skyroom in the store. As we were ordering, I mentioned to Dolores that I was running out of cash. What I meant was that we'd have to use the credit card for any more purchases.

189

Family Ties

Soon the waitress came to our table and asked little Tom if he wanted dessert.

"Are you kidding?" he said. "We don't even have enough money to pay for the meal."

༄༅༄༅༄༅

We were staying at the Minneapolis Athletic Club one time, and Jim had gone down to the lobby area where they had a little giftshop.

He was probably eight or nine years old. Pretty soon, he came back up to the room, and he had his arms full of stuffed toys. I looked at Dolores, and she looked at me. We asked where he had gotten the toys.

"Oh, it was easy," he said. "All I had to do was sign my name and 629-NR."

You could see that a life of mergers and acquisitions was in his future.

༄༅༄༅༄༅

Jimmy used to come down the steps on his way to school. "I can't stand it," he'd say. "Mom tells me to wear one thing, and I've got four other women telling me how to dress or that what I'm wearing is wrong. Have you ever seen anybody with five mothers?"

I think we had more discipline at home, and I think you saw more in the schools in those days. Around our table, one of the most frequently heard statements was, "Well, sister says" — referring to their nun teachers at school. And what sister said was the eleventh commandment. If we didn't agree with what sister said, it took some undoing to undo what sister said.

We always went to church together. If we took a trip to Minneapolis or anywhere, the kids always went with us. We did a lot of entertaining, both for business and friends, and the children always helped. I think they were fortunate to have the exposure to all these people.

༄༅༄༅༄༅

I would always have books of 25 one dollar bills put together out of new bills to give to the kids or grandkids for Christmas. Sometimes I would end up with an extra book or so.

I was walking through the International Airport in Minneapolis one day wearing a new pair of shoes that Mary Kay had given me. They were like dress moccasins.

There was this fellow who had been giving shoe shines there for many, many years. All the regulars at the airport knew him and talked to him all the time. I sat down, and right away he poked his partner and said, "Look here. Millionaire shoes."

I tried to explain to him that they were just normal shoes that you could buy in downtown Minneapolis, but he would have none of it. "Nope, I've been shining shoes for 30 years, and I've never seen shoes like these. These are millionaire's shoes."

He did his usual professional job, and I reached in my pocket for my cash, and all I had was one of those books of one dollar bills. I tore off about six of them and handed them over.

His eyes got really big, and he poked his partner again.

"Not only is this fellow a millionaire, but he prints his own money."

෩෬෩෬෩෬

We have witnessed that in other families, as the children get older, they have become more removed from their parents. They both live their own separate lives. For us, for better or worse, that's never happened. I doubt there's a day that goes by when we aren't in touch with them in some way. We've remained close. We celebrate every joy with them, but we also ride out every sorrow and every illness with them. If somebody's got a fever, we know exactly what the temperature is. We bring a lot of stress upon ourselves.

We are proud of the children. They've all done extremely well. But we worry about them and about our grandchildren. It's a riskier world now.

We got together for a family photo for Christmas 2000. There are 23 of us in our new shirts.

Family Ties

It reminds me of my mom. When she was 96 years old and dying, I was still her little boy. She was concerned about me every hour that she was alive. She had to know how I was every day. She was concerned if I was driving or taking a trip. She was the same with my brothers and with all of our families.

∽◯∽◯∽◯

There's a story behind how we named our cabin on Lake Pokegama near Grand Rapids, Minnesota.

Many years ago, my dad had been hurt in the mine. My mother didn't speak English very well, and one day she walked into the grocery store in North Hibbing and the grocer, Mr. Becchetti, said, "Pasquale will be all right. Don't worry."

My mother replied, "Oposo." She was trying to say "I hope so."

The year we were building the cabin, there were some major health problems in the family -- 11 surgeries. We were trying to find a name for the cabin, and we weren't having much luck. We were going around the table every night, but we couldn't come up with just the right name.

One day, something else happened to one of the family, and Jim said to his mother, "Oh, don't worry, she'll be all right." And Dolores said, "Oposo."

Jim said, "That's the name." And that's what we've always called it.

∽◯∽◯∽◯

We had a major fire in our house in in 1986. We were in Minneapolis at the time, and we were called back home. We got back about midnight, and, of course, there was no electricity in the house. All we could do is walk around in the dark and feel these crunchy ashes beneath our feet.

We got a room that night at the Kahler Hotel. We were just devastated. So many family pictures were gone, and other valuable things were burned. The next day we were looking over the damage to the house, and we were in such despair. One the kids said, "Do you still have that champagne in your refrigerator downstairs?" I would sometimes keep a couple of bottles there.

She said, "Well, we're all alive. Let's think of the positive side of this. It didn't all burn down, and it can all be fixed."

So we were toasting this champagne to one another, and we all had happy looks on our faces. We were having a good time.

Who should walk in but Dave Naughtin. He was there to extend his condolences for the fire he had heard about. He was the former assistant county attorney, and I'm sure they had arson cases in his day. He must have expected us all to be in great sadness, but instead we were having the time of our lives. He looked just a little suspicious. It was a good thing he was a good friend.

In the end, we rebuilt the house to its original grandeur.

∞⋙∞⋙∞⋙

We told the kids in 1999 that we didn't want a 50th wedding anniversary party. They were pretty disappointed, but I told them Dolores and I would come through the Twin Cities at Christmas and we could all get together, just the family members.

We had a nice Christmas, and the day after everybody starting heading for home. People were heading for the airport. We were staying at Barbara's house, but we had spent the morning at Jim's. We got back to Barbara's about twenty minutes to two, and at about 10 after, the doorbell rang.

A recent photo of Dolores and me.

We went to the door, and here are all the children, all the grandchildren, all dressed beautifully, lined up and down the sidewalk. At the end of the driveway is Jimmy with a chauffeur's cap and a "Driving-Miss-Daisy" long navy blue coat. At the curb is a vintage Packard car. He said, "Come on, let's go."

They had arranged for Fr. Dick Rice to be at Immaculate Heart of Mary Church on Summit Avenue in St. Paul for a mass. The kids sang, played the piano, did the readings. We were in our glory. It was absolutely unbelievable.

From there were went to a wonderful Italian restaurant in St. Paul, Pazzaluna, where they had assigned a whole staff to the private dining room. We had champagne and flowers and five courses. Jim took us back then, sitting in the back seat of this Packard, built the year we were married. The car only had 33,000 miles on it, and it was immaculate. Jim said, "This is your anniversary gift."

Family Ties

You had to see the looks on our faces.

I have it at our lake house. I've driven it several times, and I'll be driving it quite a bit in the future.

❧☙❧☙❧☙

In later years, Dolores and I have begun taking morning walks along the beautiful streets of Hibbing. Often we will end our walk with breakfast at the Sportsman Cafe where will will share a table with some of the regulars like Lance Sundquist, Roger Saccoman, and Doug Swenson. On Wednesday, we sometimes join the book club group including Mike Fay, Jim Huber, Pastor Lyle Rossing, Carol Blomberg and Tony Kuznik. These people along with such dear friends as Ed and Judy Matonich and Jeff and Cam Perrella have become very precious to us in recent years. They are like our extended family, and they have been there when we needed them.

❧☙❧☙❧☙

I think of the standard that Dolores set for the children. She never had a college education because she was taking care of the family business. She was self-taught, street smart and she became accomplished in so many endeavors and fields. She could do anything. She was just a natural. I think the standard we set for the children, unconsciously, created such a drive in them that they felt they just had to succeed. I worry about it, having instilled in them too much of a drive for achievement.

I sometimes wonder if something wasn't sacrificed in the process. This life is not a permanent thing. I've had my own regrets about being so serious at times. I have gotten into such a drive, such a determination that something's got to work out, something over which you have no control. I may have missed a lot of life.

If I could do it over again, I think I'd try to lighten up a bit and have more fun.

I see it in the children now. They just drive themselves incessantly. But they have also learned better than we did to relax, meditate, to do their best and leave the rest to God. They all have good, balanced home lives, some really model families.

I pray mostly for their health and their happiness. In the end, it doesn't really matter about wealth. What matters is how happy they've been and what kind of life they've led, and how symbolic it's been with regard to God's expectations — and whether they help make the world better for their being in it.

❧☙❧☙❧☙

It's hard for me to believe sometimes that none of the children have come back to the Iron Range. It's such a good area to raise a family. Although the economic future

Chapter Eighteen
The Equation of Life

One time we went fishing at God's Lake up in the Arctic Circle. It was July of 1957, and the ice had just gone out of the lake. We were heading in for a shore lunch, and I asked the guides to drop me on a rock off the shore. I wanted to fish for some grayling. About 125 yards away was a miniature replica of Niagara Falls. It was very picturesque. The roar of the water over the rocks was deafening.

I fished for a while by myself. The rock on which I stood was kind of slimy, though, and I slipped off it into God's Lake. The water was unbelievably cold, and I was wearing hip boots. I was shooting down, just like a rocket. I came back up out of the water, but then shot right back down again.

I shot up for the third time just like a cannon. I had all these fishing clothes on. My boots were filled with water. I was cold. I was frantic, and I looked around to discover that a canoe was approaching. One of our Indian guides had sensed the danger and was paddling over.

Dutch Weber, Bill Fagan, Dave Bruneau, Hub Shields and Babe Petroske were on shore. They actually shot a movie of me in the water. There was nothing they could do, so they just let the camera roll.

I saw the canoe, and the only thing I could think of was to grab the canoe and start crawling in. I couldn't figure out why this Indian kept batting my hands with the oar.

THE EQUATION OF LIFE

Happy times on God's Lake in 1957 with some pretty big fish. It was probably one of those rocks in the background that I slipped from. The guy to the left of me is the late Dutch Weber, one of Hibbing's most successful businessmen. Left to right are Everett Joppa, Carl Burton, Bill Fagan, Weber, myself, and Dave Bruneau.

I wasn't smart enough to realize he didn't want me to tip the canoe and have both of us in the icy water. He just wanted to pull me into shore. If we went down the falls, we would never be found.

But I wasn't about to be stopped. Somehow I crawled over the side of that 18-foot canoe and got inside without tipping it. I've always said to this day: No one is going to tell me there isn't a God, and no one is going to tell me that there aren't miracles.

It was an absolute miracle. If I tried to climb into a canoe with all that gear on a hundred more times in Side Lake on a nice summer day, I couldn't do it. I can't swim, and how could I have done that with my hip boots full of water?

My whole life flashed before me, and I was scared for days. We had a party several weeks later in Duluth with all these great pictures we'd taken and a dinner of some prize fish that we'd caught. I had a 38 lb. lake trout and a 28 lb. northern. My pals showed the movies they had taken -- shots of me in the water and shots of me naked, with all my clothes up on the line and the fire drying them out.

To this day, there's hardly a week that goes by when I don't stop to thank God and tell him that, without Him, everything that subsequently happened wouldn't have happened. I didn't save myself. It was God's will. I often wonder what's expected of me for that. What do I owe?

When I was young, I was always running to play baseball, raising money for uniforms, entering the team in tournaments, taking care of this or that. I just seemed totally dedicated to helping the public all the time.

My mother used to get peeved with me because there was wood to chop and other chores to do around the house, and I'd always say, "Well, I'll do it later." But I had to run.

In Italian, she would always yell out to me as I left on another mission, "Qualche giorno te more per la patria." She said, "Some day you're going to die for your public." She used to predict that I would die impoverished because I would do anything for my public.

Early on I had to try to balance the equation of life so that serving the public didn't become a be-all and end-all.

Algot Johnson was part of a construction firm called Piper, Drake and Johnson. It was one of the largest contracting firms in the world, and it was later renamed the Algot Johnson Construction Co. I asked him one time, "What ever happened to Piper and Drake?"

He said, "Well, Carl, just remember. The best kind of a committee in the world is a three-man committee with two members absent."

Every four years since 1962 — the year I had my shot at higher office — people would ask me if I planned to run for governor. I'd tell them that my time had passed. It's a younger person's game, I'd say. Still, once you've been in office, people assume that's going to be your goal for the rest of your life.

And the way things are going in the Legislature and the Congress, you can't blame people for feeling that way. It does seem like a lifetime profession.

But it's becoming very difficult to serve in public office, and I think we will see

The Equation of Life

more and more people serving one or two terms and then invoking their own term limits even if Congress or the legislative bodies don't. Many of the problems these days are almost insoluble. More than that, though, it's a much more difficult job nowadays. One is looked at through a microscope.

I met with Bill Frenzel, the former Congressman from Minneapolis, one time after he had left office and asked him if he was happy to be out. He said he was, and I asked why. Didn't he miss the excitement and the power and the prestige?

He said, "Well, Carl, the job is tougher, the public is meaner and the talent is leaner." There are some outstanding people in politics today, but overall the quality and dedication are diminished.

In any full-time legislature around the country, like Minnesota's, it's hard for some of the very talented people to shake loose from their families and jobs and whatnot and devote that kind of time.

In our day, it was really a delightful job. There was camaraderie on both sides. There wasn't the bickering. We weren't trying to frame anybody or anything. There wasn't the political name calling. Everything was decided on its merits.

One would be very surprised sometimes to get up and talk about a bill thought to be controversial, and before one of the people from your own faction could get up and support it, somebody from the other side of the aisle would get up and say, "I could support this bill."

That's the way the legislature should be run.

ಸಿಡಿಸಿಡಿಸಿಡಿ

I'm frustrated many times when I think of God-given abilities and what people do with them. Or what they do if they don't have them. For instance, I always wanted to be a singer.

I tried being in the church choirs, and it was pretty miserable. I did, however, get into the play "Guys and Dolls," and I got to sing a solo. I loved it. I was so sorry to see the curtain ring down after a week. People still talk about it and laugh about it. It was a real shocker that I could stand on a stage and sing a solo to a beautiful girl.

We fall into certain niches, and we realize we have certain capabilities. In the Reserve Case, and the Taconite Amendment and in bringing Hibbing Taconite to the Range, I was able to use my abilities and play a part.

But there were likewise many situations of which I was not a part. There was always an adversarial relationship between Gov. Perpich and I. And yet I was more involved and more the center of many, many things when Perpich was governor than I was later when he was out of office.

I've asked myself a number of times, though, why I did end up in the middle of things when I didn't try to be? Why do people come to me? Why do I end up in these positions? Why does the Lord put me into these circumstances and what is expected of me?

There have been times when my family has been neglected. My wife has asked, "How much more can you give of yourself?"

You tend to end up fighting a lot of battles by yourself. You can have tacit agreement among people, you can go to Chamber of Commerce meetings, you can get people to say that something must be done. But when it comes time to do something, there are very few people there to make sure it's done. A friend of mine used to say, "You can search all the public parks, but you will never find a monument to a committee."

※※※

There were times at the duck camp at Squaw Lake where the shooting was really awful. There weren't any ducks flying. I used to go down to the blind in front of our place, right across from the public landing and not too far from town, and I'd take two or three boxes of shells. I'd just shoot my gun in the air continually -- straight in the air.

Later, at church, people would come up to me and say, "You had a hell of a shoot, didn't you?" I'd say, "I don't want to talk about it. I don't want to talk about it."

"Well, how many did you get?" they'd ask.

I didn't say anything.

I did this for years. They'd say, "That lucky guy. The only ones getting any shooting are over at Squaw Lake."

Many years later, I was telling Fran Ryan and Russ Ryan, "There weren't any ducks. I just shot these shells into the air." They said, "What were you doing?"

I said, "I was just keeping up the value of the real estate."

※※※

Even though we never did too well on a lot of my entrepreneurial outings, I guess if I saw another opportunity come around I'd consider it. The basic instinct is still there.

Carl Pohlad is a good friend of mine. I've watched Jeno Paulucci. They're into their 80s, and are acting as if they're 45 or 50 and are making plans for 10 and 20 years into the future as if they were youngsters.

In a sense, I'm the same way. Maybe it's a way of denying mortality, of convincing myself that I'm keeping death from the door as long as I'm doing things and planning things that go off into the future. Maybe I'm kidding myself that I'm not going to die.

The Equation of Life

☙❧☙❧☙❧

As much as selling tires is not a romantic business, it's a service business. We're helping people. People need tires. America moves on wheels.

The real treasure of being in the tire business is the fact that we've not been tied 24 hours a day to servicing or selling a tire. It provides us with an income. It allows us to belong to many organizations and to do philanthropic things. We can carve out a niche of image and respect and power. It's the kind of power similar to the power of politics, but its more enduring because it's something they can't take away.

As long as I keep building, and as long as I have friends and do a good job, it satisfies that inner ego, the same need that drives a lot of politicians.

☙❧☙❧☙❧

Dolores and I have had great debates about what constitutes a good friend. I always remember what Abraham Lincoln said. "If you have enough friends to count on the fingers of one hand, you're a great man. If you have enough friends to count on the fingers of two hands, you're a truly great man." And I say, "Oh, hell, I don't have enough hands."

But Dolores would always say, "How many real friends do you have? I don't think you have many." And I'd say, "Oh, I've got enough."

But she has a point. She has a lot of very close friends. I guess it all comes down to the interpretation of what is a friend. She says that my history is that I became involved with older people from the time I was a small child. Even when I was 16 years old, I was involved with the Junior Chamber of Commerce.

Because I'd spend so much time with them, and we'd eat together at the Androy Roundtable, I considered them close friends. Even today, they are my friends although the ones who are not deceased are very old now.

Except for school and baseball, I separated from friends of my own age. Dolores went to school in Virginia, and there were ten gals who were inseparable. They were good students from good homes, and they did things in school. They remained in contact through all the years. In fact they still get together every year. There are six left. They mail a round-robin letter, and in all those years they've never let that letter get off schedule. Those are real friends.

So what is a friend? Is it someone to whom you say, "I need your car?" If they only had one car, would they tell you to take it? If you needed money, would they give it to you? Would they come over and babysit for you? What is a friend? We use that term loosely.

From the period of my youth, my schoolmates and I were daily friends. As I began associating with older people, and became a resident of South Hibbing and the world, I began getting involved with older people.

Some of these wonderful people were Max Edelstein, Ernie Messner, Frank Fiola, Dick Galob, Joe Taveggia, Al Strand, Bill Knudsen, George Elioff, Gene Bangs, James Abate, Helmer Olson, Alex Steele, Gus Ekola, Dr. Frank Bachnik and Aldo Boria.

There had to be at least 75 to 100 people who were instrumental in my life. They were involved in the newspaper, radio, television, business, mining, politics, religion, banking, medicine, and sports. I can't start naming names, but these people were all important in my life. We had lunch, coffee, went fishing, went on vacations, would call each other at any time.

But my wife would tell you that some of these people don't qualify as friends. Friends are people you play cards with, people you take a walk with, people you volunteer with, people who you keep up on their children and how their doing. She'd say that was the definition of a friend.

Today I would be hard-pressed to say who my very best friend was.

When Patti was graduating from college, the family decided to do a bike trip from central Minnesota to Lake Geneva, Wisconsin, to visit the Palmersheim family. Tom Palmersheim, who taught music at Hibbing Community College, was playing at a night club in Lake Geneva for the summer.

I thought my family was crazy, and I fought the bike trip all the way. I told them there was no way I was going. But they went ahead and planned and organized, and they were ready to leave in two days when I relented and said I'd go along. I figured I'd better go along to protect them.

Now you have to understand that I can't leave for work in the morning without two or three briefcases and my pockets overloaded with notes. On the bike trip, all I could take with me would have to fit in a 6-inch by 16-inch handlebar bag. It was a great lesson in how little you need to survive, have fun, get great exercise, and enjoy life.

We started out at 7 a.m. each day, and would stop at 5 p.m. or so each evening. There were motels and restaurants that catered to the bike crowd, and we met many interesting people. We biked up some hills in Wisconsin that seemed like mountains, and came down hills that required a certain amount of expertise in braking to stay under control. Every night we were so tired, but each morning we were anxious to go again.

I was amazed at how I could get by with so few clothes. It reminded me of the retreats at the Jesuit Retreat House at Lake Demontreville near the Twin Cities where you were assigned a little single room with a metal bed, metal desk and chair, wash

The Equation of Life

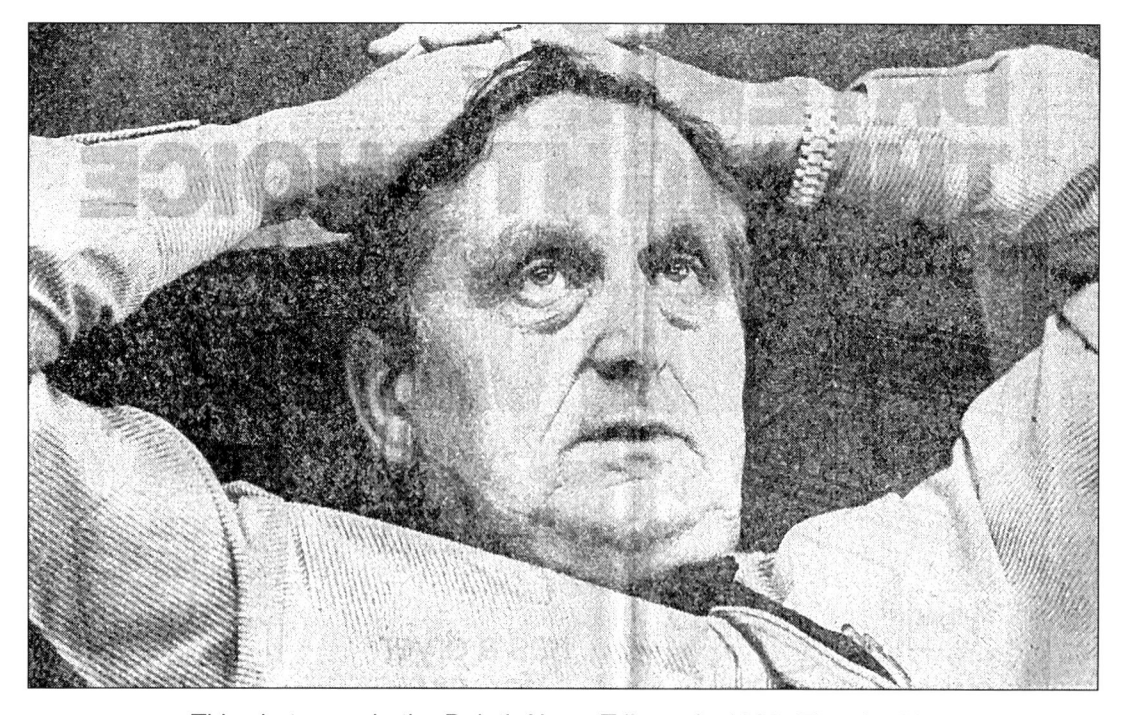

This photo was in the Duluth News-Tribune in 1982. They had interviewed me on my views of the economic recession hitting the Iron Range.

basin, a lamp, and a clothes rack. Bathrooms were shared with seven or eight other retreatants. After four days, I would hate to leave, and when I got home I realized how many useless possessions we all accumulate during a lifetime.

When we got to the Palmersheim residence, we heard them in the back yard with some neighbors enjoying some refreshments on a really hot day. We stayed in front and sent out son, Jim, around the side of the house.

Tom Palmersheim was stunned. He said, "Jim, how did you get here?" Jim said, "I biked here."

The Palmersheims roared with laughter and disbelief, at which point we all came around the house on our bikes.

They were speechless.

ಸಂಬಂಧ

I've been told that I'm probably one of the most unique sales people that has ever existed in the world because, as successful as I've been, I have to admit that no more than three times in my life — if that — have I ever asked for the order.

I make my presentation and I say "Think it over." I've never done as the book says, "Ask for the order. Don't leave without closing the order." I've not done that. I leave it to their judgment.

And it's worked.

❧❧❧

When I was in the sweepstakes for the governorship, I was in the Crystal Lounge one day about 4:30 or 5 o'clock with the after-work group. Dave Naughtin came in and said, "Hey, Carl, why would you want to be governor?"

I said, "A smart-ass question deserves a smart-ass answer. I want to be governor because you get your picture on the wall at the Capitol, and all the high school kids and everybody for ages will come by and admire you." He said, "Oh, that's what you think. All those pictures do is collect dust, and the only one the state employees clean off is the one who's currently signing the checks."

And isn't that the truth? Even the Presidents in my lifetime who were thought at the time to be so great are no longer remembered. All the world is but a stage.

❧❧❧

Albert Einstein used to say, "You can't solve the significant problems you face at the same level of thinking you had when you created them." I know in my own case, as far as food, it was too much of too many good things. It took a heart attack in 1990 to give me a wake-up call. Now, maybe people are going too far the other way with the stress on non-fat eating. The old adage of moderation in everything seems to be the best way to go about life.

❧❧❧

Maybe it's a factor of getting older, but I realize that my time is getting less. I start to try and peek into the future to see what will happen with my family. It's part of the love I have for my children.

❧❧❧

I admired George Burns, and I remember he said at one point: "In everybody's lifetime, there will be a time when you are well and a time when you are sick. You will be happy, and you will be sad. You will be rich, and you will be poor. But the only thing you will survive with is your attitude." I find it so true. If I greet people with a cheery "Good morning," they may be startled, but soon it starts to work and to spread.

The Equation of Life

As one grows older, I realize the three most important things in life start with the letter "F." No, I don't mean Fame, Fortune, Fun, or Food. I mean Faith, Family and Friends. Only when I really need someone do I find the reality of this.

We live in a fast-changing world. Technology has become a craze. Much of it is beneficial, but at the same time it tends to destroy person-to-person relationships. Electronic relationships tend to become very shallow. There is a decline in that real connection with other people. Technology is a tool, but quicker doesn't mean better. Knowledge doesn't mean wisdom.

ೲೲೲ

Happiness is being at peace with yourself, your family, your community and your creator. Happiness is an internal feeling. It can, and most often is, affected by our surroundings and circumstances. True internal happiness is strengthened by loving or giving to others -- rather than receiving.

I'm imbued with a deep daily sense of my obligation to all people, both those I know and those I may not know. I try every day to help someone, and if no one seeks it, I try to find someone or some cause that needs help.

ೲೲೲ

One of the really colorful characters on the Iron Range was Fr. Dominic Strobietto at Immaculate Conception, the Italian church in Hibbing.

He was such an idol that when he developed cancer of the throat, many Italian men, including my father, started thinking they had the same thing. I had to take my father to Dr. Joseph Leek at the Duluth Clinic to assure him that he didn't have it.

I thought that would assuage his fears, but on the way home, my dad said, "Why did Dr. Leek call you into the room alone? Why didn't he let me be there when he told

There were many colorful clergy in Hibbing through the years, and Father Dominic Strobietto took a backseat to no one.

you this?" So he still thought he had it.

One day my dad said he wanted to go visit Fr. Strobietto. He didn't drive, so he asked me to take him. They sat together for a while, and my dad offered him sympathy, and he said to him in Italian, "Father, are you afraid to die?" And Fr. Strobietto said, "Yeah, Pasquale, I'm very much afraid."

And my dad said, "Well, you've preached for years that we should not be afraid to die, that it's our graduation present, and that we'll get to be in heaven with God. If you're afraid, then what chance is there for me?"

Fr. Strobietto said, "Well, Pasquale, let me try to explain it to you. Here in my house, I've got a little wine. I have spaghetti every day. I go to the bank and post office every morning, and I stop a Panichi's Monarch Bar for a little brandy. I know what I've got. Over there in that other house, I don't know what I'll get."

※※※

One day I was standing in line for the annual spaghetti feed at Immaculate Conception Church with Yhonne Harrison. He was the town clerk and he had compiled a heroic war record. He was well-known in town.

Fr. Strobietto came in the door from the cold night, wiped the fog from his glasses, and got in line behind us. I said, "Father, you don't need to wait in line, this is your church." He said, "Oh, no, no, Carlo, I wait. I wait just like all the people." He turned to Harrison and said, "Who's this?" I introduced him, but Fr. Strobietto said he didn't know him.

I said, "Father, you should know Yhonne, he's the town clerk. He's a war hero." The priest just shook his head. I tried again, "Maybe you remember his father, he used to own the lumber yard."

"No, no, no, I just don't remember him."

Finally I said, "Well, his father was a member of the Ku Klux Klan."

Father Strobietto's eyes lit up. "Oh, now I remember. He was the third one on the white horse in the parade."

Meanwhile, Harrison was just about apoplectic. I guess that's not how he wanted his family remembered. He tried to interject something, but it was too late because by that time Fr. Strobietto was enumerating who was on the first horse, who was on the second horse, who was on the all the horses.

※※※

Fr. Strobietto used to tell the story about when he needed to go to Duluth to see the bishop. Angelo Pingatore, one of his parishioners, offered to give him a ride.

They were on their way, and Fr. Strobietto noticed they were going a little fast.

The Equation of Life

"You know, Angelo, he's a good guy," Strobietto would say. "But pretty soon we're going 75 miles an hour, and I'm afraid. I don't a feel-a good. I say, 'Angelo, You've got to slow down, you go over the speed-a-limit.'

"Angelo said, 'It's okay, father, I've got St. Christopher in the car.'

"I say, 'No, no, he get out when it's 60 miles an hour.'"

ഌഝഌഝഌഝ

And one quick one about getting older. One time at our place in Florida I was up and about in the morning. I was talking to one of the employees of the place, and he said, "Oh, I see you'll be in time for the organ recital at the pool at 10 a.m."

I told him I didn't know there would be an organ recital. In fact, I said I'd never seen an organ or any other musical instrument near the pool.

"Oh, just you wait," he said. "Just at 10 o'clock, when the residents start to gather around the pool, you can hear the organ recital: 'Oh, my kidneys. Oh, my prostate. Oh, my liver...'"

ഌഝഌഝഌഝ

Every family has problems. I went to the priest one time and told him that things were so bad that I couldn't concentrate, I couldn't sleep, I couldn't work. I told the priest that I was going to make some pledges. I was going to do something significant in the church through a major gift to the school. I thought maybe an essay contest. We'll give some sort of prize.

He said, "Carl, you're going to try and bargain? You can't bargain with God."

I said, "Oh, yeah?"

Index

A

Abe, Ernie, 58
Abate, Jimmy, 49, 201
Ackerson, Bert, 153
Aho, Rudy, 121
Albany Mine, 4
Alexander, G.H., 7
Allard, Lucille, 186
Anderson, A.B., 51, 55
Anderson, Andrew "Bus Andy," 27-30, 154-156
Anderson, Bud, 133
Anderson, Eddie "Rochester," 152-153
Anderson, Elmer, 70-74, 77-78, 81-84, 91
Anderson, Hilda, 154
Anderson, Robert, 114, 131, 134, 148-151
Anderson, Wendell, 58, 86, 103, 108, 139
Andreas, Dwayne, 79
Androy Hotel, Hibbing, 37, 41, 47, 49, 61, 203
Armstrong, Larry, 39
Arrowhead Traveler, 28-29, 30-31, 138
Atcheson, Glen, 43
Aurora, Minnesota, 79

B

Babbini, Andy, 38
Babbitt, Minnesota, 103, 107, 110
Bachnik, Dr. Frank, 201
Ball, Joe, 60
Bangs, Gene, 201
Banovetz, Matt, 109
Bantaari, Sigrid, 25
Bartlett, Tommy, 49
Beasy, Pete, 156-157
Befera, Fran, 95-97, 119, 126-128, 132-134, 160
Befera, Orfeo, 126
Beno, Vic, 140
Benzoni, Peter, 80
Berger, Ben, 123
Berklacich, Nick, 20
Berklich, Bill, 161
Berklich, Frank, 34, 156
Berklich, Liz, 161
Berlin, Billy, 39
Berman, Sanford, (Michael Dean), 26
Bernard, John T., 47
Bethlehem Steel Co., 121
Biancini, John and Jennie, 173
Bierman, Bernie, 165-166
Birkeland, Lionel, 88
Bjornson, Val, 83-84
Blatnik, John, 20, 34, 40, 46-47, 54,

207

Index

77, 90, 105, 138, 140, 141
Blatz, Jerry, 96
Blomberg, Carol, 194
Blumhardt, Keith, 25
Boentje, John and Kay, 69
Boo, Ben, 86
Boria, Aldo, 37, 173, 201
Borlaug, Norman, 105
Brice, Dr. William, 116, 119
Broad, Anthony "Funny," 156
Brooklyn, 9, 15, 21,
Bruneau, Dave, 196-197
Brunetti, Cledo, 103
Buescher, Robert and Jodi, 121
Buhl, Minnesota, 26, 38, 39, 58
Burns, George, 203
Burton, Carl, 197
Bush, George, 142
Butler Taconite Plant, 113-117, 148

Capone, Al, 153

Carey, Cathy, 184
Carey, Tom, 180
Carlson, Arne, 100, 118-120, 138
Carlson, Curt, 93
Carnegie Library, 19, 20
Carr, Hal, 138
Carter, Jimmy, 135, 147
Casagrande, Helen, 82, 171, 177
Casagrande, Mario, 64-66, 169-172, 174, 176
Casagrande, Sally Jean, 171
Chapin, Gaylord, 134, 139
Chapin, Mary, 160-161
Chapin, Tom, 139
Checci, Alfred, 138
Cher, 146
Chisholm, Minnesota, 26-27, 39, 69, 97, 140-142, 167
Chisholm Free Press, 141
Chocos, Marian, 25
Cina, Fred, 51, 59, 79, 107
Clark, Jack, 151
Clark, Mel, 36
Clayton, Donald, 72-73
Cleveland Cliffs, 109-110, 115
Clinton, William, 99
Coleman, Nick, 86
Coleraine, Minnesota, 121, 153-154, 184
Collins, Jim, 117
Cook, Chuck, 167
Cook, Dave, 96
Cook, Minnesota, 38, 40
Costanzi, Vic, 49-50
Cox, Charlie, 157
Crawford, Ed, 26
Crispigna, Kathleen, 173
Cronkite, Walter, 139
Cuyuna Range, 108
Cypress Mining, 109

Dahlberg, Carl, 166

Dahlner, Gus, 27
D'Aquila, Barbara, 146, 167, 174, 179, 182-183, 185-186, 193
D'Aquila, Bonnie Manhan, 188
D'Aquila, Carl and Dante, 184
D'Aquila, Concetta, 3-12, 15, 17, 24, 64, 191-192, 197
D'Aquila, Dolores, 48-49, 59, 65, 67, 68, 71, 82, 84-85, 90, 100, 105, 110, 123, 125-126, 129, 135, 140, 146, 147, 150, 154, 160-162, 167, 168, 169-194, 200
D'Aquila, Donna Fleming, 184

D'Aquila, Frank, 4, 5, 15, 24, 25, 27
D'Aquila, Isabella Rose, 188
D'Aquila, James, 93, 100, 137, 162, 174, 179, 182-183, 187-188, 190, 192-193, 202
D'Aquila, Lucy, 24, 64
D'Aquila, Margaret, 174, 178-179, 182-183, 186-187
D'Aquila, Mary Kay, 108, 163, 174, 179, 182-183, 185, 190
D'Aquila, Michael, 64
D'Aquila, Mike, 4, 5, 24, 25, 64
D'Aquila, Pasquale, 3-12, 16-20, 24, 25, 64, 75-76, 177-178, 192, 205-206
D'Aquila, Patricia, 163, 174, 178-179, 182-185, 201
D'Aquila, Salvatore 5
D'Aquila, Thomas, 64, 125, 160, 174, 179, 182-184, 189
Davies, Jack, 77
Davis, Dr. E.W., 53, 75
DeLoia, Joe, 134, 182-183
DeLuca, Jack, 88, 162
DeVancy, Fred, 53
Dickinson, Angie, 146
Dole, Bob, 142
Dominici, Pete, 142
Donaldson, Sam, 159
Donovan, Joe, 72
Dornack, Oscar, 151, 154
Dougherty, John, 126, 160-161
Dougherty, Mary Kay, 161
Dougherty, Tom, 134, (and Jeanne) 173, 168
Dragich, Joe, 16
Draskovich, Emil, 116, 118, 121
Drong, Jerry, 118
Drummond, E.P., 38
Duluth News Tribune, 202
Duluth Dukes, 21

Dunn, Roy, 2, 45-46
Durenburger, David, 81, 85, 142-143
Dwan, John and Mary, 168
Dyer Appraisal, 9-10
Dylan, Bob, 145-146

Edelstein, Max, 147-148, 156, 201
Edelstein, Sammy, 34
Edmond, Jerry, 154, 156
Egge, Sig, 65
Einstein, Albert, 203
Ekola, Gus, 20, 85, 156, 173, 201
Elioff, George, 201
Elmer, Minnesota, 49-50
Ely, Minnesota, 109
Enroth, Dennis, 120
Enterprise Mine, 148
Erie Mining Co., 53, 75
Eveleth, Minnesota, 96, 170
Eveleth Taconite, 114

Fagan, Bill, 196-197
Farley, John, 110
Farley, James, 25
Fay, Mike, 194
Feldman, William, 34
Fena, Jack, 169-173
Fena, John, 7, 34, 170
Fiola, Frank, 201
Firestone Tires, 67
Fish, Russell, 148
Fisher, George, 34, 54
Fleur, Marcia, 94
Flynn, Dr. Bernard, 187
Foote, Susan, 142
Ford, Gerald, 147

209

INDEX

Fragnito, Robert, 117
Freedy, Jack, 28
Freeman, Orville, 59, 70, 104
Frenzel, Bill, 198
Furlong, Porky, 151
Furness, Ed, 104

G

Gabardy, Arthur, 58

Gabor, Zsa Zsa, 146
Galob, Richard, 136, 201
Gannon, Bob, 60-61
Gannon, John, 40, 156
Garagiola, Joe, 162
Gelein, Bob, 87
Gelein, Hud, 26, 87
General Tire, 64-65
Gilbert, 43
Gillen, Arthur, 81, 84, 154
Gillen, Lois, 154
Gleason, Jim, 16
Gleason, Jim Jr., 21
Glumack, Ray, 96
Goetz, Jim, 84-85
Goodwin, John, 120
Goodyear Tires, 67, 110-111
Gorbachev, Mikhail, 93
Grand Rapids, Minnesota, 90-91, 163-164, 168, 192
Graven, Dave, 86
Graziano, Rocky, 151-153
Grcevich, Denny, 119
Great Northern Railroad, 63
Greyhound Bus Lines, 27-28
Grillo, William, 180
Guentzel, Earl, 53
Gustin, Joe, 80

H

Hall, Gus, 47

Hall, Halsey, 17, 165
Hall, Larry, 2, 44, 48, 57
Halloran, Mike, 58
Hanna Mining Company, 25, 113-121, 131, 148-151, 154
Hanson, Al, 68
Harrison, Hugh, 88
Harrison, Perry, 148
Harrison, Yhonne, 205
Hayes, Tom, 134
Head, Doug, 85-86
Healy, Don, 118
Hegstad, J.G., 23
Heiam, Dr. William, 38
Heinz, John, 142
Herbert Heinig, 62
Herrett, Art, 58
Hesburgh, Rev. Theodore, 162
Hibbing Daily Tribune, 33-35, 54, 56, 57, 69, 72, 74
Hibbing High School, 13, 23, 25-26, 33, 88, 171, 186
Hibbing Junior College, 33
Hibbing Taconite Co., 53, 75, 120, 121, 198
Hirschboeck, Jack, 26
Hitchcock, Jim, 69
Hoffman, Mike, 55
Horowitz, Harry, 41
Howell, J.N., 120
Huber, Jim, 194
Hull-Rust Mine, 6, 12
Hulstrand, Vic, 29, 49-50, 53
Humphrey, Hubert, 60, 74, 99, 105, 136-137, 140, 141
Humphrey, Muriel, 140
Hurley, Jack, 151

Hurley, Lillian, 25

I
Il Progresso, 11

Inland Mining Co., 113-114
Iron Mining, 131-132
Iron Mining, 9-10, 17-20, 30, 38, 40, 51-54, 67, 75-80, 93, 99, 103-111, 113-121

J
Jacobs, Irwin, 93

Jacobson, Wayne, 165
Jefferson School, 18, 20
Jensen, Ray, 117, 120
Johnson, Algot, 79, 197
Johnson, Charlie, 17
Johnson, Cindy, 146
Johnson, Clayton, 10
Johnson, Dennis, 118, 120
Johnson, Lyndon, 74
Johnson, Marshall, 118
Jones, Alan, 171
Jones, Wally, 135
Joppa, Everett, 197
Jyring, Jerry, 123

K
KSTP-Television, 95-96, 136, 137

Keewatin, Minnesota, 117, 166
Keith, Sandy, 71-72
Kelly, Dan, 117
Kennedy, John F., 92, 104
King, Jean Levander, 81
King, Jim, 83
King, Shirley Fredrickson, 83
Kinney, Minnesota, 58

Kitzville, Minnesota 5
Knudsen, Bill 201
Koskinen, Barney, 66
Kotonias, George, 116, 118, 120
Krueger, Al, 50
Kuusi, Clarence, 117, 120
Kuznik, Tony, 194

L
LaMothe, Gene, 65

Langley, Clarence, 45
Larson, Dr. Bill, 134, 161, 185
Larson, Marlene, 161
Larson, Paul, 184
Lauber, Harold, 156
Leahy, George, 44
Leek, Dr. Joseph, 204-205
Leetonia, Minnesota, 180
Lehtinen, Larry, 115
Leirfallom, Jarle, 81
Levander, Hap, 81
Levander, Harold, 58, 81, 83-85, 91
Levander, Iantha, 81
Levitov, Dr. Alexander, 163-164
Lewis, John L., 146
Lincoln School, 18, 20, 22
Linney, Bob, 148-150
Lomoro, Frank, 166
Lord, Jim, 108
Lord, Miles, 105-108
LTV Mining, 110, 114-115
Lund, Alvin, 104

M
MacCormick, Norman, 173

Mackay, Harvey, 46
Mackay, Jack, 46, 48,
Mader, Douglas, 187

211

INDEX

Mader, Nicholas, Meaghan and Charles, 187
Mandsager, Lute, 150
Manella, Dyke, 20
Maras, Firpo, 63
Maras, Mike and Nick, 156
Marinac, Mike, 34, 151
Marinelli, Ron and Carla, 158
Mathisen, Oscar, 64
Matonich, Ed, 134, 161, 163, 164, 194
Matonich, Judy, 161,164, 194
Maturi, Babe, 154
Mayo, Dr. Charles, 77-79
McCarthy, Eugene, 105, 141
McGolrick Institute, 15
McHardy, Sandy, 26, 151-152
McKanna, Nonnie, 86, 118
McKinnon, George, 2
McLain, Bill, 154-155
McNamara, Rev. William, 161
Meineke, Dave, 118
Merickel, Andrew, 185
Merickel, Dr. John, 183, 185
Merickel, Jonathon, 183, 185
Merklin, Barbara, 69
Merritt, Grant, 106, 108
Messner, Don, 148
Messner, Ernie, 201
Micheletti, Andy, 184
Michelin Tires, 65, 67
Miettunen, John, 25
Miller, Bibbs, 26
Mills, Wilbur, 131
Miner, Jerry, 165
Minneapolis Tribune, 96, 99
Minneapolis Star Journal, 17, 58
Minneapolis Star, 17
Minorca Mine, 114
Mondale, Walter, 105, 119, 131-135, 141, 160
Mondavi Family, 82
Mondavi, Rosa, 82
Montague, Bill, 92
Moynihan, Pat, 142
Mt. Iron, Minnesota, 38, 39
Muller, Joanne, 70
Munter, Bernard, 87
Murr, Dennis, 118, 120

Naeseth, Julie, 28
Nashwauk, Minnesota, 117
Nassau Location, 5
National Steel Corp. (NKK), 116, 119, 131
National Steel Pellet Company, 113-121
Naughtin, Dave, 161, 180, 192, 203
Naughtin, Lois, 161
Nelson, Dorothy, 73
Nelson, Emily, 156
Nelson, Gaylord, 105
Nelson, Marilyn, 93
Nickoloff, Anne, 135, 147
Nickoloff, C.A., 6-7, 80
Nickoloff, Connie, 25
Nickoloff, Robert, 80, 126, 131, 135, 147
Nides, Louie, 49
Nixon, Richard, 135, 139, 165
Nolan, Mark, 43
North Central Airlines, 138, 141, 157-158
Northshore Mining, 109-110
Northwest Airlines, 138
Nyberg, Al, 22, 157, 188

212

O

Oberstar, James, 90-91
Ogle, Art, 70
Ojala, Bill, 79
Oliver Iron Mining Co., 20
Olson, Helmer, 20, 38, 201
Ontario Mining Co., 53, 75
Owens, Dr. Ben, 25, 162-163

P

Pacific Isle Mining Co., 88
Paciotti, Jean, 161, 164
Paciotti, Dr. Vince, 126, 134, 161, 162, 164, 167
Pajunen, Ed, 134
Palmersheim, Tom, 202
Panichi, Alipio, 26, 50, 150-154
Park Addition, 9
Parson, Stuart, 165
Pasin, Anna and Antonio, 159
Paulucci, Jeno, 17, 93, 199
Pederson, Kenneth, 37
Peluso, Thomas, 121
Perrella, Jeff and Cam, 194
Perpich, George, 87
Perpich, George (Rudy's brother), 90, 95, 100
Perpich, Lola, 100
Perpich, Mary Sue, 93
Perpich, Rudy, 12, 34, 58, 69, 77, 86, 87-101, 103, 106, 109, 198
Perpich, Tony, 90-91
Pervenanze, Lawrence, 38
Peterson, C. Donald, 72-74
Peterson, Elmer, 2, 34, 51, 59, 88-89
Peterson, P.K., 45, 58, 73
Petroske, Babe, 196
Phillips, Christina, 183, 185
Phillips, Thomas Scott, 127, 183, 185
Phillips, Scott, 127, 183, 185
Pickands, Mather Co., 25, 75-76
Pillsbury, George, 118
Pillsbury, John, 81, 83-84
Pingatore, Angelo, 205-206
Pohlad, Carl, 93, 127, 158, 199
Ponikvar, Veda, 97, 137, 140-142
Power, Vic, 40, 140, 156
Prahl, Helen, 20
Pribic, Marko, 76
Proxmire, William, 105
Purse, Jim, 149

Q

Quie, Albert, 98-99, 136
Quigley, Roy, 41

R

Rantala, Helen, 25
Rather, Dan, 138-139
Reagan, Ronald, 132, 135, 142, 158
Republic Steel, 106
Reserve Mining Co., 75, 103-111, 113, 115-116, 148, 198
Rice, Curt, 161, 167
Rice, Fr. Dick, 193
Rice, Rochelle, 161
Robbie, Joe, 129
Roberts, Joe, 58
Rocchi, Matt, 151-152
Rocco, Louis, 26, 61, 150
Rockefeller, Nelson, 74
Rockne, Knute, 160
Rolvaag, Karl, 25, 70-72, 74, 77, 81
Roosevelt, Eleanor, 141
Rosen, Dr. Ralph, 48

INDEX

Rossing, Lyle, 194
Rostvold, Eddie, 148
Rothstein, Eugene and Jean Ryan, 164-165
Rukavina, Tom, 118
Rutter, Loren, 58, 61-62
Ryan, Fran and Russ, 199
Ryan, John, 150
Ryan Hotel, St. Paul, 1, 41-43, 61

S

achs, Mish, 21

St. Louis County Independent, 33
St. Paul Pioneer Press, 59, 83, 99
Saccoman, Roger, 194
Sauey, Norm and Don, 126
Schirmer, William, 34
Schmid, Ed, 105
Schwanke, Fred, 51
Scranton Mine, 4, 75-76
Seiler, Stuart and Robin, 167-168
Shaffer, Packy, 21
Shapiro, Jay, 25
Shell Tire, 65
Sher, Izzy, 68
Sheran, Robert, 53
Shields, Hub 196
Shipka, Vladimar, 59
Side Lake, Minnesota, 151, 185, 188, 196
Sikich, Rudy, 165-166
Simon, Bill, 137-138
Slattery, John, 33-34, 88, 100
Smalley, Earl and Cat, 129
Snyder, Jimmy "The Greek," 147
Solomon, Athony, 131
Sonaglia, Tom, 134
Sorvari, Mike, 40
South Agnew Mine, 180-181

Spannaus, Warren, 90, 93, 109
Spanner, Lee, 55, 65
Spensieri, Anthony, 173
Stassen, Harold, 81, 91
Steele, Alex, 20, 38, 201
Steinbrenner, George, 127-128
Steiner, George, 85
Stevens, Ted, 142
Stewart, Payne, 167
Stinson, George, 131
Strand, Al, 201
Strobietto, Rev. Dominic, 204-206
Stuhldreher, Harry, 159-160
Sundquist, Lance, 194
Susquehanna Mine, 107
Swenson, Doug, 194

T

aconite Amendment, 75-80, 198

Taddei, Al, 22
Taft, Sen. Robert, 60
Taveggia, Joe, 22, 49, 201
Teller, George, 46, 60
The National Observer, 78
Thouin, Isabel, 20
Timmerman, Art, 33, 36-37, 60
Twigg, S.E., 28, 30
Twiggy, 147

U

.S. Steel, 10

Uniroyal, 65-67

V

alentini, Bruno and Rose, 167

Valentini, Dionella, 167
Valentini, Michael, 166

214

Valentini, Nello, 167
Valeri, Nobby, 65, 110-111
Van Buren, Abigail, 147
Ventura, Jesse, 138
Vinchiaturo, Italy, 3-5, 7
Virginia, Minnesota, 83, 103, 114, 118, 135, 138, 148, 166, 169-174, 200
Vukelich, Tom, 51, 59

W

WDGY-Radio, 44-46
WDIO-Television, 94-95, 97, 128, 147, 159
WEVE Radio, 170
WMFG Radio, 26, 47, 49, 55, 56, 60, 62, 96, 158, 169, 188
Wallace, Bob, 69
Wallace, George, 135-136
Washington School, 15, 18, 20, 22, 68, 185
Weber, Dutch, 150, 196-197
Weinberg, Jack, 59
Wenberg, Vern, 186
Wheeling Steel Co., 113-114
Whitney, Dick, 148
Whitney, Wheelock, 72-73
Widstrand, Oscar, 33, 35, 40, 60
Widstrand, Paul, 60, 62
Wilcox, Claire, 165
Winemaking, 7-8
Winter, Max, 123
Wivoda, Roland, 49
Wold, Archie, 55
Woodle, Merlyn, 107, 109

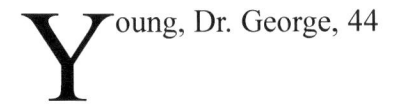

Y

Young, Dr. George, 44
Youngdahl, Reuben, 48
Youngdahl, Luther, 1, 39, 43, 45, 47-48, 136-137

Z

Zale, Tony, 151-153
Zanuck, Darryl, 152
Zeitler, Steve, 66
Zimmerman, Abe, 145-146
Zimmerman, David, 145
Zimmerman, Morris, 34, 145
Zontelli Family, 108